SEX SYMBOL

Cover Design:
Letitia Hasser, RBA Designs

Photo Credit:
Wander Aguiar Photography

Interior Design & Formatting:
Christine Borgford, Type A Formatting

Editing:
Nancy Smay at Evident Ink

ABOUT THIS BOOK

This book was previously published with a different cover under the title Take Two. It has been re-edited for this release.

Micah Preston is Hollywood's #1 sex symbol.

A rich and famous actor who has sworn off any serious relationships, the playboy is the media's favorite bachelor.

But he wasn't anybody when Maddie Bauer met him seven years ago. Then he was just the hot guy at the party who gave her an amazing orgasm and never called her again.

Now her job as a camera assistant has landed her on the set of his latest movie, and despite her vow to ignore his charm, she finds him pulling her focus.

She just has to make it through the shoot without landing in his bed. But when the legendary bad boy sets his sights on her, how can she possibly resist?

SEX SYMBOL

LAURELIN PAIGE

ONE

A NIGHTCLUB WOULD HAVE BEEN bad enough, but when Maddie Bauers heard the stereo pulsing loudly from where she stood outside the Woodland Hills house, she froze, preparing to march full stomp back to her car.

"Oh, come on." Bree flashed her puppy-dog eyes, the ones that usually got her anything and anyone.

Maddie pursed her full lips. "You said one drink, Bree. This is not one drink. This is a noise violation and disorderly conduct ticket waiting to happen."

"This is fun waiting to happen." Bree tossed her long blond hair behind her shoulder. "I know you're frigid and anti-good times, but one fucking party isn't going to kill you. As your best friend, it's my duty to tell you that you need to chillax. Have a good time."

Bree leaned closer to Maddie. "And I heard from someone who heard from someone else that the cast and crew of the latest Davenport indie might show up. That means hot celebrities." She raised her hands triumphantly above her head. "Woo hoo!"

"First of all, I couldn't care less about celebrities. Secondly, how do you know they're hot?"

Bree waggled her eyebrows. "Let's just say I heard some rumors."

Maddie groaned. "I'm so leaving."

"Come on. Don't you want to celebrate your graduation even a little bit?"

"I am perfectly happy to celebrate on our couch with a glass of red wine."

"Maddie, I hate to tell you this, but for twenty-two, you are old."

Bree had a point. Maddie had always been serious, probably too serious for her own good. But it paid off. While the rest of the students in her film class partied and fumbled their way through college, she'd graduated with several completed independent films under her belt and landed a summer internship with the Oscar-winning filmmaker Joss Beaumont. Maddie was headed for a lifelong career in the film biz and she rarely let parties or men distract her.

Bree was another story. Maddie believed the petite buxom blonde would try to sleep her way into a starring film role, a goal bound to get her into trouble sooner or later. Parties like this one could bring that trouble sooner rather than later, and leaving Bree there alone was probably not such a good idea.

Maddie sighed. "Okay, okay, I'll stay." Before Bree could squeal with happiness, Maddie gave conditions. "But you have to promise not to abandon me in some corner like you usually do. And whoever you decide to randomly hook up with, promise me you'll use a condom."

"You act like I'm such a slut." Bree pulled Maddie toward the front door of the house. "But, yes, I do have a condom. In fact, I brought two."

"Are you planning to get lucky twice?"

"No, I brought it for you."

Bree didn't abandon Maddie in the first five minutes as she usually did at parties, she waited nearly ten before she excused herself to find a drink. Bree being Bree, Maddie knew it'd be a while before they met up again.

Maddie snagged a seat on the living room sofa and busied herself with picking at her nails. She assumed a don't-bother-me posture, more out of habit than on purpose. After an hour that felt like three, she wondered if it was too soon to hunt down her roommate and declare the night over. Was she really so much of a fuddy-duddy that she wanted to leave a graduation party before midnight? Yes, she was. But it was Bree's graduation night too and she deserved to celebrate, so Maddie determined to hold out a little longer.

Taking a deep breath, she stood up, tugged the straps of her pink tank top into place and smoothed down her knee-length black cotton skirt. *Might as well try to enjoy myself.* She pushed through the crowd and found an open beer cooler near the patio doors. She grabbed a Corona, leaned against the open sliding door and peered into the backyard. Even though the party extended to the yard, there seemed to be more breathing room there.

Once she got past the crowd surrounding the doors, Maddie saw that most of the partygoers congregated in and around the pool and hot tub—many of them sans swimsuit. Definitely a scene she wanted to avoid. She stuck to the side of the house, steering clear of the pool area altogether.

On the other side of the backyard, she spied a couple making out on a porch swing. She watched as the man's deft fingers traveled up and under the woman's thin chemise. Even in the darkness, Maddie could see her shiver. The woman let out a moan of longing, and Maddie's belly ached with unexpected jealousy. It had been a while since she'd been kissed that way. *Too long.*

It didn't have to be too long, she reminded herself. That had been her choice. She could choose differently. What if she were audacious and uninhibited like Bree?

Then she wouldn't be on her way to a promising film career, that's what.

She shook off her arousal and fancies of unbridled passion, and searched for a place to hole up unbothered. She spotted a concrete sitting area with an unlit fire pit against the yard's back wall. It was dark and in shadow, and it looked deserted. She moved to claim it for herself.

Excited voices near the pool caught her attention when she'd nearly made it to the sanctuary. She glanced over, seeking the cause of the excitement. A drunken woman clothed only in a shirt and panties stepped out from the center of the spectators and onto the diving board, twirling her skirt around her finger in the air as she did.

Maddie stopped short as she made out the face of the woman. Her stomach tightened. She knew that stripper. It was Bree.

Bree sang some current popular hit at the top of her lungs, basking in the attention her display earned her. Soon she began inching her shirt up, teasing her audience as she did, until her shirt was abandoned in the pool below and Bree stood wearing only a black demi-cup bra and matching panties. The crowd cheered as she bent over provocatively, shimmying her petite behind.

"What the hell are you doing?" Maddie softly asked, willing the question to penetrate the distance between them and stop the antics of her wild friend.

"I'd say she's having a good time," a male voice said from behind her. "Giving one as well."

Maddie jolted and put her hand over her heart. She turned to find her sitting area wasn't deserted as she'd hoped. In the shadows on the stone bench behind her sat a male figure. She couldn't make out his face, but moonlight fell on his lower body revealing taut, lean muscles constrained within his tight jeans.

"Sorry. Didn't mean to startle you." He leaned forward, his face appearing out of the shadows.

She took a quick breath as her gaze met his. His dark hair, thick and tousled, framed the smooth chiseled face. Deep-set eyes peered out from under intense eyebrows. She couldn't be sure in the darkness, but she guessed his eyes were blue. Whatever color, they were piercing and her knees weakened under his stare.

"No problem," she managed. "I didn't realize there was anyone out here."

"Clearly." He grinned. "I mean, the whole allure of this area is the seclusion, right?" His smooth words combined with the slightest hint of a drawl sent an unexpected ripple of desire south of her belly.

"Right." Maddie turned back to Bree, hoping to hide the heat that was rising in her cheeks. What was wrong with her? She never reacted this way to guys, let alone one she'd just met. Perhaps the scene she'd witnessed minutes before had aroused her more than she'd realized.

"She'll be fine." The man mistook Maddie's withdrawal as concern about her stripping friend. "She has plenty of people looking out for her."

"That's what I'm afraid of." But this stranger had the right idea. It was no good worrying about Bree when she got herself in these situations. Maddie knew from experience the best course of action was to just wait it out. Bree would summon her when she could no longer handle herself.

Maddie took a swig of her Corona and turned back to the piercing eyes. Despite the nearby striptease, his gaze was fixed directly on her. "She doesn't seem to have captured *your* attention."

The man shrugged. "I prefer private shows."

An image of the kind of show Maddie could give him flashed through her mind. She quickly took another swallow of her beer, clearing her head of the deliciously inappropriate thoughts. Seriously, what had come over her?

The stranger tilted his head, as if trying to interpret her silence. "You're welcome to sit."

Her insides twisted at the thought of being close to him, wanting an accidental brush against his strong body. She dismissed her usual tendency to overthink and walked toward the stone seating. "You were looking to be alone, I wouldn't want to intrude."

"I was looking for seclusion, not necessarily to be alone."

His words possessed a teasing tone that made her shiver. She tensed as he looked her over, fully aware that he was checking her out. She'd been gifted with pretty brown eyes and nice features, and she took care of her figure, but she didn't pay attention to whether or not she was attractive to men. This man seemed pleased though, giving her a look that would usually turn her on her heels. She didn't flirt with strangers—didn't flirt much period—which was one of the reasons she avoided social gatherings such as this one.

But this man compelled her, his body drawing her like a magnet. He was so incredibly attractive, and hell, didn't she deserve a little fun on her graduation night?

"I'll take you up on the offer. To sit, I mean."

"Ah, I hadn't offered anything else." He let out a slow breath. "Yet."

Her heart raced at the implications of his statement as she sat beside him on the bench, closer than she imagined she'd ever dare. Her skirt rose as she crossed one long leg over the other and she fought the impulse to adjust it, feeling the intensity of his eyes on her thigh.

She flushed again under his gaze and realized she needed to calm the fire kindling between her legs. Seeing he held a Coors Light, she lifted her bottle in a toast. "To privacy."

He smiled, his face lighting up as he did, causing another stir in Maddie's nether parts. "To privacy." He clinked her bottle then took a sip of his own. She watched as his mouth parted around the tip of the bottle and found herself imagining the feel of his full, firm lips, wondering what he'd taste like. Her tongue darted across her teeth at the thought.

"Tell me," he said, setting his bottle down on the ground next to him, "what's a hot—I mean attractive—woman like you doing at a party like this if you're looking to be alone?"

Her heart raced at his shameless remark. "One could ask the same of you."

"Yes, they could. It's the question on everyone's mind. But I asked first."

"You aren't full of yourself at all."

He feigned seriousness. "No, not at all. If I was full of myself we would be talking about me, but I'm trying to find out about you and so you should answer the question."

Hot and charming. Delish.

"Well . . ." She wished she had some witty comeback. She settled on simply answering his question. "I was dragged here with Miss Bare-It-All over there." She nodded her head toward Bree who now only wore panties. "It's supposed to be our graduation party."

The man stiffened beside her. "Graduation?"

She laughed. "From film school. Were you worried you were coming on to a teenager?"

He leaned back, distancing himself from Maddie. "Oh, you thought I was coming on to you?"

Crap! Had the teasing only been in her mind? She opened her mouth to speak, but she stuttered, "Uh . . ."

He chuckled. "Relax. I was totally coming on to you."

She raised a brow. "Really? Or are you just keeping me from being completely humiliated?"

"No, I really was hitting on you. Come on, it was incredibly obvious."

"Yes it was. Are you still hitting on me now? Or has the moment passed?"

"Oh, no, the moment hasn't passed." He cocked his head and his eyes travelled down her body again, lingering at her low neckline. "So . . . film school," he said after a heat-filled moment. "What's your area of interest?"

Maddie barely kept herself from a fit of nervous giggles. "You never told me why you're here."

"That's boring."

"Impossible."

"Okay, you really want to know? I was also dragged here. By some of the guys I work with." He craned his neck looking around the party. "I have no idea where they are. Nor would I tell you if I saw them because they might be more attractive than I am and I wouldn't want to give myself unnecessary competition."

Maddie let her eyes explore his body. His casual white and black button-down shirt opened to mid-sternum and she could see serious pecs underneath. The bottom buttons also remained open and when he stretched his arms above his head—undoubtedly on purpose—a patch of tight abs and a trail of hair peeked out. Yum, yum, and yum. "You don't need to worry about competition."

"Seriously? Then I'm doing okay?"

"You're doing just fine." She locked eyes with him, and thoughts of him naked above her flashed through her mind. Blushing, she looked away.

"So . . ." she said, raising her eyebrows. Was she really flirting like this with a stranger?

"You never told me what area of film you studied."

As a rule, Maddie stayed away from this conversation with people she'd just met. Saying you graduated from film school in L.A. was like saying you had breakfast. It was a dull, overdone topic. But this subject was safer than her fantasy thoughts and the man's assertiveness easily drew the answer out. "Screenwriting."

He nodded.

"And directing."

He raised his eyebrows. "Hmm, now that would be fun."

"Directing?"

"Being directed by you."

Her eyes widened at his brazen comment. She quickly finished off her Corona, attempting to calm her nerves. How on earth did this stranger manage to fluster her like that? Turn her inside out so easily?

She played with the label of her empty bottle as she fought to stay on solid ground, steering away from his innuendo. "Yeah, so directing is my thing. But of course, it's difficult to break into that biz, so I'm interested in all things film at the moment. Sound, camera, you name it. Screenwriting just fell into the mix because when you're a kid growing up wanting to direct, you needed material to direct so you could practice. I've got three full-length films under my belt. Indies, but still . . . and I start an internship with an amazing film crew on Monday." She stopped, realizing she was babbling.

"I'm intrigued." He took the bottle from her and set it on the grass next to his.

Without the bottle in her hands she felt vulnerable. And was he sitting closer than he was a moment ago? She returned to her jabber, unable to organize her thoughts. "It's really not that interesting. I'll be a production assistant, the lowest of—"

"That's not what I'm intrigued with," he interrupted, his voice husky.

Maddie met his eyes and saw a flicker of desire. He wanted her, it was obvious. Why not? For one night, why not live carefree?

She tilted her head toward him and steeled herself to tempt his seduction. "Then tell me, what is intriguing you?"

In one swift move, he had her pressed against the wall, his mouth hovering above her own. The rough stone behind her barely registered as she licked her lips in anticipation of the kiss she knew was coming.

But he didn't lean in. Instead, he brought his finger to her cheek and caressed it softly. She shuddered at the electric pulses that followed his light touch as he traced her jaw line. When he reached her chin, he lifted her face up to within an inch of his mouth. She felt his breath, hot and sweet, on her face. And then his mouth was on hers, tugging at her bottom lip, teasing her until she eagerly drew him in, wrapping her arms around his neck.

The kiss built, each stroke varying in pressure and intensity. Soft nips evolved into frenzied exploration, their tongues dancing, plunging deeply and hungrily. She savored the taste of him. A rush of pleasure rippled through her and she trembled under his attentive suckling.

His mouth released hers, traveled along her jaw and down her throat, his trail of kisses searing her skin. She clung to a fistful of his thick hair while he alternately nibbled and nuzzled her neck, stoking the fire in her core. When he raised his head to reclaim her lips, she glimpsed a greedy longing in his eyes.

He pressed tighter against her and Maddie could feel the bulge of his erection against her hip. She drew in a sharp breath, and he grinned against her mouth before recapturing it in his.

Desperate to feel more of his body against her own, for him to touch her more intimately, she arched her back, pushing her chest deeper into him. He read her cue and brought his hand down over her shirt to cup her breast. He stroked his thumb firmly over her nipple until it stood up under the contact.

"Damn," he said, his tone pleased.

For once, Maddie was grateful that her chest, though on the smaller side, was firm enough to wear built-in shelf tank tops without bras.

He continued his assault on her other breast. Maddie moaned, her hips rocking up instinctively looking for something more, something her rational brain would have told her was inappropriate to seek from a man she'd just met. Hell, she didn't even know his name. But her rational thought was lost within the flood of passion brought on by his equally fervent ardor.

She raised her hips again, and this time he responded by moving his hand to the inside of her upper leg. Softly, he caressed her thigh, journeying up slowly until he reached her panties. She gasped as his fingers moved underneath the elastic and found her taut bud. *Holy fuck!* She relaxed her legs to give him better access, letting him know she wanted more.

And man, did he deliver. With the pad of his finger, he stroked and swirled her tender flesh. Expertly, he increased the pressure to her swollen bundle of nerves until she was lost in glorious sensation. His mouth recaptured hers, swallowing her cry of pleasure as wave after wave of ecstasy crashed through her, and she shuddered uncontrollably.

His kissing slowed, and when she had calmed enough to resume a modicum of control, he pulled his lips away and rested his forehead against hers. "Would you join me somewhere even more private?" he asked, his engorged shaft still pressing hot against her hip.

Yes, yes, a million times yes! Even in the afterglow of her release, she desired him, longed to bring him to his own climax. Still panting, she opened her mouth to answer when a not-too-far-off voice interrupted her.

"Maddie! Maddie! Is that you?"

Bree.

Maddie turned from the handsome stranger and saw her near-naked friend peering at her from a few feet away.

"It *is* you!" Bree squealed. "I'm so, so, so, so happy I found you. I really think you need to take me—"

Bree's sentence was cut off as she vomited all over the lawn.

The man shook his head. "I see you're needed . . . Maddie, is it?"

"I . . . I'm . . ." She felt torn between responsibility and recklessness. She wanted to leave Bree to figure out her own mess rather than give up this magnificent creature in her arms. Maybe it would teach her a lesson. But Bree was in no condition to handle herself. Maddie sighed with frustration.

"I totally understand." He released her from his embrace. "I won't say I'm not disappointed—very disappointed—but I understand."

"I'm sorry. Truly sorry." She stood reluctantly, and glowered at Bree, now on her hands and knees sobbing. Maddie readjusted her skirt and took a step toward the pathetic creature.

"Wait." He grabbed her hand. "Can I see you sometime?"

Maddie tilted her head to stare back at him. "Really? You don't have to—"

"I know I don't. I want to."

She broke into a grin. "Give me your phone." He did and she typed her information into his contacts then handed it back.

"Thanks." He nodded toward Bree. "Let me help you with her."

"No," Maddie said quickly. His questioning look prompted her to explain. "It's just, I'd rather remember you right there, not fumbling around with my idiot drunk friend." Plus she couldn't subject him to dealing with Bree, especially with the hard-on she knew he still sported.

"Got it." He adjusted himself. "Just as long as you are remembering me."

"Oh, I could never forget." She sighed to accent her point. He winked and she turned again to leave when a thought crossed her mind. She spun back to him. "Hey, I don't know—"

"Micah," he said, accurately predicting what she was going to say. "I'm Micah."

"Nice to meet you, Micah." She rolled the name off her lips, relishing the feel of it in her mouth. Then she gave him one last longing look before she left to help Bree.

TWO

____

MICAH PRESTON COULDN'T DECIDE IF he was irritated or glad to be left waiting in Stu Steeling's front office for so long. On the one hand, he'd already been sitting there for more than half an hour. If this was any indication of the sort of attention he'd receive if Stu signed him as a client, he should bail now. Except Stu Steeling was the best publicity and image manager in Hollywood. Getting an appointment with him was nearly impossible, let alone getting a contract. And Stu had called Micah's agent for this meeting, which was why Micah didn't just up and walk out.

On the other hand, the wait gave him a chance to compose himself and focus before his interview.

Who was he kidding? He couldn't focus, not one bit. His mind kept returning to the night before and the leggy brunette who had gasped and moaned so beautifully at his touch. *Maddie.* He could still taste her on his tongue.

He hadn't wanted to attend the wrap party for his indie film. Not that he was averse to a good time, but his meeting with Stu was bright and early, and his agent had recommended that Micah stay sober and well-rested.

"You'll never get a chance like this with Steeling again," his agent Priscilla had said. "If he signs you, you will go from unknown indie films to big studio features. I swear it. He can make or break your acting career."

So Micah had done a quick walk around the wrap party, making sure he said goodbye to the people he wasn't sure he'd see again. Then, not wanting to be totally uncool and leave before midnight, he grabbed a beer and found a quiet spot to relax.

That was when he'd spotted her, making her way through the crowd with such purpose and direction, it seemed as if she was coming to join him. She'd stopped to survey the spectacle at the pool and he'd had a perfect view of her long legs and firm behind. An image of her bent naked in front of him had flashed through his mind and his cock was twitching before she even turned around. When he did see her face—her perfectly plump lips, her deep chocolate eyes—he knew he had to touch her, taste her, feel her against him. And that he did.

He closed his lids as he remembered.

It was a good thing their encounter was interrupted. He hadn't enjoyed going home blue-balled, but he'd been minutes away from taking her fast and hard in an empty bathroom in his producer's house, and she deserved something more than a hot round of Wham-Bam-Thank-You-Ma'am. Micah wanted to give her that something more, and he planned to take her out on a real date and end up in a bedroom, nice and proper.

Not for the first time that morning, he pulled out his phone and stared at her contact information, trying to decide if he'd seem too eager if he sent her a text. Hell, he didn't care if he sounded eager—he *was* eager—to know her, to touch her again.

He began composing a text when the receptionist called his name.

"Mr. Steeling will see you now."

Micah saved the draft and pocketed his phone. He'd have to save his fantasies for later—now it was time to focus on the biggest moment of his career.

A few minutes later, Micah found himself seated across from Stu Steeling, who perched behind an immaculate mahogany desk.

"I'm going to get right to the point," Stu said after they greeted each other. "I'm not much for small talk—it's a waste of time, and in this business, time is money. I've seen your work. You're talented, there's no question about that. And you're good-looking. Priscilla tells me you've been working with her for . . ." he paused to study a small notepad he'd pulled from his pocket. " . . . seven years. Most people would say you should have hit it big by now if you were ever going to, but I'm not most people. How old are you?"

"Twenty-four."

Stu's forehead creased. "Twenty-four is older than I like to start with clients, but it's not a deal-breaker. It just means that if you agree to work with me, you'll have to really commit to the guidelines I set out for you, and I mean commit, one-hundred percent, no fucking around. Building an image in Hollywood is not impossible, but it takes dedication and hard work. It's grueling and not recommended for the faint of heart. What do you say?"

"I'm not opposed to hard work." Micah had just finished three indie films in a period of just as many months, and was not any worse for the wear. He was tempted to agree to whatever Stu had in mind, no questions asked, but decided to play it cool and aloof. "Though I'd like to know exactly what you propose before I can commit to anything."

"Excellent—a young man interested in the details before signing on. You don't know how many people fail that part of this interview. "

Micah hid any reaction, grateful for he didn't jump on Stu's offer. He sat back in his chair, and waited for Stu to proceed.

"I'll expect you to work on project after project. There are no breaks when you're climbing the ladder. I will push you to audition, audition, audition. You'll be so tired, you'll want to kill me. But that should all go without saying."

"It does."

"Now here's the tough stuff: First and foremost, no drugs, no drunk driving, no excessive Lindsay Lohan-type partying. I don't care if you smoke a little weed now and then, but if you're ever caught with anything harder than that—and you're always caught—I'll drop you immediately. Clear?"

Easy peasy. "I'm clean. I'm not even a big drinker."

"Perfect. Next, you need to get to a voice teacher. You got the acting chops, but your speech isn't as clear as it could be. You have a bit of a mid-western dialect at times."

Micah hadn't heard that one in a while, but he knew where it came from. "I grew up in Kansas. I moved here at thirteen when my parents got divorced."

"Yeah, that's in your speech. It's actually somewhat endearing, but it doesn't work for every character and from what I've seen, you don't ever vary it."

"I'll get a voice teacher. I'm glad to learn more acting tools."

"Good. I've got someone I work with who's excellent. She'll come to you, so you can train while you're working." Stu made a note on his pad.

"We need to get you a personal trainer—the kind who's going to whip your ass and make you puke after every session. I know you're in pretty good shape now, but we need to see a six-pack when you take off your shirt, and from the footage I got from Dirk Davenport, you've only got a four-pack."

Micah knew that was coming. He hadn't worked as hard at the gym as he could have, but no one ever complained about his naturally well-built physique before. He also hadn't made it into a feature film yet. Maybe his body could use some work.

"Speaking of Davenport," Stu said without waiting for Micah to agree to a trainer, "he's a great director and I admire him. He knows how to cast pretty boys who can also act. But there's a reason he's never made it past his indie film status. Gay films are just not mainstream. You're not gay are you?"

"No," Micah said, thinking about Maddie again. "Definitely not."

"Perfect. Not that there's anything wrong with being gay. I'm all for equal rights and all that bullshit, but we've got to be honest—the actors who are hot right now are straight. I hope as much as anyone that that changes soon, but for now, that's the formula for success. Don't get me wrong, this gay indie is going to look great on your resume. Especially since you're straight—it shows you can act. But now we need to focus on your heterosexuality. Do you have a girlfriend/fiancé/wife?"

Micah wasn't sure how Stu wanted him to answer. He'd played gay on film—not anything porn-like, just some kissing. It was no big deal—he was acting. Maybe Stu wanted him to have a girlfriend to combat that image. But he didn't have a girlfriend at the moment. Not yet, anyway. He went for the truthful answer. "Nope, I'm completely single."

"Terrific! It's much easier to sell a single young actor than one that's attached. The women all want to believe they have a shot with you and the girlfriend thing just gets in the way. I'm not suggesting you cut out sex—you can have as many fuck flings as you like. Hell, that usually works in your favor. Every gossip rag is dying to tie you to someone. It's great publicity.

"Not that we can't work things out if you do hook up with someone long term. But, I'm telling you man-to-man, it's not easy to manage love and a career. Women mess with your time and emotions. They pout every time you have to spend weeks away on a shoot or heaven forbid, have to do an onscreen kiss. And you can never tell if they're into you or your money. Keep the strings unattached and you're better off. Just a suggestion from a guy who's been around."

Micah opened his mouth to comment, but didn't know what to say. Show biz and relationships . . . boy, did he know something about that. Stu's advice wasn't half bad.

"Anyway, kid, if you're serious, I'll sign you today. Keep your nose clean, work on your trade, don't get distracted, and I promise that I'll make you a star. I'm sure you know I've got an excellent track record and no one's ever been–"

He was interrupted by his phone ringing. He pushed the speaker button and the receptionist's voice filled the room. "Brad Licht is on the phone. He said to interrupt."

"Great, send the call back." Stu pressed the speaker button again and the receptionist was gone. "Micah, I have to take this. It'll be just a minute."

Stu picked up the phone's handset and pushed the flashing button on his console before Micah could agree. "Hey, Brad. What's up?"

Micah was curious about Stu's conversation. Brad Licht was a famous actor and client of Stu's. Witnessing Stu's interaction with him would be a great indicator of what kind of relationships he had with his clients.

But instead, Micah's mind wandered to Stu's advice on women. It wasn't a new thought—Micah had toyed with the idea of remaining single before. He'd witnessed his parents' marriage go up in flames when his mother decided to run off to California, hoping to get a break into the biz herself. She didn't succeed as she'd hoped, and she always blamed her ex for holding her back when she was younger.

And though she never said it out loud, Micah knew that being a mother had held her back as well. She'd been a good actress. She could have made a name for herself if she'd had fewer responsibilities and obligations. Eventually she gave up and threw her energy into Micah and his career instead.

Micah's dad never got over the split. He pined for his wife until his death of a heart attack at forty-eight. And as much as it pained Micah, he knew his father never approved of his son's decision to be an actor because of all the grief it had caused their family.

Yeah, Stu made a good argument. No strings, no burdens—it was definitely the way to go. Even though he sometimes yearned for a more substantial relationship, Micah could be happy as a playboy.

Of course, there was Maddie. He'd just met her and, hell, he knew hardly anything about her, but his attraction to her ran deep. He was certain that if he saw her again he'd want to see her again and again and again. She couldn't be just a fuck fling, as Stu had put it, though fantasies of fucking her kept dancing through his mind. It would be best if he cut things off before they went any further. Leave it as the hot memory it was.

He pulled his cell out of his pocket, and reread the draft of the text he had composed to Maddie. *"I'm remembering your moans. When can I make you mo—"*

Now, he deleted the unfinished message. Then, he went to his contacts and scrolled to the info she'd entered the night before: *"Maddie from the party, 310–555–0557."* He paused before he moved his finger over the delete button and pressed it.

"Are you sure you want to delete this contact?" his screen flashed. He hesitated. Maybe he was overreacting. Just because his parents hadn't

worked out . . .

"Christ, Brad, divorced?" Stu said into the phone. Until now, Stu hadn't said much and his sudden outburst drew Micah's attention. "I knew that chick was just after your money."

Stu paused. "Look, I'm real sorry to hear that. I'll get Pam to spin it to the press however you want me to. It's funny, I was just saying to another client that relationships in Hollywood are tough."

Stu gave a knowing wink and Micah's mind was made up. He looked back at his phone, still flashing: *"Are you sure you want to delete this contact?"*

Micah pushed *"Yes."* And Maddie from the party was erased from his phone. Erased from his life.

SEVEN YEARS LATER

THREE

____

MADDIE STEPPED OFF THE ESCALATOR at Denver International Airport and followed the crowd in front of her to baggage claim. She'd never been to this airport, but she easily found carousel four where the monitors showed her flight's luggage would arrive soon. While she waited, she pulled her phone from her purse and turned off the airplane mode. Immediately it buzzed with a text.

"Tell me when u get in. Meet ur driver by the West Terminal doors."

It was from Bree. Maddie responded. *"Just arrived."* She pushed send and wondered for the hundredth time that morning, how did she get talked into this again? She replayed Bree's frantic call from the day before in her mind.

"We need you, Maddie," Bree had said. "The assistant camera operator broke his tailbone and needs surgery so we need another assistant pronto for location. We're already six weeks into shoot. I know you swore off working with Beaumont, and I'd never ask you, but Adam only wants you. You can totally name your price and you'll get it."

Even though more than six years had passed, Maddie still felt the sting of the Joss Beaumont disaster that had effectively ended all her hopes of being a Hollywood director. Thank goodness she had mad skills in other areas of film, though he never treated her with respect again. On set, he treated her like his own private valet and coffee runner and then blamed her for not being around when he needed her. He might be one of the country's top directors, but as far as she was concerned, he was an ass.

Despite her dislike of Beaumont, Maddie was very fond of Adam LaForgeon, one of Beaumont's regular camera operators. Old enough to be her father, Adam had taken her under his wing on the first film she'd done as an intern seven years before. He'd stood by her through what Maddie liked to now refer to as the Beaumont Fiasco. Soon she was working as Adam's main assistant, joining him on all his projects. She would have been on this shoot from the beginning if Beaumont hadn't been directing.

Adam respected Maddie's hatred of the pompous director and would have never requested her unless he was desperate. He'd stuck by her when she was desperate. How could she turn him down?

And she owed Bree, too. Maddie was the main reason Bree worked as Beaumont's personal assistant. Bree shared Maddie's dislike of the asshole, but she belonged to the keep-your-enemies-closer camp. She claimed that working for "the fucker" might help Maddie. Besides, since sleeping her way to the top hadn't worked as well as Bree'd planned—a series of nude photos and an accidental adult film ended that—working for a big-time director seemed a great way to get into the Hollywood scene from another angle. Unfortunately, several years later she only had P.A. on her legit resume and Maddie remained a camera assistant.

So here Maddie was, less than twenty-four hours after Bree's phone call, at the Denver airport waiting to claim her hastily packed suitcase with absolutely no information about the movie she'd be working on except that it was midway through production.

The carousel whirred into motion and Maddie's burgundy suitcase with the rainbow ribbon on the zipper pull was the first bag to sail down the ramp. She grabbed it, pulled up the handle and wheeled it behind her while she looked for her transportation. She spotted her driver near the doors to parking holding a flimsy white piece of paper with the name *Madalyn Bauers* scrawled across it. He had short clean-cut blonde hair, a baby smooth face and was built like a wrestler. Young. Definitely an intern or production assistant.

"Hey," Maddie said as she approached him. Her phone buzzed in her hand, probably with a response from Bree, but she ignored it. "You're looking for me. I'm Madalyn Bauers. Well, Maddie."

"Then you are correct; I am looking for you," the young man said. He held out his hand in greeting. "I'm Sam, and I'm your ride."

"Awesome." Maddie didn't miss the innuendo. "I can't believe you went to this much trouble. I could have taken a cab."

"Honestly, I'm here to pick up one of the actors. He landed about fifteen minutes before you. You just got lucky with your timing." Sam gave a sly smile. "Or I got lucky."

Oh cute, he was flirting. She responded with a hesitant smile.

"I just gotta let the crew know I got you and then I'll grab your bags."

While Sam made his phone call, Maddie read Bree's text. *And all is good?*

So far, Maddie replied. Pretending to still look at her phone, she covertly checked out her driver. *Hmm, not bad.* Good-looking, but too young. And blonds weren't usually a hot-button for her. But still, there was possibility.

"Okay, all set. I can take your bag for you." Sam pocketed his phone and reached for Maddie's carry-on.

"Oh, thanks. Where's the actor?"

"He's around here. Went to get a coffee or a newspaper or something. He should be easy to spot." Sam craned his neck looking around the terminal. "Yeah, there he is. Looks like he got noticed." He motioned with his head toward a group of people a dozen or so yards away. "You know talent, they always have an entourage."

Maddie followed Sam's gesture. She could see the back of the actor wearing tight jeans and a casual blue sports jacket. Damn, the jacket obscured any ass-checking, but she'd bet money his booty was capital-F fine. He was signing autographs for four women surrounding him. Nearby she saw a muscleman, arms crossed, wearing sunglasses, jeans, and a T-shirt. He appeared aloof, but Maddie noticed how he watched the crowd. *So this guy warrants a bodyguard.* "Who is it anyway?" she asked.

Before Sam could answer, the actor and his bodyguard turned away from the groupies and started toward them. Maddie's heart began to race. Simultaneously her stomach dropped. She knew that wavy dark brown hair, those deep-set blue eyes, and those perfectly formed lips.

"Micah Preston," Sam and Maddie said in unison.

Wow. She was stunned.

It had been forever since she'd thought of Micah Preston as anything more than a Hollywood icon. Yes, he'd transfixed her in their brief encounter years ago and she'd dared to hope she would see him again for more than a week after that. When he didn't call, she was disappointed, but what could she do besides move on? She hadn't even known his full name.

Nearly a year after their encounter, she'd come face-to-face with him on the cover of her *Entertainment Weekly*. *Micah Preston, Break-Out Sensation*, it had read. Then he was everywhere, on every magazine cover, in every movie. As hot and handsome as he'd been the night they met, his face on the screen sending Maddie's heart into palpitations.

But seeing Micah everywhere in such a different context than the one she knew him from made it easy to distance herself from him. And the more she learned about him, the less she cared for him. Especially disgusting was the fact that Micah Preston was a playboy. In every picture the paparazzi took, he had a different stunningly gorgeous broad on his arm. Though Maddie had been easily seduced by him, she'd never done anything like that before or since. Apparently it was Micah's M.O. Typical actor. And she, like most technical crew, had learned early in her career to stay clear of the talent. Their egos generally left little room for anyone else.

Still, as Micah and his bodyguard approached her, a strange nervousness overtook her. She usually didn't care much about making an impression, but she wished she'd had time to look in a mirror. She was in stupid sweats, a ratty tank top, and no bra—her comfy traveling clothes, for heaven's sake. And now she was going to be face-to-face with a man who'd made her orgasm with his fingers. Would he be embarrassed that he'd hooked up with the likes of her? And what would she say to him?

How on earth would she manage to not sound like a bumbling idiot? *Lord, strike me down now.*

"Hey, man," Sam said. "Looks like we're ready to go. This is—"

"Madalyn Bauers," Micah finished, his eyes on her. At least, she thought his eyes were on her. She couldn't quite tell through the sunglasses he had slid onto his face after leaving his fans.

Maddie's heart flip-flopped at his attention and the way he said her name. It rolled off his tongue like music. "Um, hi."

"You two already know each other?" Sam asked.

Micah shook his head and pointed to the sign Sam was still holding with Madalyn's name scrawled on it. "I just assumed."

Maddie swallowed. He didn't remember her. Most goddamned adventurous night of her life and he didn't even remember her. Sure he'd had a million girls since her, but she thought he'd at least think there was something familiar about her. *Well, that sucks.*

Refusing to show her disappointment, she held up her chin and thrust out her hand. "Actually, it's Maddie. Pleasure to finally work with you, Mr. Preston."

"Mr. Preston? It's Micah." He grasped her hand firmly. "And that guy is, Fu—um, Chris, my bodyguard."

Maddie carefully kept the shock of Micah's touch from her face. And did he hold her hand a little too long, or was that her imagination? Whichever, it felt nice.

"Micah it is." He let go of her hand and a fleeting thought of never washing it again crossed her mind.

What am I, a school girl? She was totally being ridiculous. Yes, seeing Micah again made her dizzy and warm in all the right places, but he was nothing more than a random boy who'd felt her up years ago at a wild party and never called afterwards. Nothing to be excited about now.

She turned to Sam, avoiding Micah's face as she pivoted. "Are we ready to go? I'd love to settle in and get to the set. I'm sure Adam could use me as soon as possible."

"Sure thing. Let's motor. I'm not parked too far."

On the walk to short-term parking, Maddie stayed with Sam so she wouldn't have to watch Micah's backside tease her. Behind her, she heard him on his phone, but she couldn't help putting a little sway into her own stride in case he might be eyeing her.

"Ha ha, got some fries with that shake?" Chris asked, strolling up behind her.

Crap. She blushed.

He leaned in so only she could hear him. "Don't worry about it. Common occurrence with Micah. I don't even think some chicks notice they do it."

She didn't know how to respond. "Thanks for, uh, pointing out my shimmy, Chris."

"No prob. And everyone calls me Fudge."

"Fudge. Awesome."

When they reached the vehicle, Maddie caught a glimpse of her reflection in the window as Sam loaded the bags into the trunk of the blue SUV. Her long brown hair was piled in a mess on top of her head. Her sunglasses, thankfully, hid the circles under her eyes and the red spot on the side of her nose that she knew from experience was the beginning of a zit. She looked, well, jet-lagged. She removed the scrunchee from her hair and finger-combed through her tresses before pulling it into a ponytail, a minor improvement. Maybe it was best that Micah didn't remember her.

"Here, I got that for you." Sam pulled open the back door for her.

"Thanks." Chris, er, Fudge, had already taken the front passenger seat. That left Maddie in back with Micah. *Shit.* She should have moved faster. Sighing, she climbed into the backseat and let Sam shut her door.

As soon as she was seated, Maddie pulled out her phone. Bree was so going to get it. She knew all about Maddie's encounter with Micah seven years before, even though Maddie hadn't told her initially. Leave it to Bree's crazy eye for all-things-hot-guy-related to spot Micah in a movie trailer sometime later.

"Didn't you totally get it on with him at our graduation party?" she'd said.

So much for Bree being too drunk to realize what was going on.

Maddie had spilled the details—all the details—how he made her body sing, how she hadn't known his full name, how he hadn't called afterward. Bree knew full well that Maddie would have wanted to know he'd be on this shoot.

Maddie's text said it all. *"Micah freakin Preston???!!!??? You are so dead . . ."*

She dropped her phone onto her lap and leaned against the passenger door, leaving as much space as possible between her and the spot where Micah would sit. He slid into the backseat next to her, his thigh muscles bulging through his tight pants. God, he was positively scrumptious. No wonder half the women in America had a crush on him.

"Okay, I'm getting in the car now so I've gotta go, Mom." Micah wrapped up his phone call. "Uh huh. Bye."

Damn. Now she might actually have to talk to him. At least she no longer had to wonder who was on the other side of his phone call. Not because she was envious, just curious.

Pathetic, Maddie. Real pathetic.

Micah pocketed his phone and stretched out, his limbs landing only a few inches from her body. She felt the warmth exuding from his body, and suddenly the backseat was ten times more cramped than it had a minute before. Hopefully it would be a short trip to the hotel. "How long is the drive?"

"About an hour," Sam replied, starting the car.

Maddie let out a slow breath. A whole hour. Maybe she could pretend to sleep. She leaned her head against the window. A sudden buzzing in her lap made her jump.

She felt Micah's eyes on her as she read her text. *"If I told you, it wouldn't have been as fun right now."*

"It's not at all fun right now!"

Bree's next text came almost instantly. *"Why????"*

"He doesn't remember me." She paused, looking at the words before she pushed send. Did he really forget her? Did he have no inkling of familiarity?

She risked a full glance at him and found he was still staring at her. At her look, he perched his sunglasses on top of his head. "So, who are you?"

Yeah, he really didn't remember her. Why should he? She was a nobody. She wondered if she would have remembered him if he hadn't become Mr. Superstar. Yes, she would. He was totally unforgettable. And he knew how cool he was. He'd gotten cocky. A lot of the famous actors did. Too bad.

She hit send on her phone as she answered him. "Uh . . . Maddie."

"Right. Maddie-not-Madalyn- Bauers. Got that. I meant what are you doing on the show? I don't remember seeing you on the set in L.A." He scanned her bedraggled body. "And believe me, I would have noticed."

"Oh." Maddie blushed. Cocky, but still had the charm. Self-conscious, she tugged on her tank top. "No, I wasn't in L.A. I'm taking over as first camera assistant."

"Cool. You're much better looking than Carson. What happened to him anyway?"

Sam answered for her. "Carson got here a day before shoot started and broke his tailbone trying to do some fancy dirt biking."

"Ha, that totally sounds like him," Fudge said. "That crazy motherfucker."

Sam made eye contact with Maddie in his rearview mirror. "Maddie's supposed to be an amazing camera assistant. Adam requested her. Had nothing but good things to say."

She felt warm from the praise. "I'm right here, you know. Don't need to talk about me in third person." She reluctantly slid her own sunglasses off and faced Micah. "I'm Adam's usual assistant. He has to say nice things about me."

She studied him. In the years since she'd last seen him he'd changed his look often depending on his film roles. Now he sported the scruffy-Micah look—sexy stubble covered his face and his hair was longer and unkempt in a totally hot way. Her fingers curled into the upholstery as she imagined how they'd feel running through his hair.

Micah furrowed his brow. "How come you weren't here from the beginning?"

"I had some personal issues with . . . someone . . . working on the show." In this business you couldn't badmouth anyone without serious repercussions.

He leaned toward her. "Did those issues resolve somehow?"

Her body ignited from his close proximity. *Stupid female hormones.* Beaumont seemed much less of a problem now that she had Micah to cope with. She simultaneously wanted to scoot nearer and shrink into the car's interior. She did neither. "I'm learning to deal."

He looked at her carefully, then reached over and casually pushed aside a stray hair from her face, his finger brushing her cheek. "Hmm, let me know how that goes."

Maddie shivered under his touch. "Thanks," she managed to whisper. Was he hitting on her? Maybe he hit on all girls the minute he met them. He did have a reputation. Or maybe she was just wishing he was hitting on her.

No, she wasn't wishing he was hitting on her. That would be trouble. He was just so attractive it was hard to remember that.

She needed a distraction. "What exactly is this movie about, anyway? I didn't get a chance to read a script."

"It's great," Sam said. "You'll love it. It's a heist movie—g"

"It's a romance," Micah interrupted, his eyes never leaving Maddie. "There's kissing."

"—and a romance," Sam conceded. "A bunch of friends take on a small mountain gambling town, then have to hide in the great outdoors."

Fudge looked up from whatever he was doing on his iPhone. "It's Affleck's *The Town* meets the west."

Micah shook his head. "It is not."

"Whatever, dude." Fudge pulled a set of earphones out of his jeans pockets and stuck them into his phone. "I'm gonna nap. Is that cool?"

"I'm sure we'll be safe on the ride from DIA to Golden." Micah bent his leg and Maddie realized if she relaxed just a little, their knees would bump. "Besides, the windows are tinted. No one can see in."

She couldn't help herself; she relaxed, silently gasping at the light contact.

Did he respond by moving his leg against hers? No, he'd only bumped her as he bent over to fiddle with his bag. The brush sent tingles through her lower belly. She had to close her eyes to regain focus.

Unaware of the desire running rampant in the backseat, Sam continued with his lowdown of the film. "Most of the cast already arrived. Heather Wainwright. And Pierce Bartlett and Bray Morgan. And Josh Gibbs plays the cop."

Maddie couldn't pass up the opportunity to turn Micah's earlier question back on him. "So who are you?"

He smiled. "Touché. I'm the love interest, of course." He tapped his finger on her knee as he said "of course." Even through her sweat pants, Maddie felt the electricity of his touch.

"Of course." Maddie's traitor face returned the smile. The glimmer in his eye made her warm between the thighs. She blinked and looked away, hoping her flushed face didn't give away her indecent thoughts.

What the crap was she doing? Even if he wasn't flirting, she was, and she shouldn't be. She couldn't get sucked into Micah again, even though the idea of sucking and Micah fit deliciously together in her mind.

She tried to stay on topic. "Good cast," she said, though she couldn't even recall who Sam had mentioned. *Focus, focus.*

"They're excellent." Sam's upbeat attitude seemed to be his signature trait. "Great cast, awesome script. They shot all the interiors in L.A. and now we're doing the exteriors in Golden. It's beautiful up there. " Sam met her eyes again in the rear view mirror. "Not the most beautiful thing I've seen all day, but still pretty breathtaking."

Oh no, could she please have some wine with the cheese? Still, Sam could prove to be a way to keep her mind off the tall, dark and, oh-my-God-hot specimen sitting next to her. And he was definitely flirting, while Micah was probably just being Micah. She gave Sam a small wink. "You'll have to show me around."

His face lit up. "I will."

Micah pulled his leg away—deliberately? She couldn't tell, but his retreat blew through her like a cold draft. He covered a yawn with his hand and pulled down the armrest between their seats and closed his eyes. "Sam, is it? Are we all staying in the same hotel?"

"No. You and the other actors are up the mountain a bit. The rest of us are staying in a Comfort Inn."

"Good," Micah said, his eyes still closed. "I prefer the cast and crew separated. I hope you're dropping me off first."

"Certainly." The ever-cheerful Sam seemed only slightly downtrodden by the superiority in Micah's tone.

Maddie's insides echoed the same disappointment. Who knew Micah Preston was such a jerk? Had he been that guy when she'd first met him? Or had he become that way with fame and money? Whichever, he was bad news. Now if someone could convince her body . . .

Her phone buzzed with a text. *"He doesn't remember u? So no replays of your night together?"*

"Not a chance. So over him."

It was only partially a lie. He still made her insides hot and bothered like no one had in a long time, but he was cocky, a player, and had forgotten her. Three strikes against him. Maddie had never been a sports fan, but she was pretty sure that three strikes meant you were out.

FOUR

HER.

Even with his eyes closed he still saw her face.

Micah had spotted her talking to Sam by baggage claim and, though it took him a moment, he knew there was something familiar about her big dark eyes, high cheekbones and long legs, hidden beneath her baggy sweats. And that perky bosom of hers that peeked out above the low neckline of her tank top—he'd definitely fondled those tits before. But when?

He was so distracted trying to place her that he hadn't even minded signing autographs for fans. He'd needed those couple of minutes to gather himself.

It wasn't until he'd seen her up close, her hair all mussed and cheeks flushed like a woman after a night of pleasure, that he suddenly remembered her. *Maddie from the party.* Oh, yeah. That chick.

If he remembered correctly, that party was before he'd even signed with Stu. He had to be careful or she'd want to hook up again. Women from his past didn't ever want anything except his fame and fortune. Hell, women in his present only wanted that. He decided it best to pretend he didn't remember her at all.

She remembered him, though. It was obvious. Recognition spread over her face the minute he said her name. Her eyes glimmered with hopefulness.

Then the spark left and letdown settled on her features. He could have thrown her a bone then, given her a hint that he knew her, but he didn't.

Yeah, he was an asshole.

Then he was stuffed in the SUV with her, drowning in her unique smell, and memories of their evening together crashed over him like a giant wave—her tentative flirting, his smooth moves, that apple-pear body spray she used, the one she still wore now. He hadn't done anything big at that point. She hadn't even known he was an actor. And still, she'd let him kiss her and touch her. Very intimately.

Was she the last woman he'd kissed before he'd become known? Too many years and women had passed for him to be sure. Maybe she wasn't, but she reminded him of that time. A time before he doubted the sincerity of every compliment, when his pick-up lines were meant to start relationships, not just get some for the night.

Now no pick-up lines were necessary at all. He could bag a girl with a flash of his famous smile. And though having models, co-stars, and willing fans lined up at his bedroom door was out-of-this-world awesome, it got boring. Hot sex wasn't the same as just talking and flirting and connecting with a woman. How long had it been since he'd done that?

What if he could recapture those days? With her. With Maddie. They still had chemistry. He could cut the sexual tension in the backseat with a knife. He felt her lean into his leg. He got it. He wanted to touch her too. And he did—a brush of her cheek, a hand on her knee. It wouldn't take much to get her alone and underneath him.

But then she flirted with that overly chipper butt-kisser Sam, and he remembered—he wasn't *that* guy. He wasn't the guy who was in it for the long haul. Micah was a movie star. He was into girls for a minute. He couldn't recapture the days before his fame and that was the price he'd paid. Even if he tried to get involved with a woman, he could never trust her intentions with him. He'd chosen this life, made a very deliberate decision of career over love.

And getting tangled up with a girl like Maddie Bauers, a girl from the days when he *was* that guy, wasn't what he needed.

What he needed was to get to his room and take a cold shower. He crossed his hands low in his lap to hide his stiff bulge, and shut his eyes, attempting sleep. Or, at least the pretense.

"Hey, Micah." Fudge paused. "Dude?"

His bodyguard's insistent tone pulled Micah out of his pretend sleep. "What?"

"Look out your window. The mountains are dope. Why do we only come out here in the winter?"

"Because you think sliding down a mountain on a surfboard is fun." But he leaned forward to look at the scenery through the front window. Fudge was right, it was gorgeous. "We'll do some sight-seeing while we're here, okay?"

"You should invite Lulu."

He swallowed a sigh. "Maybe." Lulu was his mother. Lucille actually, but he and his friends had always referred to her as Lulu.

"Come on, she'd love it out here."

"I'll think about it." She would love it. His mother had a thing for nature and Micah flew her out to many of his more picturesque locations.

It was just that, though he adored his mom, she also brought him down. She'd remained single since she'd flown off to California when he was twelve, and Micah worried about her being alone. He couldn't help but worry she was sad and, maybe lonely.

Sometimes it made him question his own decision to be alone.

But then he'd remind himself that he was nothing like Lulu. She'd given up love for a career and it hadn't worked out. Micah's sacrifice *had* worked out. He had the life most people only dreamed of. He had the life *he'd* dreamed of. He didn't want for anything.

Well, almost anything.

He snuck a peek behind him at Maddie. He'd moved nearer to her to look out the window, but didn't have the luck of brushing against her again. Now he saw why. She was leaning against her window, her beautiful body pressed against the door, away from him. Thick irritation emanated from her like a barrier between them. It was so thick it bordered on loathing.

Good. Hate him. It would make it easier to avoid her if she were also avoiding him.

He sat back in his seat and closed his eyes again. It was simpler now to fight any urge to make amends with Maddie. Now that he saw how turned off by him she was, he had no desire to ease the tension between them.

He closed his eyes again and succeeded in putting her out of his mind until they pulled up in front of his hotel. As Sam retrieved his luggage from the trunk, Micah stole one more glance at the brunette beauty beside him before he stepped out of the car. Only then did he realize that Maddie's expression didn't read as angry—it read as hurt.

Aw, shit. That wasn't what he was going for at all.

He should have left it at that, painful as it was to see her distressed. But he couldn't stand it. He swallowed. "Hey, Maddie Bauers." She looked up at him, her eyes big with curiosity. "I got to know Adam when we were filming in L.A. He's the best cameraman I've ever worked with. You must be pretty stellar to get his recommendation. Welcome aboard."

"Thanks," she said softly.

That wasn't so bad. He remained professional, yet seemed to lift her spirits. Problem was, the smile she gave him had his cock jumping again. He shifted, hoping she didn't notice as he stepped from the car.

Fudge joined Micah at the bellhop station. He chuckled at the star as Micah watched the SUV pull away down the mountain.

"What?" Micah asked.

"Nothing." But the amusement remained on his face.

Damn. Fudge knew Micah too well. He was much more than an employee. The two had met in middle school when Fudge stood up for Micah after a bully had teased him about a commercial he'd appeared in. They'd been good friends ever since. Half the reason Micah employed him was for the company. The life of a famous Hollywood bachelor wasn't as friend-filled as many people thought.

Not much later, Micah tipped the bellhop and closed the door behind him in his room. He threw his jacket over a chair and crossed to the large windows. The small town didn't have the luxury hotels Micah usually stayed in, but the view from his room—a breathtaking landscape of mountains and wildflowers—couldn't be topped. He took a moment to memorize the scene, wondering if Fudge had a similar view from his room across the hall.

Maybe he would invite Lulu. She'd go ga-ga over this place.

And maybe being with her would make them both feel less lonely.

With a sigh, he drew the fire curtains. Heavy window coverings were one of his best friends. They shut out zoom lenses and the prying eyes of fans.

He rummaged through his carry-on for his iPad and stretched out on his king-sized bed. Checking his email, he found his schedule for the next day. Seven a.m. call time. That left almost thirteen hours before he would see Maddie again.

Had he really just calculated that? Yes, yes he had.

He ran his hand over his stubbly chin, deciding how to handle his Maddie thoughts. The night was still young. He could try to find a pretty young fan in the hotel bar, someone willing to suck off a star just so she could brag to her friends.

Or he could try to find *her*.

No, bad idea. Instead, he used her newly discovered last name to look for her on Facebook. He didn't have an account himself, just a fan page his publicist maintained, but he knew his way around the site.

He found Maddie's profile easily. Her privacy settings didn't allow him to see her wall, but her photos were set for public view. There were only two, but they were enough. The first was a simple headshot, her long gorgeous brown hair pulled back in a ponytail, her smile slight and professional. This was the one she currently had set as her profile picture.

The other, though, was the one that Micah zoomed in on. It was a candid shot taken with the ocean as a backdrop. Maddie held her loose hair out of her face with one hand while the other hung loosely at her side. The modest tankini showed off her body and verified what Micah had suspected, that her legs were gorgeous and never ending.

His dick throbbed as he ran his finger over the screen, tracing the curve of her breast. He pretended he could remember the feel of it under his hands, her nipple taut against the thin fabric of her top. How she'd moaned and responded to his touch.

God, it was too much. He propped the iPad on the pillow next to him and undid his jeans, releasing his straining erection. With long strokes from root to crown, he fisted his pulsing shaft, fantasizing it was her mouth sucking and taking him in. Slowly she would tease him, licking along the thick nerve that ran the length of his penis. Then she'd curve her lips tightly around his tip and draw him in, inch by inch, her hands massaging his balls as she bobbed her head up and down.

He closed his eyes, imagining his busy hand was tangled in her hair. With a low grunt, hot fluid spurted over his fist, and still he pumped, not wanting the fantasy to end, while he came and came and came.

Afterwards, he basked in the pleasure of release, knowing from experience it would soon fade to a lonely ache. He looked at Maddie's picture one more time, then turned his tablet off and made his way to clean up.

In the bathroom, as the dullness crept in, he stared at his reflection and groaned.

Fuck.

He'd spent the last seven years at the top of his game, focused on his career. He'd been tempted into love by the hottest women, offered the best drugs and the sweetest of sins, and he'd always resisted. No hesitation or doubt.

But now he faced six weeks on set with a woman who once upon a time didn't care about what or who he was.

Maddie Bauers just might be his undoing.

FIVE

MICAH SAT IN HIS DIRECTOR'S chair, script in hand, trying his damnedest to get his lines down for the day's scene. He was usually great at memorization, but in the three days since he'd arrived on set in Colorado, his concentration had gone to shit. He blamed it on the mountains, told Beaumont he hadn't adjusted to the altitude yet.

But it was her. Maddie was there, everywhere, every day. Her job as camera assistant kept her on set at all times. Focus puller was the term for her crew position. Focus puller was right—she pulled his focus any time she was within a hundred feet of him. Most the time she was closer than that. Her job kept her near the camera, and since the camera was always in his face, so was she.

Maddie barely acknowledged Micah while she worked. She stayed out of the way during blocking and took all her camera measurements with the stand-ins. If she noticed he had missed a mark, she informed Adam instead of telling Micah directly, which was what she should do. And it was what he had wanted. But it drove him crazy—having her so close, yet so ambivalent about him.

Not that he was going out of his way to talk to her either. It took all his willpower not to find an excuse to touch her or strike up a casual conversation, but he'd managed so far. To the detriment of his concentration.

He looked at his watch for the fourth time in ten minutes. His co-star,

Heather, was exactly forty minutes late for call. She had a reputation for being unreliable, but this was the first time in several weeks that she'd blown call time. It was unprofessional, and a lesser star would have been blacklisted a long time ago. But this was Heather Wainwright, the top female actress in Hollywood. She could do whatever she wanted.

He sighed as he turned back to his script. He really wasn't that pissed at the blonde diva—he didn't mind the delay. He needed to work on his lines. No, his irritation came from the brunette camera assistant.

Without lifting his head, he glanced sideways toward her. She was in video village, the area set up with monitors from all the cameras. Beaumont, Adam, and Joe, the show's assistant director, stood talking with her, probably planning what to do about the scenes they were supposed to be filming. He smiled at her outfit, black jeans and a tank top, a black button-down shirt over it. The black absorbed light rather than reflected it onto the actors. It was supposed to help her fade into the darkness, but Micah didn't think Maddie could fade into anything. She shone, vibrant and gorgeous at all times, no matter what she wore. It surprised him that every guy wasn't falling all over her. She was hands-down the most beautiful woman on the set. Probably the most beautiful woman in the state, and no one, except that yuppie assistant Sam, seemed to notice.

Christ, he was absolutely pathetic. Pining over a woman? Maybe he should be making romantic comedies. Or movies for Lifetime, since he totally seemed to have lost his balls.

"Chin up!" Darla, his makeup artist, fluttered over him, applying powder to his face. "Sugar, you keep sweating off all your makeup. Why don't you sit under the tent where it's cooler until they're ready to shoot your scene?"

He shook his head. That's where video village was—where Maddie was. "No, I'm fine here."

"But you're getting too much sun, sweetie." Darla mothered Micah, which was why he liked working with her.

Today it irritated him. "I said I'm fine."

"He can't stand to be too near the hottie that's assisting Adam," Fudge said. "He's gotta bit of a crush."

"What the—? That's not true."

"Then I guess the hard-on you've been sportin' since the airport is from that cheerleader assistant, Sam." Fudge flipped a page casually in the magazine he was reading.

"You've been checking out my dick, man? That's just weird." Of course Fudge would have noticed Micah's behavior regarding Maddie. But he didn't have to bring it up in front of his makeup artist. Better yet, he didn't have to bring it up at all.

Darla laughed. "Oh, honey, you don't need to be embarrassed. I've been working with you for five years now and this is the first time I've ever seen you so unfocused. It's a nice change. You should go talk to her."

"It's not—" Micah cut himself off and then started again at a more reasonable volume. "It's not the girl. It's the altitude."

"Whatever you need to tell yourself, sweetie." Amusement sparkled in Darla's eyes.

Fudge tossed his magazine on the grass. "What I don't understand is why you don't just hit it and get it over with."

Now that was a good question.

Micah thought about it as Darla patted more powder over his face. Why the hell not? They had the chemistry. So she reminded him of the past. That didn't have to interfere with his present. And he was already distracted by her. Wasn't that what his no-strings rule was meant to avoid?

But he'd already been an ass to her. Who knew if she'd even be receptive? All right. If she showed some interest then he'd consider pursuing it.

"By the way, that girl jogs by the hotel every morning," Fudge said. "Her hotel's about two miles away. It's funny she chooses that same route."

Hmm. That sure made it sound like she was interested.

"I need more coffee." Micah stood, rolling his script under his arm and grabbing his still half-full coffee mug from his cup holder. It was a lame excuse, but he couldn't bring himself to say outright that he planned to corner Maddie.

"I can get it for you," Darla offered.

"No, I'm getting it." Micah heard Darla and Fudge chuckling at him as he made his way toward the main tent. Yeah, who was he kidding? They knew where he was headed.

He didn't have far to walk before reaching the tent. Generally only a few members of the cast and crew hung out in the video village, but since the show was at a standstill without Heather, more people were around than usual.

Seeing that Maddie was still conversing with Beaumont, Adam, and Joe, Micah slipped behind her to the coffee center. A whiff of apples caught on the breeze, a scent he'd learned to recognize as Maddie's. Was it her shampoo, her lotion? It drove him mad. He glanced at her, his cock stirring at the view of her curvy hips and round behind. God, she was beautiful. He could strip her naked and fuck her right then and there. Maybe that would help his concentration.

The sound of his name pulled him from his lustful thoughts.

"We could shoot Micah's close-ups," Joe said. "That could keep us rolling at least."

"Maybe that's the way to go," Beaumont said. Then, noticing Micah, he said, "Hey, Preston. We're going to shoot your CUs now."

His stomach clenched, hoping his lines were ready. On the bright side, he'd be on set with Maddie.

"That's fine," Maddie said, "but I need to get new focus calculations first from the blocking change you just made."

Micah could let a stand-in do the set-up like he usually did and continue working on his lines, but he'd decided he wanted to be near Maddie, and be near Maddie he would be. "Sounds good. I'm ready."

For the first time since he'd joined them, Maddie acknowledged him. Her dark eyes glimmered as they connected with his gaze. "Oh, you don't need to . . ."

He winked. "It's no problem. Let's go."

———— ◆ ————

HE'D WINKED AT HER.

One wink and her knees were jelly as they walked to the set. Thank God the A.D. had his ear while they walked so Maddie could give all her attention to putting one foot in front of the other.

Though she'd been disappointed that he'd forgotten her and disgusted by his superiority complex, the days that had followed had shown Micah to be less of a dick than she'd thought after the car ride. He actually seemed charming and an all-around good guy. But not to her. He hadn't even spoken to her, but she'd watched him interact with the other actors and crew.

A couple of times she'd caught him eyeing her. Was that burning, hungry stare her imagination? She hadn't noticed him ogling any other female crew members. But maybe that was because she didn't want to notice.

What she wanted was to hate him, but working with him had only brought about a crush. A silly, stupid, fangirl-type crush. Her insides got all twisty and her palms got sweaty every time she was within ten feet of him. She'd found the only way to deal with her unwanted emotions was to avoid him as much as possible. She got her focus calculations from the stand-ins and stayed in the shadows like a good camera assistant was supposed to.

But one wink and he was drawing her out with his stupid hot-actor charm, making her feel self-conscious in her boring black outfit.

Dammit all to hell.

Then there was Beaumont. Fortunately so far he'd been his typical asshole self, and Maddie had been prepared for that. He'd greeted her the first day as if she were a new intern he couldn't be bothered with even though he knew her well. He showed his dislike for her in passive-aggressive ways. Three times he'd argued with her about her measurements in front of the entire cast and crew. Twice he'd actually taken over focusing for her. Once he'd sent her for coffee. The rest of the time he directed from his chair at video village, and Maddie didn't have to deal with him at all. Like now, thank God. He stayed behind as Joe, Adam, and Micah walked to set.

That meant, for now, she just had to deal with Micah.

She could handle it. Totally. No biggie.

"Okay," she said when they'd reached the set.

"Okay." His lips curled up in a slight smile. *Oh, his beautiful lips . . .*

"Are you on your mark now?" She refused to look him in the eye, hoping he didn't see the shakiness in her hands as she pulled her tape measure from the clip on her belt.

"Yes." She felt his gaze as she did some quick mental calculations.

"Yep, they moved you quite a bit." She handed him the end of her measure. "Do you mind?"

"Not at all." He brushed her skin when he took it. His touch sent a chill through her body and she dropped the measure on his foot.

"Shit." She squatted down for it. As she stood, her forearm accidentally bumped him. Bumped him *there.* And he felt sort of stiff. Oh God, was he hard? *Don't look, don't look.* Before she could stop herself she glanced and there it was, detectable because she was so close, his growing erection. She froze, gaping.

"Enjoying the view?" Micah asked, his voice low and suggestive.

"Oh my God!" Maddie jumped up, shielding her eyes with her hand. Her face flushed crimson. "Oh my God, oh my God, I'm so sorry."

Micah laughed. "Hell, Maddie, I didn't know you were interested."

Interested? That was the understatement of the century.

"I'm . . . I'm . . ." She moved her hand to her mouth, trying to stifle her nervous giggles. "I'm so embarrassed," she said when she could speak.

Micah grinned. "I'm not."

"You have absolutely no reason to be, believe me." Did she really just say that? She flushed even deeper.

His smile widened.

She was mortified—brushing his penis was bad, staring at his crotch was worse. Complimenting his size . . . ? She wanted to crawl into a hole and stay there until the whole damn production was wrapped.

Added to her humiliation and confusing her thoughts was the response of her own body to his obvious desire. Lust spread through her limbs like wildfire. She wanted to touch him, to stroke him, to bring him to release. And why was he turned on anyway? She was the only female on set at the moment. *Oh, shit.* The realization that he was like *that* because of *her* both thrilled and terrified her. Mostly thrilled her.

Which was why she was terrified.

She turned away from him, looking for an escape, and wondered if anyone witnessed their interaction. No, thank goodness, because everyone's attention was on her other nightmare approaching the set—Beaumont.

"I just talked to Heather's assistant," Beaumont said when he arrived. "She'll be ready in twenty."

Joe furrowed his brows. "Is it even worth it to try to get Micah's shots done?"

"Actually," Micah interjected, "I need to run my lines." His voice so close behind her sent another wave of goosebumps up her arms.

Beaumont nodded. "Good idea. You've been a little rusty the last few days. I know, I know, the altitude makes me fuzzy too. Maddie, go help Micah with his lines."

"Um, there's probably someone else who would be better suited—" She couldn't. She needed to be far away from Micah right now, not close and interactive.

Besides, who did Joss Beaumont think she was? Running lines was a job for a production assistant—Sam should be doing this—not first camera assistant. She should be taking care of the camera. Hell, she should be directing the goddamned film, not helping the star with his memorization.

"You can read, can't you?"

Maddie burned at Beaumont's words. Was it possible to hate him more?

She took a deep breath to control her anger. "Of course I can read."

"Then you'll do just fine."

She pivoted away from the director before she said anything she couldn't take back. "Give me your script, Micah. Where do you want to start?"

Micah handed her his rolled-up script. "Let's go to my trailer. It's easier to concentrate without all—" he waved his hand at the people around them, "—this."

"Sure." Her voice was tight. "Fine."

But it was far from fine. Alone in his trailer with Micah Preston and his hard-on? Lord, help her.

SIX

MADDIE FUMED AS SHE FOLLOWED Micah to his trailer. She didn't know if she was fuming more at Beaumont's blatant patronization or at herself for being so affected by an actor. She did know it was easier to keep walking if she concentrated on being mad rather than the butterflies swirling around in her tummy. It didn't help that she had to watch Micah's sexy swagger as she tailed him. As if she wasn't frustrated enough.

She huffed out a breath of angry air. Micah over his shoulder. "Are you okay back there?"

Her throat tightened. "Fine."

Micah climbed the three steps of his trailer and opened the door, holding it for Maddie to walk past. His trailer was one of the nicest ones she'd been in. The countertops were brown-and-cream-speckled granite. The stainless steel appliances sparkled under the abundant recessed lights. The eating area featured a soft brown leather bench curved around a light oak round table. Three barstools rounded the other side, providing additional seating. Farther down the trailer, a small leather loveseat faced a flat-screen television.

And there was the sleeping area at the back of the trailer. Maddie didn't even let that register for fear of the dirty thoughts that would flood her mind.

Micah closed the door, bringing Maddie back from not thinking about tumbling around on his bed. "Look, I really appreciate you doing this. I know it isn't your job."

Maddie ran her hand across her face before she turned toward him. Damn, he was so good-looking. His deep blue eyes stared at her intently and her mask of fury became impossible to maintain under his gaze.

"I'm sorry." She amazed herself at the steadiness of her voice. "It's not you who's got me riled up." Not only him, anyway.

"Good. I was afraid you were upset about . . . well, you know."

Oh God. Was he really bringing up the penis incident? "Oh no. I'd blocked that from my memory. Most successfully until you reminded me." She hadn't really forgotten. Not at all. In fact, she wondered if he was still stiff.

"Bummer to hear I'm so forgettable."

"Oh it's not forgettable." She just said his cock wasn't forgettable. "I mean, I really didn't forget it." *Fuck!* "I mean . . ." She took a deep breath, trying to gain control of the words coming out of her mouth. "Are you trying to make me turn as red as possible? Because I think this is the max I can go."

He laughed. "Maybe just a little. I'm sorry, I couldn't help myself. I shouldn't have teased on the heels of your moment with Beaumont. He can be . . . how shall I put it? Intolerable." Micah offered an understanding smile.

Maddie's knees went weak. His smile was like sunshine. What had they been talking about? Oh yeah, Micah's prick. No, their prick director. "Beaumont's trying, at best."

"Do you think he realizes it?"

"Realizes what? That everyone hates him? That he's an incredible asshole? That I want to smash my tape measure in his face?" She shouldn't have said any of that. She lowered her eyes knowing she'd crossed a line. And to avoid the yummy movie star's gaze. He hadn't taken his eyes off her since they'd entered the trailer.

Micah laughed, a sound that made Maddie's legs quiver. "You said it better than I would have."

"You should forget I said it at all. It was horribly unprofessional."

He winked. Again. And her body jolted in response. Again. He had to stop doing that.

"Forgotten already." He leaned back against the granite counter, and Maddie's gaze dipped to his thigh muscles pressing through the material of his jeans. She wondered what they'd feel like pressed against her. *Incredible.*

Stop it! She had to get her mind back on track. She turned away from him and unrolled the script clutched in her hand. "So what page do we start on?" Her damp hands shook as she flipped through the pages.

Micah crossed behind her to peer over her shoulder. He moved his mouth near her ear. "Top of forty-seven."

His breath tickled her and Maddie's hands were no longer the only thing damp. She shivered.

"It's the kissing scene," he added softly.

She stifled a yelp. *Crap.* It *was* the kissing scene. How had she forgotten? She needed a momentary escape. "Uh, can I use your bathroom? I had way too much coffee this morning."

Micah laughed, enjoying her reaction. He took the script from her, his forearm brushing the side of her breast as he did. "Go ahead. I'll be waiting."

She hurried to the back of the trailer, trying to ignore the taunt in his words, the brush of his arm, and the aching in her hardened nipples. Oh so much to ignore.

Once she'd closed the door of the bathroom, she took a deep breath. Why was she so smitten with this guy? He was just a guy. Yes, he was a big time actor, but she'd never been star struck before. Especially not over a guy who was such a cad. Besides, just because she was into him didn't mean he was into her. And if he was, that meant nothing. *He's a player.* The jumbo box of condoms next to his hotel key on the bathroom counter was an excellent reminder.

Seriously? A box of condoms? Who did he plan on banging in Golden, Colorado?

Certainly not her. No siree. No matter how flirtatious they got, no matter what her body seemed to want—she had more respect for herself than that.

Maddie took one more deep breath, leaned over and flushed the toilet, keeping up the pretense that she'd needed to pee. Then she spritzed her face with cold water. She wasn't any calmer, but she'd have to fake it. She couldn't stay in the bathroom all day hiding from the hottie—correction—co-worker in the other room.

"Here you go," Micah said as she returned, handing her the script opened to a page about halfway in. "Top of that page there." He had resumed leaning against the counter.

Maddie took the script and leaned against the counter opposite him, refusing to pay any attention to his thighs this time. Nope, she would not look. She scanned the page instead. The dialogue seemed harmless enough. She could get through this. No problem.

"You start," she said when he didn't begin.

"I know." A hint of something—longing, maybe—marked his tone.

She looked up from the script and found him staring at her. Again. What was he doing? Getting into character? Trying to remember his first line? Whatever he was doing, it made Maddie warm and fuzzy as he ran his eyes up and down her body. *Shit.* She was a goner.

After what seemed like an eternity, he began. *"I thought you'd be out here. Getting ready to take off with our share of the loot?"*

Maddie moved her eyes back to the script for her line. *"No. I just needed some air."*

"Yeah," he huffed. *"Like I can believe anything that comes out of your mouth."*

"I haven't lied to you." Maddie kept her reading stiff. She wasn't a great actor to begin with, and the last thing she needed was to get lost in this scene.

"Sure, you haven't." Micah took a step toward her. Oh for the love of whatever was holy, he was running the scene's movement too. That meant they were going to get real close, real soon. Certainly he planned to stop before the kiss. Right?

Maddie lost her place on the page, thinking about his lips on hers.

Wondering how his scruff would feel against her face. Her voice was weak when she spoke again. *"I haven't. If I'd wanted the money, I would've left last night, not in broad daylight. And if you're really that worried about it, maybe you should just keep track of your share yourself."*

He took another step toward her. Maddie swallowed, wishing the cabin weren't so narrow. She had nowhere to retreat.

"Maybe I should keep it all. Not too many—"

Maddie jumped on his mistake. "You forgot, 'Permanently. You know—'"

"Shit. Let me start that again." He took a step back then walked toward her again as he began the line. *"Maybe I should keep it all. Permanently. You know, I've been thinking. Not too many people would notice if you weren't around anymore. It would leave less of a headache to worry about dragging your ass with us across these mountains. And I wouldn't have to be concerned that you'd whore my brother out of his share."*

"Fuck you." Yeah, *fuck you,* she repeated in her head. *Fuck you hard and long and*—oh no, this was not going well.

"Not if you were the last woman on earth." Micah closed the distance between them and leaned his arm on the cabinet behind her head. Wow, he was so close, so unbelievably . . . close. Her eyes travelled to his arm propped near her, his perfectly formed bicep tempting her fingers to touch it.

She resisted. Barely. He smelled of coffee and makeup and sweat, and something so entirely Micah, causing the warmth between her legs to heat up another couple of degrees.

Maddie brought the script up to her face as if to place a barricade between them. Her next line came out in a whisper. *"I hate you."*

Micah curled his lip. His oh-so-sexy-lip. *"Say that again?"*

"I hate you." Man, these lines were hitting close to home.

Micah put his other arm up, trapping her. *"Again. Say it again."*

"I hate you. I hate you. I. Hate. You." She lowered the script. Here Micah was supposed to cut her—well Heather, off with a kiss. He didn't, though.

That's a good thing, Maddie reminded herself despite the desire pulsing through her veins.

But he also didn't move away. He kept her ensnared underneath him. His eyes clouded as though he was conflicted, and then they lowered to her mouth, and her heartbeat doubled its pace.

"Uh, that was really good," she squeaked. "Do you want to run it again?"

"I got what I needed." His words sounded tight and gruff.

"You did?" The intensity in his eyes, the closeness of his body—*Kiss me. Kiss me!*

Micah's eyes cleared. "Almost." As though he heard her silent plea, his lips covered hers. He plunged his tongue inside her mouth, insisting that she open up to him.

For one brief millisecond, Maddie considered pushing him away. She moved her hands to his chest to do so, but the hard pecs under her palms and the increasing demand of his kiss shattered her will. What was so bad about kissing him, anyway? Ignoring the hundred alarms going off in her brain that told her she wouldn't think that if she weren't so distracted by hormones and pheromones, and just plain old regular moans—was that her making that sound?—she closed her fingers around his shirt to pull him closer.

His hands moved to cradle her face, helping him access the deepest recesses of her mouth. His facial hair burned deliciously against her lip and chin as days of pent-up longing released under his possessive strokes. This—she wanted this, like she wanted nothing else. She'd fantasized about it whenever she saw him kiss someone else on screen, tried to remember how his lips had felt, but all of her dreams and memories dwindled in the reality of this. She didn't care if this was all she got, it would be enough.

That wasn't true. She wanted more. The fire between her thighs longed to be quenched. She wanted him, naked and inside her on that narrow expanse of bed at the other end of the trailer.

Micah pressed the length of his body against hers and she felt his own desire long and hard against her hip. *Yep, still stiff.* She moaned, his erection kindling the blaze between her legs. She reached her hands around his neck drawing him deeper still into their kiss.

He broke his mouth away from hers and circled her nose with his own. With ragged breath he murmured, "You taste so good. Exactly the way I remember." And then he caught her lips again, his tongue resuming its exploration.

Through her delirium and the exquisite sensations of his oral probing, she fought to grasp the meaning of his words. Something about her tasting good, which was nice, but also that she tasted the way he remembered.

Um, what?

Maddie pulled her head back, breaking the kiss. "Wait," she said, halting him before he repossessed her lips. "You remember?"

Micah smiled and nuzzled his forehead against her own. "How could I forget, *Maddie from the party?*" He replaced his forehead with his lips, kissing down the side of her face to her cheek.

His touch felt wonderful, electric, and she knew it was only a matter of seconds before she'd be lost to him again. But she wanted to understand. With more strength than she knew she had, she returned her hands to his chest and pushed. "Hold on."

Micah groaned but stepped back.

She waited until her panting was under control before she spoke, a million questions racing through her head. "I don't get it. Why did you say you didn't remember?"

Micah ran his hand through his hair. "I don't know. I just did." She raised a brow, urging him to continue. "I didn't want you to assume anything."

"Like assume what?"

"Like . . . that we'd pick up where we left off. Or whatever." His eyes shifted with unease.

But she didn't care if he felt uncomfortable. She folded her arms over her chest. "So it's okay if you wanted to pick things up where we left off, but not if I wanted to?"

"No. Not like that."

"What if I didn't want you to assume anything about me?"

"Then you were free to pretend you didn't remember me. Which you did. Or you could have rejected my advances. Which you didn't." He crossed back to her, resting his hands on her elbows. "It's just . . . different . . . for me. I have to be careful with women. Because I'm. . . . you know."

She shrugged him off. "An arrogant asshole? Or a movie star? Because right now they seem to be one and the same."

"Maddie . . ."

She cut him off with an upraised hand. "No, no, I get it. No need to explain. You're a famous actor." Could she help it if the word actor sounded like a curse on her lips? "You call the shots."

"Maddie, you're blowing this out of proportion."

"Except I run the camera. So technically, I call the shots. At least I'm calling this one." She turned toward the door, ready to bolt. The idea that he held all the power irked her. Just because he was famous? No, she didn't go for that. He was a regular guy like everyone else.

He reached after her, but a knock at his trailer door brought his hands back to his side. He groaned. "Yes?"

"They're ready for you on set," Sam's voice bellowed through the door.

Micah screwed up his face in frustration. "Okay. Be right there." To Maddie he said, "Can we please talk about this later?"

"There's nothing left to say." She opened the trailer door. Before she left, she turned back to the disheveled man staring after her. "I'll send your makeup artist. You need a touch-up."

SEVEN

I T TOOK THE ENTIRE WALK back to set for Maddie's heartbeat to settle down to its regular pulse rate. Even then, her head still spun from her Micah encounter.

What the fuck just happened? No, don't think about it. Think about work.

Except there wasn't any work for her to do. She'd adjusted her focuses earlier with the stand-ins and Adam didn't need anything from her at the moment. She watched as Joe walked Heather through the blocking on the lone cabin where the scene took place. It was a beautiful location. The aromatic purple grape-like flowers—Maddie didn't know their name—mixed with the tall green and yellow grasses against the rustic wood of the log home, creating a quite visually appealing setting. It would look good on film. Especially when the ruggedly handsome Micah was added to the scene, leaning back against the rough post of the deck, thighs hard and . . .

Stop!

But she couldn't stop thinking about it. Micah Preston had kissed her. He *kissed* her. And he had been into it. And he had wanted more. Then, did she end things? Yes, she was pretty sure she had. Was that really what she wanted? Yes, yes it was. There must be a good reason, though she couldn't manage to think what it was. All she could think of were his lips, his hands, his bulging pants . . .

No, stop it, stop it, stop it!

Think about something else. Usually, she spent dead time on set working on her own movie, editing on her laptop. But her computer bag was in the crew's trailer and that was too close to Micah's trailer.

Micah's trailer . . .

She pulled out her phone and scanned her Facebook newsfeed for distraction. Nothing interesting. She was tempted to update her status, but was afraid "Just made out with Micah Preston and am now lost in thoughts of him naked against me" was an inappropriate post. Though it would probably garner several "likes."

She pocketed her phone and looked up to see Micah, complete with fresh makeup, strolling onto the set. Even with several yards between them, he met her eyes and an undercurrent of electricity rushed through her. She tapped her foot to direct the frenzied energy somewhere. Did he do this to every woman or just her? Probably all women. She wasn't special. But there he was, maintaining eye contact, looking at her with— what? Yearning?

"Let's talk," he mouthed to her.

She was confused. Should she talk to him? Why did he even want to talk to her? He was into women for a quick roll in the hay, and if he thought that was what he was getting from her, then he had another think coming.

But that yearning look he gave her . . . Maybe he wanted something different from her. Something more.

Right. And fairies were real and rainbows had pots of gold at the end of them.

She wished she were invisible, wished she could fade into the background like she usually did. She closed her eyes, as if it could make her disappear. When she opened them, Micah had moved his attention to his scene partner. The absence of his gaze chilled her. Despite how easily she'd pulled herself from his embrace, she wanted him; there was no doubt of that. Wanted him so much she practically needed a change of panties whenever he was in the room.

It was possible she'd been too hard on him. So he'd pretended to not remember her. That was shitty. But he was right—she hadn't let on that she remembered him either.

It was his reasons for pretending that bothered her. That he'd thought she'd want to take advantage of him just because he was a famous actor. He had some superiority complex.

Except, maybe most women did that to him. Assumed things about him or showed an interest because he was who he was. She should give him a break.

But that just illuminated the whole reason she shouldn't get involved with him in the first place. He was an actor. A famous actor. And his life was, as he said, different. One main highlight being the rapid-fire way he went through women. All of it suggested that Micah was just a whole jumbled up mess of stuff not to get involved in.

She was stupid for being attracted to him in the first place. It was the memory of him she desired—a fun night in the past. That was all.

Well, and he was super hot. And famous. And charming.

And he'd kissed her!

This was so not like her. She was usually cool and collected and together, but Micah fuddled her up too much to sort out on her own.

Maddie pulled out her cell phone again and typed a text to Bree. *"He remembers me after all."*

"Yes! What did he say?!!?"

"He kissed me." She shook her head not believing the words as she typed them. She rubbed her fingers across her swollen lips while she waited for Bree's response, remembering the feel of his mouth on hers.

"OMG. Did you jump him???"

"No!" Maybe she shouldn't have included the exclamation point. After all, she was considering it.

"R U gonna???"

"Idk, that's why I'm texting you." Maddie typed, then paused. *"That would be bad. Right?"*

Long minutes passed before Bree's response arrived. *"It'd probly b real good. Even though he'd break ur <3."*

Maddie scowled. That was a bit dramatic. Just because she had a tendency to fall in love with every guy she slept with when she was in college didn't mean she still did. She was older and wiser now. Probably. *"Whatev."*

Her phone buzzed Bree's incoming text before Maddie could return the slider. *"And make you cry."*

Maddie's scowl deepened. Was she really so fragile that she couldn't sleep with a guy and not have it mean anything? She didn't have to be. She could sleep with him and not become a weeping willow. Sleep with him and not be affected.

Rephrase that, sleep with him and only be physically affected. An important distinction, as she liked the delicious effect he had on her body.

"We're ready to shoot," Joe said, interrupting Maddie's thoughts of her and Micah rolling around in the grassy meadow in front of them, sans clothes. "Places!"

Maddie cleared her head of the ridiculous fantasy she shouldn't have been having in the first place and started toward the camera, toward Micah. She squatted on the dolly at the side of the camera. "Sound rolling," Chloe, the sound technician, called from her cart.

Sam stepped in front of the camera and read the clapboard. "Scene twenty-two, take one."

Adam shifted as he adjusted the camera. Maddie held her position, rolling with the dolly as the second assistant moved them along the track, circling into the scene.

Micah began his lines, the very lines Maddie had read with him. As she watched him surrender to his performance, her body tingled. Not just in the usual physically turned-on way, but in the artistically turned-on way. He was really a good actor. She hadn't paid attention before, trying her best not to notice him on the days since she'd arrived in Colorado. But now she saw it, saw how his whole body took on his character, his voice and movement changing into a persona very different from the man she had swapped spit with less than thirty minutes before. Yet at the same time, he was Micah Preston, more exposed and unveiled than she'd ever seen him.

Holy crap, she was gaga over him.

Her confession settled on her as she followed the camera, adjusting the focus at the appropriate times.

Until Micah began walking toward Heather, and Maddie's chest began throbbing.

Painfully throbbing.

She knew what came next—the kiss—and she didn't want to see anymore, didn't want to watch Micah's mouth possess another woman's. But she had to watch, it was her job. So she did, the ache increasing with each passing second. By the time Micah wrapped his arms around Heather and leaned in for the kiss, the stab of jealousy was so sharp Maddie wondered if she was having a heart attack.

Impulsively, Maddie closed her eyes, blocking out the action before her.

"Cut!" Joe called out and Maddie's eyes flew open, realizing he'd ended before the scene was finished.

Shit. She'd missed her final focus. *Shit, shit, shit!* She peered up at Adam, who was listening to Beaumont on his own headset. He looked down at Maddie questioningly.

"I missed it," Maddie said softly. This wasn't like her. She never missed.

"Adam, Maddie?" Joe asked. "What was with that last focus?"

"Miscalculation," Adam said, not pointing out Maddie's error in front of everyone. "We got it now. Sorry."

"Let's take it again." Joe's irritation sounded in his voice. "Reset."

Dammit, Maddie thought as she helped the second assistant roll the camera dolly back to its starting position on the track. This, *this* was why she couldn't get mixed up with Micah Preston. She couldn't even watch him act a scene with a fellow cast member without being overcome with jealousy. Without screwing up her job—a job that she was usually perfect at. Surely if anything more happened with him, this feeling would only get worse. Right now it was already horrible. Achingly, maddeningly, horrible.

Maddie avoided Micah's eyes as his makeup artist came in to retouch his lips. She took the free moment to pull out her phone and type a final text to Bree. *"I'm not gonna jump him."*

"4 the best. Luvs!"

Was it for the best? She thought she'd feel better but her decision seemed hollow. She swallowed hard, steeling herself for the second take of the scene.

"Wait," Joe said, his right hand lifted in a halting gesture. With his other hand, he pressed his headset tighter against his ear, listening to an order from Beaumont. After a minute, he pointed to Micah. "Micah, Beaumont wants to move your initial mark to here." Joe tapped a spot on the ground with the toe of his foot. "Bruce, the light isn't hitting the new mark. Can you arm it in, please?"

A lighting adjustment and a change in blocking. She'd have to refocus too.

She took a deep breath as she crossed to the mega-fine actor, blushing as she remembered the last time she'd calculated a focus for him.

"Hey," Micah said.

"Hey." She didn't meet his eyes, didn't ask him to hold her measure, but instead put it on the ground at his feet. She felt rather than saw him pick up the end. "Thanks," she muttered. She walked the steps back to the camera and wrote down the new measurements then pushed the button to pull the length in, but it didn't budge. She glanced back at Micah who still held tightly to the end. *Seriously?*

She trudged back to him. "Can I have it back, please?"

He crossed his arms, burying the edge against his chest. "Will you talk to me?"

Heather broke into a laugh a few feet away, pulling Maddie's attention. Her eyes narrowed as she glared at the actress flirting with Joe, still bristling from having just watched Heather make out with her man. *Whoops!* Not her man. Definitely not her man.

Micah studied Maddie. "What's with you and Heather? That look could shoot daggers."

She bent her head, hoping to hide her irrational envy. "Nothing. Can I have my measure?"

"No, that wasn't a nothing look. That was most certainly something."

He pursed his lips. "Hmm. Anger? No. Jealousy."

Her cheeks went warm. "My measure, please."

"Maddie, you're blushing. You *are* jealous." He peered over at Heather and the crew. "You can't be into any of those guys. At least, I hope not, because you're way out of their league. Is it . . ." His face broke into an electric smile. "Are you jealous of her and me?"

She burned with irritation. "Oh my God, you're so full of yourself." It was true, but that he thought it was true was downright narcissistic.

"I'm right." He uncrossed his arms and stroked her chin, the end of the measure held tightly in his other hand. Goosebumps rose on her arms as his finger moved across her skin. "No need to be jealous, Maddie. That was acting. Not like our kiss."

She couldn't help herself. She moved her eyes to his crotch where his hard-on was evident. "Looked like it had the same effect." She meant to insult him with her words, but after she said them she realized she'd just confirmed his accusation. Man, she was so much better with dialogue when she had a chance to write and rewrite. Spitting it out in real time was incredibly more challenging.

Micah chuckled. "You're adorable when you're jealous. And this," he removed his hand from her face and waved it over his pelvis, "is still from you, baby."

Her insides twisted at his endearment. "I can't believe I blue-balled you again," she muttered, mostly to herself.

"Again? Oh, yeah. That night . . ." His brow rose. "Now if you're interested in paying me back . . ." His eyes glimmered with his tease.

They stared at each other for several heated seconds. Then he let go of the end of the measure. It snapped back into the metal compact Maddie held in her hand, but her eyes never left his. Softly, he said, "Talk to me?"

She clipped the measure on her belt and chewed on her chapped lip, dry from the Colorado environment and the intense assault it had undergone earlier. She did owe him for leaving him unfulfilled the night they met. Of course she wasn't expected to pay him back, but that evening with him . . . she'd had a really good time. She'd let loose in a way she never did, and though she couldn't get involved with Micah Preston, she did appreciate the bold, sexy girl he'd found in her back then.

Maybe she could relive it just once more and return the favor at the same time. It might prompt him to leave her alone. An idea formed in her head.

"Okay." She couldn't believe she was doing this—should she actually be doing this? "A bunch of the crew is going to the bar next to our hotel after wrap tonight. You're welcome to join. Maybe we can talk there?"

"I'd like that." He moved his mouth near her ear, his breath on her skin raising all the hairs on her arms. "Don't be jealous," he whispered. "If it's convincing, it's because I'm thinking of you."

Her pulse sped up.

"Places!" Joe called.

Maddie started toward the camera, surprised that his words had relaxed her. Not enough to make him and her a possibility, but enough to get through the work day. "Just remember, Micah," she said over her shoulder. "Paybacks are a bitch."

She ignored his puzzled look as she rubbed ChapStick over her lips, smacking them deliberately for his benefit. Tonight, he'd understand. Tonight, she was paying back what she owed.

EIGHT

MICAH VACILLATED ABOUT WHAT TIME he should arrive at the bar. He didn't want to seem too eager, and he knew the crew had at another hour of clean-up after he was dismissed from the set at nine.

He decided to shoot for eleven, filling his time with a light dinner in his room while he ran lines, followed by a shower to scrub his makeup and the lingering scent of Heather Wainwright from his body. Not that Heather was unappealing. They had good chemistry, having hooked up a few times over the years. Now Heather almost seemed repulsive after he'd had the sweet taste of Maddie in his mouth.

Ah, Maddie Bauers. Thoughts of her roused his cock. He mentally repeated her name over and over while he took care of his hard-on in the shower, recalling her fingers in his hair and her firm breasts pressed against his chest.

Jesus, this woman had a hold on him. And if he played his cards right, he hoped to have a hold of her too, preferably naked. Perhaps even later that night.

After he'd finished cleaning up, Micah dressed in tight dark jeans, a white T-shirt and a thin gray button-down shirt. He met Fudge in the lobby and they hailed a cab to the Golden Well, the bar next to the crew's hotel.

The Golden Well was brightly lit and crowded. Micah stood with his bodyguard near the door while he scanned the room, hoping not to be spotted by any fans. He preferred dimly-lit restaurants and exclusive nightclubs, and he felt awkward and exposed, but his resolve to see Maddie was not diminished.

Fudge seemed to share his displaced feelings. "Why are we here again? You never hang with the crew."

"I should try something different." He hated the way Fudge's words made him sound snobby. Really it was the nature of the business—different call times and jobs on set—that created different social circles for production crew and actors.

Fudge shook his head. "It's her, isn't it?"

"No. Not at all. Who?"

"Fuck, Micah. Just bang her and get it over with."

Micah frowned. "I'm not going to bang her. God, don't be so crude." Banging implied hard and fast, and though Micah imagined some of that with Maddie, he was also counting on long and slow.

"You're pathetic."

Micah turned his attention back to the crowd. "You don't have to be here. I gave you the night off."

"What else am I going to do?"

Micah spotted the back of a brunette head, hair pulled into a neat, high ponytail, and he knew it was Maddie. His breath caught as she turned to—what? Look for him?—and their eyes met. She was so beautiful. He could stare at her face for hours.

"Isn't that the A.D. over there?" Fudge didn't realize Micah had already seen her.

There were a dozen or so people sitting around the tables with Maddie, but Micah didn't register any of their faces. "Yeah, it's her. Them."

He moved toward where she sat in the back of the bar as if pulled by a string. He vaguely sensed the recognition of a couple as he passed their table, heard the hushed whispers that often accompanied his outings—"Isn't that the guy in that superhero movie?" "Isn't that Micah Preston?" But he ignored them, his full attention on the lovely woman in front of him.

As he got closer, she smiled, and Micah's dick twitched. He couldn't remember the last time a girl turned him on so easily.

"Well, look who's here," Joe said, not hiding his surprise.

Greetings passed through the group. Micah recognized a handful of them—a couple of P.A.s, the sound crew, Bruce from lighting. In all they occupied three tables.

The petite, punky sound technician—maybe her name was Claire?—was the only one to give him pause about the appropriateness of his presence. "Wow. Are we being graced with the company of 'the talent'? What made you decide to join the lowly likes of the crew?"

"I hear you have the best parties," Micah said smoothly.

"Right you are." She lifted her beer. "Good to have you."

"Good to be here." *Chloe.* That was her name. And she preferred to be called the Sound Goddess according to her introduction at the first cast and crew meeting. Fudge took the empty seat next to her.

"Hey, Fudge. Micah." Sam raised a hand in greeting.

Micah glanced at the boyish P.A. sitting next to Maddie, much closer to her than he needed to be. "Hi . . . Shawn is it?"

"Sam."

"Aw, sorry. That's right," Micah said, unapologetically. "Mind if I sit?" He gestured to an empty chair to the left of Sam and directly across from Maddie.

"That's where Leila was sitting, but I think she left already, didn't she?"

Micah didn't know who Leila was, but several members of the group affirmed that she had indeed left. He nodded, stealing a glimpse of Maddie's bosom as he sat. She had removed the button-down shirt she wore earlier over her tank top, giving a much-improved view of her goods.

"How did you know we were out tonight?" Sam asked, after Micah had gotten the waitress's attention and ordered a Guinness. "Not that you're not welcome. The crew said the actors didn't usually come out."

"I don't usually. But I was invited." He wanted to brag that it was Maddie who had extended the invitation, scream it across the bar, but he didn't need gossip to spread through the crew about he and the leggy brunette sitting across from him.

"I invited him," Maddie said, not seeming to care about the rumor mill. "Beaumont had me running lines today, can you believe it? No offense, Micah—"

"None at all."

"—And it just sort of came up." She stopped, blushing, and Micah wondered if she was recalling, as he was, exactly what had *come up* between them earlier that day.

"Beaumont's got his head up his ass," Joe said, possibly already drunk. "I'm sorry he did that shit to you. You're too damn good at your job to be expected to waste your time on that fucking shit. No offense, Micah."

Micah raised a hand to say it was okay and focused on Maddie's response.

"It's fine. Whatever." Maddie blew it off, but he could clearly see it bothered her.

"I can't believe Beaumont doesn't respect you more," Sam offered. "Doesn't he realize you're qualified to be running the camera? Why aren't you a camera operator, anyway? You have the resume for it."

Envy squeezed Micah's chest. He wished he knew these things about Maddie. He wished he knew these sorts of things about anyone. He was rarely close enough to anyone for long enough to learn what they were good at, what their dreams were.

Maddie sighed. "Camera's not my end goal."

Micah stilled, remembering again the night they'd met. She'd wanted to direct and write, wasn't that it? Though he was curious whether or not she still had that dream, he couldn't bring himself to ask. Those were the kind of jobs that a guy like him could arrange for a girl like her. And he didn't want to put himself in the position to be taken advantage of. Again.

But Sam asked. "What do you want to do?"

Micah braced himself for her answer.

But she didn't give one. She just shrugged. "Not camera."

Micah forced himself to relax. Why did he always have to be so mistrustful? Just because he'd had a past girlfriend—someone he thought he loved—use him for his connections, didn't mean that all women would. But how could he ever get close enough to a woman to test that theory out?

He couldn't. That's why he didn't try.

And he wasn't trying now. He was simply fooling around with a co-worker, something he'd done many times before. He bided his time, drinking his beer and enjoying the crew's banter and talk about their real lives. Particularly, he focused on the angel in front of him, realizing that this unique venture into her world provided more insight about who she was as a person than any encounter he'd had with her so far. Before long, he determined she was a workaholic, unappreciated by her boss, and exceptionally passionate about her craft.

He also recognized that she wasn't the type to hook up with men she barely knew. This awareness both delighted and saddened him. He wondered why she'd made an exception for him. And would she be willing to do it again?

Only one way to find out. At a lull in the conversation, he put on his best smile and said, "So, what are your plans for the day off tomorrow?"

"I'd love to find a way to Breckenridge." Maddie leaned back in her chair, giving an even better view of her amazing tits. A bit on the small side, but definitely real, a nice change from what Micah was used to. "The Breckenridge Film Fest is going on this weekend. I'd like to catch it."

"That's not even a film festival," Joe said, his words slurred. "It's a festival of crap. It's like a fake film festival of crap."

Maddie laughed. Damn, it was the sweetest sound Micah had heard in a long time. "I know. But I like film. Period. You never know when you're going to find a gem."

Micah grinned. "Agreed." Hitting California film festivals used to be a favorite past time of his. He couldn't remember the last time he went to anything indie. "I got my current agent from the Topanga Film Festival."

"*The Mission's Warrior*. Like I said, a gem."

He was impressed and in awe. Not many people had ever heard of that early film of his, let alone seen it.

"It had its weaknesses," she continued. "Mainly the script. The directing was solid and the cast was really strong." She blushed. "In my opinion, anyway."

Her pink skin and sweet praise stirred his hardened cock. He wanted to take her, right then and there, no care for everyone around him. But he'd settle for a day at the film festival. He'd rent a car and it would be just the two of them, sharing their love of movies. He'd ask her as soon as they were alone.

"I'll take you," Sam said. Every muscle in Micah's body tensed. "Breckenridge is beautiful and only a couple of hours from here. I'd love to show it to you."

Micah resisted the urge to punch him. *Say no, Maddie,* he willed silently. *Say no.*

But Maddie's face broke into a grin. "Really? Thanks."

"Awesome. We can work out the deets before we leave. Right now I want to get in a game of pool before Chloe heads out. She thinks she can beat me. But she totally can't." He stood and pushed his chair in. "Did you hear that, Chloe Barfoot? I'm gonna whoop your ass!"

Chloe stood as well, her small frame barely reaching Sam's chest. "Like hell you are. It's on."

"This I gotta see," Fudge said.

Micah frowned as Sam leaned over Maddie to grab his beer. He couldn't be certain but he was pretty sure that Sam was sneaking his own peek at Maddie's bosom.

"Come cheer me on?" Sam asked.

Now Micah was certain. Sam was totally looking. Who wouldn't sneak a peek? Maddie's breasts were excellent—firm, round, perky—and if Sam was sneaking peeks tonight, God knew what he'd try to do to them tomorrow. Micah couldn't stand the thought. As soon as he could get a damn minute alone with her he'd tell her not to go. Though now she'd likely go to the pool tables to be the douchebag's personal cheerleader.

But she surprised him. "I'll cheer you from here."

Micah didn't bother to hide his satisfaction.

After a moment of shuffling chairs and gathering beer bottles, most of the table had dispersed to watch the game.

Maddie flashed a mischievous grin. "We're alone."

Hmm. He liked the tone of this conversation. Too bad they weren't really alone. He was very aware of the waitress eyeing him, and the couple in the booth behind him, and the woman at the bar. "Mostly."

"Mostly enough." She took a deep breath—was she nervous?—and slid herself over to the chair Sam had occupied. "I'm glad. I need to give you something."

"You do?" Micah's curiosity piqued as Maddie took a long swig, finishing off her Corona. Then she dug in her pocket for her ChapStick. He watched entranced as she applied it leisurely to her full, pink lips, just as he had seen her do so many times on set. Thank God for the dry weather.

When she'd finished with her lips, she began to rub the ChapStick liberally over her left hand.

He raised an eyebrow. What the hell was she doing?

He was answered by the approach of her hand underneath the table where his cock throbbed painfully in his jeans. His jaw dropped as she undid his zipper and freed his aching member, her eyes never leaving his. Well, this wasn't characteristic of the Maddie he thought he'd begun to figure out. *What a nice surprise.*

Maddie circled his penis with her lubricated hand, eliciting a gasp. *A nice surprise indeed.*

"So, Micah, I've been meaning to ask you—why so many women in your life?"

Micah blinked several times before answering, not sure he could converse with her hand on his dick. With effort, he managed, "I have a very strict no-strings rule. Relationships in Hollywood are near impossible."

"That's pessimistic." Slowly, Maddie began to move her hand up his shaft from the root to head of his member, driving a shiver down his spine. "There are plenty of actors who have girlfriends in Hollywood."

Micah put his palms down on the table and stilled himself. "Hardly any of those work out. And the no-girlfriend thing has kept me focused. It's gotten me to the top."

She met his stare full on, a glint in her eyes. Her hand slid back down to base camp. Ho.Ly. Fuck.

"Maybe you got to the top because you're talented." Again, Maddie moved her hand up his shaft, dragging her thumb along the thick vein on the underside of his cock.

He suppressed a groan. "Talent means nothing in Hollywood." Was he even making sense? It was so hard to concentrate on words.

"And lucky." She paused then moved her hand over his head in lazy circles before sliding it back down his shaft.

He gritted his teeth. "I am *very* lucky."

"And incredibly hot." She pumped quickly once before returning to her unhurried drag up his member. Micah almost blew his load right then.

He sucked in a haggard breath, amazed that her words could have an additional effect on him. "You think I'm hot?"

"I think you aren't bad on the eyes." She repeated the pattern, circling his head, then moving her hand down again.

"No, you said hot." She pumped twice this time, then followed with a slow tug up. "Incredibly . . . hot." *This* was incredibly hot. So . . . incredibly . . . hot . . . Sure, he'd had hand jobs in public before, but usually in darkened, private corners, not at a table with co-workers. Certainly not from reserved serious types such as Maddie. It was totally, thrillingly, unexpected.

"And what do you do if you fall in love?" Three quick pumps. His cock felt like steel; he'd never been so hard.

"That would be tricky. To fall in love." He could only produce short sentences. "When you only spend. One night with someone." Though if you asked him right then he'd likely say he loved this woman. He definitely loved what she did to him, what she was doing to him.

Her eyes clouded, but her hand didn't stop moving, continuing her rhythmic pattern. Her voice was quieter when she continued. "You've never considered breaking your rule?"

He'd done more than consider it. He'd broken it hardcore. And that fiasco did nothing but enforce his no-love stance.

But his answer to Maddie was much simpler, though it came out strained. "No. I don't. That rule got me here. I *love* it here." He was close. So close. A few more strokes and he would be done for.

Her eyes darkened. Was that hurt? Disappointment? He couldn't tell and he was too consumed with what she was doing to him to fully register meaning in her expression.

She leaned over giving him a perfect view of her round breasts and pumped four times fast. It was her final harsh whisper that threw him over the edge. "You would have gotten *here* anyway."

Micah brought his hand to his mouth to stifle his moan as he exploded into her hand. Even as he came, he wanted more, knew that this would not be nearly enough. Maddie Bauers was completely and utterly under his skin.

NINE

MICAH CLOSED HIS EYES AS Maddie caught the hot fluid with a cloth napkin. She cleaned him up, wiped off her hand, balled the napkin and threw it onto the table. She'd never done anything like that—ever—and she was unexpectedly roused.

But she was also resolved. She'd needed to give this to Micah, to even the score and put a cap on their night from the past. Their most recent conversation confirmed again that messing around with him would lead to nothing but heartache. He was in love with his career. Why she even bothered to argue it with him, she didn't know. "You would have gotten where you are in Hollywood, too. Don't kid yourself that a woman would have held you back."

Micah paused to calm his breathing as he tucked himself back into his pants. "I don't believe that."

"What about Lulu?" She was taking a stab in the dark, but she'd heard Fudge and Micah talking about the woman during the car ride from the airport. It was evident Micah had feelings for the woman, whoever she was.

"Lulu?" Micah laughed. "Lulu has never held me back, though she's a major factor in my decision to not date. But it's not for the reasons you'd think." He paused. "Lulu's my mother."

"Oh." She blushed. "Whoops. I thought I'd stumbled on a woman you were seeing on a regular basis."

"Good guess. I do see her on a regular basis after all. But she's honestly the only woman I can say that about."

She sat back in her chair, attempting to put everything in perspective. He was a player. A self-declared gigolo. At least he didn't deny it.

And she couldn't deny that she was mildly interested. More than mildly. More like wildly.

But she knew herself. She was too into him already. It wouldn't take much to make her fall for him. As Bree had said, he would make her cry.

She sighed and then leveled an even stare at him. "I can't date you, Micah."

His eyes hinted amusement. "Who said anything about dating?"

"And I definitely can't do that with you."

He leaned forward, challenge written all over his face. "Why not?"

"Are you serious? To just be a random number in a group of women? A notch in your bedpost that doesn't mean anything?"

Micah put his hand over hers, his touch burned like fire on her skin. "You wouldn't be random. You're Maddie from the party."

"God, Micah, that's just . . . gross." She slid her hand out from under his. "I'm not against one-night stands in general, but you said it before. You're different. You'd be different."

Micah leaned forward and placed his hand on her leg under the table sending electric shocks throughout her body. "If by different you mean the most insanely hot, wicked pleasure you've ever felt, then yes, I'll agree."

His fingers moved in circles on her leg, and her mind filled with unwanted images of the insanely hot wicked pleasure Micah promised.

Shaking the fantasies out of her head, she removed his hand from her thigh. "Though I imagine what you say is true . . ." He winked at her and she had to look away. "That's not what I meant. Most hook-ups you can love and leave. But not you. I'd see you everywhere after and I'm not talking about in person. And it would make me a major hypocrite. I don't approve of how you use women like Kleenex—"

"Hey, no one's ever complained."

"I'm sure they haven't." His cavalier attitude about the whole thing just reinforced her decision. "And I'm sure you aren't used to hearing these words, but I'm not interested, Micah. Not in the least."

Okay, that was a lie, but he didn't need to know that.

Micah fixed a somber stare on her for several long seconds and she began to wonder if he knew she was exaggerating her disinterest. But finally he said, "It's too bad you feel that way."

She took the last swallow of her beer, trying to drown the cloud that had settled around them. She hadn't meant to take this to such a serious place. It wasn't like they were breaking up. Strange how it felt like they were. "Hey, you were fun." She patted his knee to lighten the mood. And to get in one last grope.

Micah grabbed her hand and moved it to the growing package in his pants. "I can still be fun."

"Oh no, no, no." She pulled her hand away blocking out the knowledge that he was hard again, suppressing thoughts of what she could do with that knowledge.

"Then what was all this?" He waved his hand, referring to Maddie's under-table gift.

Shit. She'd given him the wrong idea. That hadn't been her intent. She was trying to end things. Not make him want more. "I owed you."

"You really didn't."

She threw his words back at him. "I don't believe that." All right, maybe she'd done it just as much for herself as him. To give herself closure. Or maybe to prove something, that she wasn't a prude, that she could make a move like that without getting attached. Hell, she wasn't quite sure why she'd done it. Micah confused her so much she had no idea why she did anything anymore. In fact, if he asked her again, she might go to bed with him now.

Micah sighed. Was he really going to give up this easily? She was both relieved and disappointed. "I guess I have to settle for friends."

She scoffed. Friends? That was ridiculous. He didn't know the first thing about her, didn't even seem interested in her beyond the physical. "We're not friends."

"We could be friends." He rubbed his leg against her lower calf, sending tingles up her spine.

Besides, his version of friends didn't seem the same as hers. She pulled her leg out of his reach. "No we can't. You can't even keep your hands to yourself."

"I can, and my hands aren't even touching you." He waved his fingers in the air to further his point.

"Whatever." He was flustering her. As always. "Your feet, your hands, your things!"

Micah grinned. "Are you sure you want that? My *things* are awfully fun."

She flushed. "We are totally not friends." She didn't even want to be friends with him—spend more time with him, so she could crush on him even harder? No way.

Micah sat forward, suddenly serious. "Look, we have to spend the rest of the shoot together. Work together every day. And that means you might drop your tape measure in front of me and I might get all turned on and we have to be able to laugh about it like friends."

He was getting cute. She needed another drink.

"Or Beaumont might want you to run lines. I still have a sex scene coming up. What if you get sent in to help with that?"

"I won't." Fuck no. She'd be naked within half a page. She signaled the waitress for another round.

"You won't be sent or you won't help?" He propped his elbow on the table and set his chin in his hand.

She glared at him and then melted at his boyish expression. God help her. She kept up her protest, hoping he hadn't noticed her crumbling resolve. "Well I might be sent, but I'm not helping."

"What? That isn't any kind of friend to be."

She covered her eyes with her hands, hiding her amusement. "Because we're not friends."

When she removed her hands she found him grinning at her. He gave a half-wink. *Oh, for the love of God.* He knew he'd won her over.

His ocean-blue eyes sparkled. "You say that, but you don't mean it. I'm fun. Even when I keep my *things* to myself."

"All right, all right!" She sighed. "Friends."

He sat back, basking in his win. "Awesome."

Maybe they *could* be friends. She liked talking with him and hadn't felt so relaxed in . . . she couldn't even remember how long. She enjoyed his banter, almost as much as she enjoyed his hands on her.

No, she couldn't think about that. They were friends.

The waitress delivered their beers, lingering to stare at the Hollywood star. Micah appeared not to notice. He raised his own beer and clinked Maddie's bottle. "To newfound friendship."

"Yeah, yeah, yeah." She took a swallow.

"Now that we're buds," Micah said, setting his glass down. "I have to tell you: do not go on a date with that P.A. scum."

Here it was. She'd known friendship wouldn't work. "It's not a date."

Micah nodded toward the pool tables where Sam and Chloe appeared to be nearing the end of their game. "He thinks it is."

"It's not." Though she wasn't exactly sure that was true. "And it's none of your business."

He cocked his head. "We're friends. Friends don't let friends date douchebags."

Again with the cute. He had charm down to a science. "He is not a douchebag. And I want to go to Breckenridge."

"Let me take you."

Maddie paused momentarily thrown by his abrupt sincerity. "First of all, no. That would not be a good idea." *Not a good idea at all.* "Secondly, Sam's from here. He's a perfect guide."

Micah scowled. "He's a douchebag."

"At least he's not a playboy." Low blow and she knew it.

He flinched slightly. "You don't know that. He doesn't want to show you Breckenridge. He wants to show you what's in his pants. And I guarantee it's not much."

"Whatever, Micah." She was not going back to a conversation about pants. That only led to thoughts of what was inside Micah's pants. And she had already thought about—and *touched,* God, did she really do that?—his love muscle way too much for one night. Correction, too much period.

And now she was thinking about his dick again, hard and inside her. Did she really have to give this up?

It was as if he sensed her resolve breaking. "Come on, I'd make it fun." He gave his most devilish grin—the one that made Maddie weak in the knees and slippery in her panties. He lowered his voice as Sam and a few of the spectators returned to the table. "I think I've demonstrated that in the past, haven't I?"

Maddie's belly tightened at the soft, seductive quality of his voice. *Dammit.* She had planned for the evening to go one way: hand job then blow off. Instead he had complicated things with "just friends," wandering hands, and an invitation to spend their day off together. She no longer had a hold on what was up or down with Micah Preston. What she did know was that a daytrip spent with Sam would pale in comparison to one spent with the hot piece of meat next to her, though Sam would certainly be safer. Well, somewhat safer—he would likely make advances of his own, but Maddie could handle him. Not necessarily true with Micah. She was befuddled.

"I totally thought she had you," Fudge said. "Excellent final play!"

"Thanks, man." Sam took the seat Maddie had occupied before.

Maddie sat back in her chair, distancing herself from Micah. "So you won?"

"I kicked her four-foot-eight ass."

"Four-foot-eight and a half, thank you very much," Chloe corrected.

"Next time, I'd love to have you there to cheer me on." Sam put his hand over Maddie's on the table.

Ah, crap. He was totally into her. And going alone with him to the film festival would likely give him ideas about them as a couple, which would totally be misleading because she was not jumping baby-face Sam. No, she couldn't do that to him.

But it was Micah who made her decide to compromise. She glanced at him when Sam took her hand, expecting to see an "I-told-you-so" look on his face. Instead, he'd let his mask slip for the slightest of moments and underneath the hot actor exterior she saw a lonely, yearning man.

It tugged at her heart and before she could think too much about it she slipped her hand out from under Sam's and said, "Hey, I hope you don't mind, but I invited Micah to go with us to the festival tomorrow."

"And Fudge," Micah said, not missing a beat. He winked at her.

"Yes, and Fudge. That's not a problem is it?"

"Uh no, of course not." Sam's disappointment was evident but he recovered quickly. "Is there anyone else who wants to go? I can seat one more."

"Hell, I'll go," Chloe said. "We could take the van I rented. I could fit one more."

Joe stood, wobbling as he did. "Awesome. I'll join you. Which means I need to get to bed. I might have had a little more to drink than I thought."

The bunch agreed to call it a night. Phone numbers were exchanged and specific times set for those meeting in the morning. Maddie trembled as she handed her phone to Micah for him to enter his info. *His number!* She tried not to let that thought excite her.

The waitress brought over the final tab. Micah grabbed it first, then pulled out a gold American Express and returned it to her.

"It's on me," he said.

Surprised and grateful "thank you's" passed among the lot. "Thanks, man, that was really nice of you," Sam said. "You're welcome back any time."

"It's no problem. The waitress wanted my autograph anyway but couldn't get the nerve to ask. Now she'll have it."

So he had noticed the waitress. Sure Micah had more money than God, but treating everyone was a nice gesture and Maddie saved her own acknowledgement until she had his full attention. "Thank you."

He nodded and she felt his eyes as she stood, grabbing her purse from where it hung on the back of Sam's chair. She waved and started out of the bar.

Before she'd made it to the street, her phone buzzed with a text from *Micah from the party.* She grinned at his entry then read his text. *"No, Maddie. Thank you."*

She wasn't sure if he was thanking her for Breckenridge or the hand job, probably the latter. What struck her was the effort he was making to get her . . . it made her tummy swirl with a storm of butterflies.

But it also made her dizzy and disoriented. Why her? She'd said no, more than once. If he was really only interested in a lay, why was he still trying to win her? Was it the thrill of the chase? Had her refusal read to him as playing hard to get?

It was the uncertainty and the fear of leading him into pursuing her more that kept her from responding to his message. Instead, she closed his text and pretended she could put the man out of her head as easily as she stowed her phone in her pocket.

TEN

"THE LAST ONE INTRIGUED ME," Maddie said as they neared the venue of the next movie they planned to see. Out of the three films they'd seen so far, the last had been the only one halfway decent. Still, she was having fun with Joe, Chloe, Sam, and even Fudge and Micah. As promised, Breckenridge was beautiful, and she enjoyed getting in touch with what other artists were doing. Such days never failed to inspire her.

"Agreed," Joe said, walking into the old movie theater. "It wasn't exceptional, but it had something."

"It was sort of creepy," Fudge said, holding the door for Maddie.

"It was brave," she said walking in to the lobby.

"The satire was perfect," Micah chimed in behind her. "Clearly influenced by Bret Easton Ellis."

Maddie faced him. "Ellis? I'd say more Elio Petri."

"I've never even heard of Elee Peteri or whoever." Chloe rubbed at her mouth. "My God, it's so dry here. Does anyone have any lip shit?"

"No, definitely Ellis," Micah insisted, removing his baseball cap and pushing his sunglasses to his head. "I think Maddie has some ChapStick."

Maddie blushed, ignoring the glint in his eye and the memory of her hand on his privates as she dug into her purse for her ChapStick. "It's almost gone, but take it." She handed the tube to Chloe. She turned back to Micah, not letting the intimate flashback interrupt the debate. "*American Psycho* would never have existed without films like *Investigation of a Citizen above Suspicion*."

"But I guarantee you that—" Micah pulled his crumpled program from his back pocket and flipped until he found what he was looking for, "—Todd Nichols never in his life saw a Petri film, or Z or *Salo*, for that matter, so I'm calling Todd's influence Ellis."

Maddie pursed her lips. Few people could keep up with her on film history. Even in the biz she never ceased to be surprised by how many people had no idea about the background of their art. Micah's ability to intelligently and convincingly hold his end of the debate warmed her core. "Just because the artist is unaware of the influence doesn't mean it isn't valid," she argued, less forcefully than before.

"I think you're mistaking influence with roots."

"I got the tickets," Sam cut in. Maddie hadn't noticed he'd gone to the ticket counter. "This one's popular. We need to get in if we want to find seats."

"Lead the way," she said. Thankfully, Sam wasn't acting weird after the drive up. In the backseat of the van where he sat with Maddie, he'd taken her hand. Maddie had pulled away, gently but definitively, and shaken her head. He got the point. If only Micah could be so easily dealt with. Except maybe he had been. He hadn't made any moves on her the whole day. Maybe he meant what he said about being just friends.

"Oh my God, Micah Preston!" A female voice came from a group next to them. "Can we have your autograph?"

Fans. They'd been lucky so far not to be noticed, but Micah had worn his cap and sunglasses for most of the day. Now, with them removed, he was recognizable.

Maddie stood close enough to him to hear his soft sigh. The admirers saw nothing but his bright smile. "Sure!" He stuck his cap into the back pocket of his jeans. "Do you have a pen?"

They didn't, but Maddie did. She handed him one from her purse, vaguely aware of someone snapping a cell phone picture as she did.

"Micah, what are you doing in Colorado?" another of the girls asked.

"We're shooting a film near Golden."

"Cool! Do you need any extras?"

"I wish." Micah was polite, charming even. "But it's about a bunch of outlaws hiding in the mountains. Small cast. Hey, I'd love to stay and chat, but my friends are waiting." He returned Maddie's pen.

"That wasn't so bad," she said as they joined the rest of their group at the theater doors.

"No, but they took our picture. That gets online and the rumors will begin about you and me."

You and me. Her heart sung. How nice that sounded.

"That's our one pic, Maddie," he teased. "We'll have to be more careful in the future."

She shivered at the thoughts those words elicited of sneaking around, avoiding paparazzi and fans. It was an unexpected turn on. Maybe a secret affair with Micah wouldn't be so bad. But then there'd be the inevitable break-up and that would just suck.

At the door they surrendered their tickets to the usher and entered the theater. Sam had predicted correctly—the room was packed and available seating was sparse. Finding six seats together would be impossible.

"There's four," Fudge said pointing to an area near the front.

"You guys take them," Micah said. "Maddie and I will sit back here. She doesn't realize I've already won our film debate, and I'm sure she has a few more impressive yet irrelevant bits of trivia to throw at me." He winked at her.

Before anyone could argue, Micah ushered her into the two seats on the aisle of the very back row. It was an older theater, one without stadium seating, and the exit lay just behind them.

"You're terrible," Maddie said as she sat down, though she was secretly thrilled to be alone with him.

"What, why? I said it was impressive trivia."

She glared. "Not that."

"Oh, separating you and Sam? You said it wasn't a date."

"It isn't. But do you really think it's fair to stick him with your bodyguard?"

"Hmm." He considered a moment. "Nah, they're fine." He pressed his knee against hers. Was it on purpose? Maybe he had equally been turned on by thoughts of a secret relationship. Or maybe he had been waiting to get her alone. "They can get to know each other."

She willed herself to stay strong, but leaned into his leg anyway. "Like we're getting to know each other?"

He relaxed at her response. "I hope not—I mean, do you think Sam is . . . ? I'm positive Fudge's on our team, but Sam . . ."

She laughed. God, he was charming. "Shut up. Sam is not gay."

"You sound like you know from experience."

"You sound jealous."

"I don't get jealous." He took her hand. "I get what I want."

Her hand in his felt warm and tingly, quite unlike when Sam had played the same move. He began stroking her slowly with his thumb and her skin burned under his touch. Nearby giggling drew her attention to the fans from the lobby seated across the aisle. She reluctantly pulled her hand away. "Stop it. I don't need people thinking I'm hooking up with you."

"Why? Am I that repulsive?"

"No. You're perfect." *Too perfect.* "Besides, we're just buds, remember?"

Micah stretched his arm around the back of her seat, leaned in and whispered in her ear. "Haven't you heard of friends with benefits?" His mouth at her ear stirred her blood, arousing her instantly so that the lazy circles his fingers drew on her bare shoulder were almost too intense to bear.

She shifted in her chair, crossing her legs. "I'm beginning to think that's the only kind of friends you have."

"That is simply not true. I have lots of friends I don't sleep with."

"Female friends."

"Still not true. Well, mostly not."

"You're impossible." Visions of women upon women lined up at his bedroom door filled her mind. Her stomach sank at the thought. How many women had he had? Hundreds? Thousands?

"No, I'm perfect. You said it yourself." Still stroking her shoulder, Micah's other hand moved to play with the edge of her skirt hem.

All her senses heightened, she trembled. He was a lion and she was his prey, helpless under his gaze, his touch, even his artsy intellect reduced her to a puddle.

In utter defiance of her body's arousal she said, "I'm not going to sleep with you." At least her brain still worked.

He smirked. "Who said I wanted to?"

"You've been trying to get in my panties since yesterday."

"No way. You're totally reading me wrong. I'm just being nice."

"If that were true, you'd think you could keep your hands off me."

"Yeah, you'd think that. You just have such soft skin." He moved his hand from her skirt to trace the line of her leg down to her knee with his thumb, leaving a trail of goose flesh in its wake. "I appreciate the feel of soft, silky skin."

She tugged at her skirt, pulling it further over her bare thighs. "As long as that's all it is, feel away."

"Did I mention I also appreciate the feel of perky breasts?" The arm around her lowered and he brushed the side of her bosom with his fingers.

She shrugged his hand away. "Ha ha. How about you appreciate them from a distance?"

"Fine, be that way." He abruptly removed his hands from her body, leaving her chilled. He leaned back. "Hey, can we talk about something besides your beautiful breasts?"

"Sure. You're the one who brought them up."

"I did do that. But I sort of feel like you wanted me to. You know, you're keeping them right out in front." She felt his gaze searing on her cleavage. "I'm thinking they like the attention." He pointed to her nipples, pebbled under his stare.

Maddie blushed. "Hey, the air conditioning is chilly in here." Damn her lightweight cotton bra, it hid nothing. She crossed her hands, attempting to suppress the ache of her breasts, sensitive with the want of his lips on them, kissing and pulling, fulfilling their need to be touched.

"Whew, that's better. I can concentrate."

"Awesome." She couldn't, still imagining, dreaming—hoping—for his mouth on her tender skin. For the love of all that was holy, why did he do this to her? And why wasn't the movie starting? "What did you want to talk about?"

"That douchebag, Sam—"

"He's not a douchebag—"

"He is, but let's not argue." He put his finger to her lips. "I don't think you should get involved with him."

"Oh really, and why is that?" Her voice came out breathy, all her effort put into not drawing his finger into her mouth as he swept it across her lips.

"Because he's a douchebag."

She pushed his hand away. "You think you're so adorable and charming that everyone's unworthy in comparison. Why do you care, anyway, if I'm with a douchebag? I mean, with Sam?"

"See that? Freudian slip. He's a douchebag and you know it. And I care because, well, think of it as a public service. You could do much better."

"Like you?"

"Excellent example! Because I am, as you said, adorable and charming."

She groaned. "No, I didn't say that. What you are is an ass. You tell me not to get involved with someone, someone who potentially could be a real fixture in my life if I gave it a chance, simply so you can tease me by touching and fondling me and getting me all hot and bothered when I've made it clear I don't want that."

The next thing she knew, Micah had pulled her from her seat to the dark recesses of the hall behind them. He held her against the wall, pinning her arms with his own, and growled more than spoke. "I make you hot and bothered?"

Maddie's voice came out small and thin. "You know you do."

"Well, here I am. Does it really seem like I'm only teasing?" He leaned in and she closed her eyes, waiting for his kiss. But he stopped just short of her mouth. He circled her face with his own, barely grazing her with his nose. His breath tickled and awakened her as it touched her neck, her ear, her skin. She was on fire, molten lava, and she needed more, needed him. Involuntarily she arched her back, wanting him against her.

Taking her cue, he pressed against her tightly, meeting her body in all the right places.

She gasped as she felt his desire, hard and throbbing against her belly. More, more, she wanted more, needed him on her, inside her.

Behind them the movie roared into action, shocking her to her senses. What was she doing? She pushed him away and ran into the empty lobby of the theater, blinking as her eyes adjusted to the light.

She heard Micah follow her and she turned on him, angry. "What is it you want from me?"

"You." He took a step toward her. "I want you."

"For today? For a week?"

He shrugged. "For the rest of the production schedule?"

Her chest ached. That he could be so cavalier about the inevitable brevity of a relationship with her fueled her anger. "Yeah, no. I can't do that with you, Micah. I'm not pretending I'm virtuous or that I haven't had flings that only lasted the duration of shoot. Not many, but, you know, some. But I'm not looking for that now." She softened. "I'm not looking for that with you. I can't be just another notch in your bedpost." Her voice cracked. "I like you too much for that." She felt naked, exposed from her declaration.

His eyes turned distant. "I can't offer anything but that."

"I know." She did know, but it hurt to be reminded. Which was exactly the reason she had to be finished with the never-ending Micah flirtation. Here and now. "That's why it can't happen." She swallowed. "And if you keep pushing me, Micah, you'll win." She heard him inhale. "But you'll break me."

His shoulders fell, his poise collapsing. "That's not what I want. I don't want to break you."

"Then this—" She gestured between them. "This . . . has to stop."

"All right." He put his hands up in a surrender position, his eyes filled with bewilderment. "It's stopped. Promise."

"Thank you," she choked. She rubbed at her eyes before any tears could fall. *Stupid girl tears.* "Now, if you don't mind, I want to see this film."

She didn't wait to see if he followed as she returned to the theater. She marched down to where the others were seated and tapped Fudge's shoulder. "Please trade me seats," she whispered.

Once Fudge relinquished it, Maddie sank into the chair, thankful for the sad subject of the movie so she could cry and hug herself without any questions.

ELEVEN

MICAH HAD MANAGED THE BEST acting week of his life. Unfortunately none of the great acting was on camera. Yes, he'd filmed several scenes that week, and they'd been decent, but the most convincing work he did was when the camera wasn't rolling, when he pretended that he was unaffected by Maddie Bauers.

He hadn't talked to her in several days—since the day in Breckenridge—and he certainly hadn't touched her. He'd promised he'd stop— stop what? Pursuing her and flirting with her, he supposed. The only way he knew how was to avoid her completely. He'd stayed away from her at the catering tent and let his stand-in take his measurements to be sure he wouldn't have to address her. He ignored her name on the call sheet and her number in his phone, unwilling to go so far as to erase her contact info. Sure, he was in a foul mood every moment of every day, but remarkably, no one but Fudge seemed to notice. Either he was a better actor than he thought, or his mood just blended in with the rest of the cast and crew, who were edgy from a week of night shoots.

Micah stifled a yawn.

"Am I boring you?" Beaumont asked. It'd been a long day and the director was coaching the main actors for the next evening's scenes.

"Sorry. It's been a long day."

"It has. Well, I'm done with you, anyhow. You're on fire, kid. Keep it up. Any questions?"

Micah shook his head. Truth was he hadn't been listening to most of what his director had said. Early in the conversation Beaumont had begun picking on the crew, had even thrown a vague insult toward the camera crew, and Micah became distracted. Were all his directors such pricks when it came to the production staff? He hadn't paid attention in the past. Why did he notice now? Was it because Beaumont was especially prickish or because one of the crew members was Maddie?

It was totally Maddie. How could anyone work with her and not notice her passion and drive? He knew Adam noticed. And Joe. And Sam. How did Beaumont miss it? Micah had paid careful attention to her work whenever he watched the dailies—the raw footage from a day's shoot. So many times he and the other actors would miss their marks, improvising their blocking, and Maddie's expertise kept everything in focus, time after time. Why didn't Beaumont know that? He sat in video village for nearly every take, watching from the monitors, directing over a headset, but surely Joe and Adam told him. Still, the director acted like he had no clue what Maddie did to cover for the cast.

Micah yawned again.

Beaumont patted him on the back. "Get some sleep. Next week we're back to day shoots. We're all struggling, but we'll get through."

Yeah, right. This week video village had been set up inside the cabin. Beaumont got to sit in comfort while his cast and crew slapped at bugs and waded through stickers in the meadow and the woods outside in the dark. Hardly seemed like Beaumont was struggling.

But Micah nodded and looked at his watch before picking up his messenger bag. Four in the morning. No wonder he felt so out of it.

He bid goodnight to Beaumont and the actors still conversing around the table in the cabin dining area and walked into the main room. At the front door, he glanced at the monitors that made up video village in the corner. Maddie sat there, her back to him.

Alone and unnoticed, he took the opportunity to feast his eyes on her for the first time in days. Her dark brown hair was swept up into an untidy bun, long tendrils hanging down her neck—her long, graceful neck—curling around the cord of the headphones she wore. She'd discarded her overshirt and Micah could see the thin, baby-blue strap of her bra peeking around the edge of her tank. He relished the times she bared her firm, strong arms and her sun-darkened flawless skin. He longed to touch her, run his hands over her shoulders, feel his arms around her.

But that was a fantasy for another life.

What caught his attention now were the images on the thirty-inch monitor she sat behind. Picturesque shots of a young couple filled the screen. The woman knelt in a red wagon, her arms spread as the man raced down the street, pulling her behind him. Both laughed, the camera catching the pure and exquisite joy of such a simple moment. It was shot as the sun was setting, and beams of light reflected off the camera lens, creating a whimsical effect. Micah was enthralled.

He moved closer to watch over Maddie's shoulder. Eventually, he was unable to contain his curiosity. "What is it?"

She jumped and swiveled toward him. "Oh my God, you scared me." She removed her headphones and hung them around her neck. "We have a production meeting in a bit. Joe said I could use the monitor until then. Are you guys done?"

She wouldn't meet his eyes. God, what he'd done to her that she couldn't even look at him. "I'm done. Beaumont's still with the others. But I meant, what are you watching?"

"Oh, I . . . it's just something I've been working on." She hit a button on her laptop and the screen froze.

"Don't stop it. Please." Maddie shrugged and restarted the film from the beginning of the section. "*Working on,*" Micah repeated, his eyes not leaving the screen. "Editing . . . ? Directing . . . ?"

"Both."

"Beautiful," he whispered.

"What?"

He cleared his throat. "It's beautiful. I can't hear any sound, don't even know the storyline and I'm totally drawn in. The images are so vivid. The lighting is perfect. The quality is excellent. Digital film?"

"Yes, I shot it on RED."

"*You* shot it? Gorgeous." Man, he wished he could've seen that. The idea of her behind a camera was a total turn-on, mentally and physically. First, she'd look hot on a camera dolly. Hell, when didn't she look hot? But more profoundly, he'd always admired people who ran camera. They dared to see the world in front of them in such a way that it created an exact story. It was much easier to act—totally self-absorbed—than it was to see everything completely outside of yourself.

He realized then that she probably saw him. Saw him in a way that few women ever did, with her photographer's eye and her crazy insight and her brief glimpse of him in his youth. It scared him.

He shook away the thought and focused on the screen. When he spoke again it was as if he hadn't been quiet for several minutes. "But it's not just that, it's the editing. Those jump cuts are awesome."

Her eyes widened. "They take forever to put together."

"I bet. But it's worth it. It reminds me of Soderbergh. Or early Aronofsky."

"Really? I was going for Godard, but I'll take Soderbergh and Aronofsky any day."

"Godard," he chuckled. "Of course. Back to the roots. Yes, I see the influence of *Breathless.*"

She smiled, meeting his eyes for the first time in the conversation. The sudden connection shocked him and they both looked away quickly.

"What's the story?" he asked, returning to the film.

"Young woman stuck in a mundane life. She becomes obsessed with wanting to fly."

"To fly?" He wasn't expecting that.

"A symbolism of her desire to be free. Free to do what she wants, free to follow her heart, her dreams."

"She's you."

She didn't reply and he realized from her downcast eyes that he'd said something too personal.

He moved back to safer ground. "What are you doing with it? Is it a short?"

"It's full-length." She stretched and leaned back in her chair. "I'm slowly putting it together whenever I have down time. I worked like crazy for years to save up for production and then I hired some friends real cheap and took some time off to shoot. That's what I was doing while you were filming in L.A.."

So that's why she joined the crew late. "And when it's finished?"

"I don't know. Enter it in festivals maybe." She sighed. "It's hard to find time to work on it. I don't know when it will be done. If I could afford more time off . . ."

Her voice trailed off and Micah felt the yearning in her unspoken words. Not for the first time in his life he recognized how lucky he'd been to "make it" in the business, so to say. It hadn't been easy, but some people—many people—didn't ever get the chances he had. They worked and struggled and hit brick wall after brick wall. What obstacles had Maddie come up against?

He could help her, if he wanted to. He shouldn't, he'd been burned before. But he could.

He leaned back against the arm of the leather sofa. "Have you tried to get some backers?"

She shifted, looking uncomfortable. "Uh, no."

"Why not?"

She shook her head. "Um, I just . . . I wouldn't find anyone who'd invest. Trust me."

He was puzzled by her response. Maddie worked with a lot of big names. Surely she could get interest from the directors she knew alone. Maybe she was scared. He could understand that. But she didn't need to be. "It's good, Maddie."

She laughed, the light sound awakening his cock. "You don't know that. You saw two minutes."

He held his messenger bag in front of him to hide the protrusion in his pants. "More like ten. I was watching long before I said anything."

She looked up at him through her long eyelashes, her eyes seeking affirmation, and suddenly he felt like a total dick. He'd pestered her and flirted with her, as if the most important thing in her life could be getting laid by Micah Preston. But all Maddie wanted was someone to tell her she was good.

He swallowed, then said the words he knew he shouldn't. "I'd back it."

She rolled her eyes. "Ha, thanks."

Another woman would have taken advantage of his attraction to her and tried to weasel money out of him. But Maddie didn't even take it when he offered. Was that her game? Was she playing him slowly?

No, he didn't believe that. She hadn't ever meant for him to see her film.

He tried again. "I'm serious."

"Ah no, that's not a good idea." Her defenses were up. He was surprised she'd let them down at all. Didn't she realize how weak he was? How hard it was for him to uphold his promise to leave her alone? Defense mode was a good thing.

"Okay, if you don't want my money, which I have plenty of and have been looking to invest in production opportunities, I totally understand. But I can hook you up with other producers."

She swiveled in her chair and met his eyes again. She held his gaze for several long seconds. Finally she spoke. "Don't be nice to me, it confuses me."

He grinned. "Sorry. I won't let it happen again." She returned his smile and he had to force himself not to wrap her up in his arms. Why did he have to be such a shit with her? Maybe he could try to be something different with her. Could attempt a real relationship.

But even if her hesitancy wasn't from fear, his was. He was scared. A big fat chicken. And he didn't see that changing anytime soon.

He straightened and pulled his bag to his shoulder. "Consider the offer, okay?"

She turned back to her computer. "Okay."

"You don't mean that, do you?"

A small smile crossed her lips. "No, not really. Now go away."

He scrutinized her, studying the soft features of her face, wishing he could get inside her head. She was proud, but not haughty, simultaneously strong and fragile. She longed to be free, to fly, so to speak, in her own way, but refused to take a handout. It was so refreshing in the world of show business, where so many people were pompous self-serving assholes. He loved that about her.

Though he shouldn't be loving anything about Maddie. That completely broke his no-strings rule.

She shifted in her chair under his long stare. "What?"

"Just . . . you never cease to amaze me, Maddie from the party." He walked toward the door, refusing to look back at her. He knew if he did, he wouldn't be able to turn away from her again.

TWELVE

M ADDIE WAS PISSED.

After a whole week of avoiding any Micah drama, he had to go and wreck it in the sweetest way possible with compliments and praise and long intense gazes. Seriously? What the hell was she supposed to do with that?

It had been bad enough when her attraction was all sexual, her body betraying everything her mind commanded. But after her encounter with him the night before when he'd said all those nice things about her film and had recognized very private things about her in her art, she had fallen, smack, head-over-heels for the guy. And that flippin' sucked.

Now, like any lovesick fool, she could think of nothing but him. She kept searching for him during setup, kept looking off toward his trailer. Even that afternoon during her daily run, which usually distracted and calmed her, she could not rid her mind of Micah, Micah, Micah. Of course, it didn't help that she continued her running course past his hotel. Because it was the best view, she told herself. *Yeah, right.* Damn, she had it bad.

Just get through the next two nights, she thought as she prepared her calculations with the stand-in. Two last nights of shooting before a whole day off. Then they'd be back to day shoots and everything would be clearer in the sunlight.

Getting through tonight wouldn't be easy, though. The scene they were shooting took place around a campfire. The unsteady light source was sure to play tricks on the focus and the dark night made it difficult for actors to hit their marks correctly. She threw herself into the preparations, double and triple checking each measurement, trying to foresee any possible change that might arise during filming. By the time the actors were due to arrive she thought she actually had a good handle on the situation.

But then Micah appeared on set and she was a goner. He wore baggy jeans that hung on his hips in a way that got her juices flowing, and he had no shirt. *God, he had no shirt! Was that in the script?* She'd never seen his bare chest in-person—and it was a pretty sight. His stomach was perfectly sculpted, his pecs rock-hard. The small trail of hair at his navel caused her core to clench. She longed to trace it with her fingers. Who was she kidding? She longed to trace it with her tongue.

Damn Micah Preston and his hot body.

Yep, she was completely pissed.

When Micah took his place by the campfire, it was even worse. His blue eyes smoldered in the low light, and the flames, as they licked and furled unpredictably, seemed to echo the unstable electric pulses deep in her belly. He wound her up so tight and distracted her so thoroughly, how could she possibly make it through the evening's filming?

And that was only the beginning of the disastrous shoot.

By the time they made it through one full take, there had already been three false starts and two "cuts" because of lighting issues. Beaumont had to be throwing a fit. Maddie was glad he was directing over the headset so she didn't have to witness his displeasure. Even Joe, normally easy-going and laid back, didn't bother to hide the tension, snapping and barking the directions he relayed to the cast and crew. Before an hour had gone by, everyone was in as foul a mood as Maddie.

With all the problems, the thing that continued to piss Maddie off the most was the actors. Well, one actor, who kept missing his mark. Micah had run his blocking perfectly during the run-through, but in every take thereafter he stopped his movement in the wrong spot. If he'd be consistent with the mistake it wouldn't be that big of a deal, but it wasn't even the same wrong spot. With the unpredictable fire, Maddie found it impossible to adjust to his mistakes.

"We're out of focus," Maddie told Adam in between takes. "Micah isn't hitting his mark."

Adam nodded and called Joe over, repeating Maddie's concern.

"Micah," Joe called out. "Where are you stopping on that line? Can you show me?"

Micah stood on his mark and Maddie ran the calculations again. He was in the right spot. Maybe she'd been the one who was wrong.

But when the camera rolled, he missed it again. And again.

"What's going on, Maddie?" Adam asked after another nine takes. "Beaumont is going off saying none of the shots are in focus."

Maddie cringed. She wished she had a headset so she could tell Beaumont he needed to take up the issue with his actor. "Micah's still not hitting his mark."

"Are you sure?"

"Yes, I'm sure!" She usually didn't get defensive with Adam, but this seriously wasn't her fault. And Micah knew where he was supposed to land for his monologue. He hit it whenever they called him on it. So why did he keep fucking it up? Was he *trying* to piss her off?

Adam relayed the message to Beaumont over his headset.

"Micah, can you hit that mark again?" Joe said. "We're still having a focus issue."

Adam ran the shot then asked over the headset, "Was that good?" He listened then said to Maddie. "It's good just like that."

Maddie scowled. "Then get him to hit that when he actually runs the scene and we'll be golden."

"Okay, Micah," Joe said. "You have to hit that exact spot or we can't get the shot."

"Got it," Micah said. *Did he just roll his eyes?* Maddie wasn't sure in the dark.

They ran the scene again with the same results: Micah missed his mark and the shot was blurry.

"Cut!" Joe said. "Hold for five. Beaumont's on his way down."

Maddie groaned. Beaumont only came to the set if he was really ticked-off. Just what she needed—to be the source of his ticked-offedness. He'd already ended any chances of her being a director in Hollywood. Would he now blacklist her as a camera assistant as well?

When Beaumont arrived he marched directly up to Adam and Maddie. "What is the goddamned problem?"

It wasn't her place to talk to the director about actor issues so she swallowed the response she wanted to give and let Adam speak.

"Micah's been missing his mark," he answered, a lot more patiently than Maddie would have.

Beaumont called the actor over. "Hey, the crew says you're having trouble hitting your mark."

Micah's eye twitched. "I'm not. I've hit it every time."

Weeks of sexual frustration fed her work frustration and Maddie's anger spiraled out of control. "You have not! You keep walking right past it!"

"Maddie," Adam warned. The crew did not address actors. That was the director's job.

Micah narrowed his eyes, but didn't look at Maddie. "Look, run it again. It will be perfect. Like it's been the last twenty times. You can see for yourself."

Beaumont considered. Then he turned to Adam. "You run focus, I'll shoot."

Adam took Maddie's place while Beaumont climbed behind the camera. They ran the scene again. Just like Micah said it would be, the scene was perfect. Maddie fumed. They ran the scene two more times with the same results. Finally, Beaumont called it a wrap.

Maddie watched as the crew began to clean up, frozen in her anger and humiliation and guilt. Adam—wonderful Adam who stood behind her and mentored her for years—pulled down to do her job because Micah Preston decided to be a dick. At least, that's the only logical conclusion she could think of.

She turned to the cameraman. "Adam," she said, holding back angry tears. "He didn't hit his marks when I was on focus, I don't know why—"

"You know what, Maddie?" Adam interrupted, his voice low and rough. "I don't care what the problem is or was or the why, but I'm telling you right now it better be fixed by the time you return to this set. I will not stand for that shit when I'm on camera, not even with you. You hear me?"

Adam had never spoken so harshly to her before. And the reason he was angry wasn't even her fault.

"Now, get off my set. I don't want to see you until call tomorrow."

Dismissed from set. She had to set Micah straight. She spun around searching and spotted him walking towards the trailers.

"Micah?" She ran after him. She caught up with him as he approached his trailer from the back. "Micah?"

He turned to face her, an impatient expression on his face.

"What the hell was that?" she asked.

"What the hell was what?"

"Don't play dumb with me. You missed your mark, and what's more, I think you did it on purpose."

"I did not."

"You did! And when Beaumont took over you got it perfect. Which made me look like shit. What I don't get is why."

"I don't know what you're talking about. I did the scene the same each time. If you're feeling insecure about your work, that's fine, but to blame it on me is real low."

"Fuck you, Micah."

"Whatever, Maddie." He turned to walk away.

Her fury escalated. "Wait, I'm not done."

He pivoted back on her. "By all means, Maddie, go ahead."

Anger flooded her, so much that she shook. She pointed an unsteady finger at him. "You." She stepped toward him, gathering her strength. "You're such an actor. You charm and you play and you get into my head and jerk around with my emotions and my body. One minute you don't remember me and you're rude and arrogant and then you're thoughtful and intellectual and complimentary, all the time parading around with your hot body and please-touch-me six-pack abs. Then you're kissing me and stroking me, but oh, oh, oh wait! Nothing can come of this because, you know, 'I have rules.'"

He snorted. "This coming from Miss Leave-Me-Alone-While-I-Give-A-Hand-Job-Under-The-Table?"

Maddie had never felt so outraged in her life. She rushed at him, placed her hands on his bare chest and shoved with all her strength.

It felt so good to unleash her fury, she raised her arms to shove him again. But he grabbed her at her wrists before she could. Then he pulled her to him. In an instant, he was on her—his mouth, his tongue—kissing her with a fire and passion she'd never felt in a kiss before.

And she responded with equal fervor, her fingers clawing his rock-hard pecs. It was all-consuming, her pent-up desire met with his, and she was immediately lost in his touch, his taste, his scent of sweat and makeup and campfire. Two weeks and seven years of longing had led to this moment and she no longer cared about what would happen after, just the now. She couldn't get enough; she wanted him. All of him.

Micah wanted more too. He pushed her against the backside of the trailer, pinning her with his leg, the now familiar ridge in his pants, hard against her thigh while he fumbled at the buttons of her shirt. She was vaguely aware of her shirt falling to the ground as he undid the closure of her jeans, releasing the edge of her tank top. Then his hand was underneath her top, caressing her breast. She leaned into his palm and moaned against his lips. His other hand moved lower, slipping under the band of her panties to reach the center of her want. Skillfully he touched her, circling his thumb against her sensitive bud, sending electric shocks throughout her body.

And then he went even lower. First he eased one finger into her. *Ecstasy.* She almost came undone right then as she clenched around him, wet and hot. He pulled out and she arched to follow him, not wanting him to stop. He met her motion with two fingers, plunged deeper this time, all the while rubbing her clit.

He continued to finger her, massaging her in and out, while she struggled with the fly of his pants, freeing his hard, thick staff. She stroked him as he throbbed in her hand, causing him to utter a deep, lustful groan.

Somewhere in her head her conscience tugged for her attention, shouting at her to stop and think about what was happening. She was about to *do it* with Micah Preston pressed up against the back of his trailer. Was this really how she wanted sex with him to go? In a public place where anyone could walk by at any minute? Did he even have a condom? She sure as hell didn't.

But her body's heightened sense of arousal drowned out any common sense. Clutching his back, she wrapped a leg around his waist and he removed his hand from her breast to help hold her up. His other hand left her southern region, the sudden absence of his probing almost painful, and he lifted her other leg around him.

Condom! Her conscience screamed at her.

Then all thoughts and sensations were interrupted by the sound of voices and approaching footsteps.

"Fuck!" Micah slapped the back of the trailer, dropping her gently as he did.

She bent over for several seconds, her hands resting on her thighs, before her breathing slowed. She could hear Micah next to her, breath also ragged as he fumbled with his zipper. She found herself able to move again just in time for Sam and Chloe to round the side of the trailer.

"Micah," Sam said as Maddie turned away and fumbled with her pants. "Beaumont's looking for you to go through those shots."

"Yeah?" Micah stepped in between Sam and Maddie, shielding her as she straightened herself.

It almost made her laugh. She'd left visible scratches on his still bare chest and he was hiding her for propriety's sake?

Besides, his action didn't impress her. She was hot for him, yes, but with the passion of the moment gone, her anger returned full force, rolling through her like an avalanche. What the fuck was she doing kissing the man who had screwed with her on set? Did she have zero self-respect? Had her usual professional demeanor disappeared just because Micah had some sort of magnetic pull on her vagina?

No more. She had said this before, but now she meant it. She had to mean it if she wanted to keep working in her field. First thing tomorrow she would lodge a complaint. Not that Beaumont would care, but if she told Joe, maybe he could control his actor. She grabbed her shirt off the ground and brushed past Sam and Micah.

"Hold on a minute, Sam. Maddie!" She kept walking and Micah called again. "Maddie!"

She didn't turn around, couldn't turn around, but put her hand out to her side in a wave as she continued walking away from the trailers, away from the heart-crushingly gorgeous man behind her.

THIRTEEN

MICAH CROUCHED IN THE TREES, watching as Maddie ran up the road by his hotel. He'd spotted her when she was still a speck at the bottom of the hill and knew it was her, recognized the movement of her body from seeing her run around on set. He watched through the dark lenses of his sunglasses, enraptured as she neared him, her firm legs striding easily up the hill, her breasts bouncing rhythmically in her light blue sports bra. His cock stiffened at the sight. *Fuck.* That was going to make his next move real uncomfortable.

After she passed him he counted to three before he pulled his baseball cap lower on his head and jogged to catch up with her.

"Hey," he said when he'd reached her side.

She pulled her ear buds out and looked at him. Realizing who he was, she jolted. "Are you fucking kidding me?"

Yeah, she was pissed. He knew she was. He'd tried to find her before he left set the night before with no success. He'd called her cell phone. No answer. He'd called her room. Again, no answer. When he awoke that morning he had tried again. Still no answer. She was avoiding him. Why was he surprised? He had seriously fucked up with his behavior on set.

He had to talk to her, had to apologize, and since she was avoiding him, he'd have to resort to other methods. Including running. "What? I'm just getting some exercise. Enjoying the scenery."

"Then you can do it someplace far away from me." She looked both ways down the street then started toward the other side.

"Wait." He grabbed her wrist.

Yanking her arm away, Maddie turned on him, venom in her voice. "Don't touch me!"

"Sorry, sorry!" Her response to him—as if his touch was loathsome—felt like a knife in his chest. "I'm sorry. I need to talk to you. This is the only way I knew how."

She shook her head, her jaw set firm. She didn't speak but resumed running her original course.

Micah took that as a good sign and fell into a run beside her. As he adjusted to her stride—a punishing pace at this altitude—he tried to think of what to say. He had thought the right words would just come, that he'd be able to explain his actions. But now that he was with her, all he could think about was what had happened after the shoot, when her body was beneath his and his mouth and hands were everywhere on her.

And then she was gone, leaving him with her scent in his nose and a hard-on in his pants. When he spoke, that was what he asked about. "What happened?"

"When? When you fucked with my focuses?"

Even though she didn't look directly at him, he felt the daggers in her eyes. She had been mad last night too, but then they had kissed and so much more—didn't that mean anything?

"Did you really think that groping me against your trailer changed that you pretty nearly lost me my job?"

Shit, did she just read his mind? Truth was he'd hoped that kiss changed everything. Obviously not. He had to come clean. "Okay." He spoke in short sentences, the only way he could speak as they climbed the mountain. "I missed my mark."

"On purpose?"

He didn't do it on purpose, at first. It was dark and he was distracted, as usual, by Maddie, who was ignoring him. So missing it was a natural mistake. But after that . . . He lowered his eyes. "Yes. I missed it on purpose." There. He'd confessed. Why was that so hard? She already knew. "I'm sorry."

She stopped running, her ponytail hitting her in the face as she spun on him. "You're sorry?" She stepped toward him, hands balled at her hips. "That's all you have to say?"

He raised his brows. "I'm very sorry?"

She whipped away from him and started walking up the mountain road. "You're such an ass. You ask me to respect your career but you can't respect mine?"

Man, she was hot when she was angry. Hotter than anyone had a right to be.

He followed her, grateful for the easier pace. "I know, I know. It was shitty."

She didn't speak and he felt helpless in her silence. He wished to God he could take back his actions, wished he could go back to—to what? Avoiding her? Ignoring her? Chasing her?

He'd been a shit to her all around. He removed his glasses and hung them on his shirt. "I'm really very sorry," he said softly.

She glared at him sideways. "Why?"

He creased his brow. "Why am I sorry?"

"Why did you do it?" She swallowed and he suspected she was choking back a sob. "That was one of the absolute meanest things any-one's ever done to me."

His heart dove into his stomach. He could deal with her anger, but her pain tore him to pieces. "I know. God, Maddie, I know." He ran his hand through his hair trying to divert the frustration at himself into the action. He had hurt her. *Fuck!* Hurt her bad.

He hadn't given her a reason and she was waiting. "I don't know why."

Actually he did know why. He saw how his mistake affected her. How an easy little change in his blocking got her up-in-arms and made her pay attention to him. He knew she was getting heat for it, that he was messing with her in a way that was not only unprofessional, but also seriously shitty. But he couldn't help himself. He craved her attention, and he'd take it any way he could. "I guess I wanted you to notice me."

She glared at him full on. "Notice you? You narcissistic little fucker." She turned her attention back to the road in front of her. After several steps she said, "Like I'm not completely one hundred percent aware of your presence at any given moment?"

He grinned. "You are?"

"Don't," she snapped. "Don't be cute."

He erased the glee from his face and took a deep breath. "Look, you'd been ignoring me all week. And after the night with your movie, I thought maybe things would be different since, you know, we'd talked and . . ."

"And for once you didn't try to get down my pants?"

Well . . . "Yes."

"Wow, you deserve some sort of award for that. Were you pissed that I didn't acknowledge your accomplishment?"

"No, Maddie, I'm pissed that I can't be with you." He stopped walking, stunned at his honesty. She stilled too but didn't face him, which was for the best. It was easier to say what he needed to without the anger shooting from her gaze.

"Maddie, I want you more than anything. I am so . . ." What? He searched for the words. "Turned on by you. All of you, your mind, your art." He moved his eyes down her form. "Your body. It's killing me that you won't give me the time of day."

She rolled her eyes. "I bet it's a first for you."

"Yes."

She shook her head and resumed running.

He followed, thinking about what he'd just said. "I mean . . ." He wasn't used to women saying no to him, but that wasn't why he liked her. "I'm not attracted to you," he panted, "because you keep turning me down," he panted again, the increasing incline making it hard to carry a conversation. "If that's what you're insinuating." A stitch dug in his side. He put his hand on his waist to ease the ache. "Hey, can we just . . . walk?"

Maddie knit her brow. "What's the matter with you?"

"I'm . . ." God, this was embarrassing. "I'm not a great runner. "

"What do you mean? You're totally in shape. See? I notice you."

He bit back a smile. "I strength train. And I run on a treadmill. A treadmill that's totally flat."

"That's lame." She sighed, slowing her pace. "I guess walking is fine. Though I enjoyed seeing you struggle." Her lips curved slightly.

"I deserve that." Her candor made him hopeful. He continued in her path of truthfulness. "But trust me I'm always struggling around you."

The smile that had hinted before now settled on her face.

Good. They were making progress. Though they still had miles to go. "I feel horrible about last night. I'm buried under the weight of regret, Maddie, and I don't know how to come up for air." He paused, uncomfortable with how exposed he felt. "I was an asshole. I can't bear that it might mean I never have another chance with you. What can I do, baby?" The endearment was a slip but he didn't regret it when he saw the pleased glimmer in her eye.

"Tell Beaumont," she said without hesitation.

"Of course. I'll tell him tonight."

"He isn't on set tonight. He's out for some Beaumont-y thing. Joe's running the shoot."

"Then I'll tell Joe."

She pinned him with her stare. "No, it has to be Beaumont."

"Then I'll tell him first thing the next time I see him. I swear to God."

"And promise to never ever do anything like that again."

"Cross my heart and hope to die." Never. He would never hurt her like that again, not on purpose.

"Okay." She relaxed. "All right. Thank you."

Micah let out a breath he hadn't realized he'd been holding. They walked in silence for several seconds while he gathered up his courage to say what he had to say next. "But, Maddie, that won't fix everything. We have to deal with this." He waved his hand back and forth between them. "With whatever is going on between us. Because it's not going away." He returned the scowl she gave him. "Don't look at me like you don't know what I'm talking about."

Her eyes narrowed. "And what exactly do you propose? Just fuck and get it over with?"

His balls throbbed at the suggestion of sex. "I was going to say one date, but, yeah."

She shook her head, her ponytail catching on her shoulder. "I can't believe I'm listening to this."

He exhaled slowly, worried that he was losing ground.

She turned on him before he could formulate a new plan. "Why me, Micah? If it's not my repeated no's that have you intrigued, what is it? Why not one of the million other girls you know would kill for a night with you? Why me?"

That question. God, it was impossible to answer. He'd asked himself the same thing over and over since the airport and hadn't come up with anything he could quite explain.

But now, for her, because she needed to know, he tried. "You remember that night?" He waited for her to nod. "Back then you liked me. At least, I think you did. And it wasn't because I had money or a big name. It was me."

He shook his head, not believing how completely exposed he was making himself for her. For a woman.

But as scary as it was, he wanted to be that exposed. "Now, when I'm kissing you, I'm kissing her—the woman who wanted to kiss that no-name-guy-from-the-wrap-party. And you don't seem to give a shit about the Micah Preston stuff."

"That was a wrap party? Huh. I had no idea." She kicked at the gravel with her toe, her eyes fixed on the ground.

It drove him crazy that she wasn't looking him, that he couldn't read her features, couldn't see what she was thinking. "Yeah. For a Davenport film I'd just finished."

"Hmm." Finally she met his eyes. "Micah, that's a really sweet sentiment. And I'm sure I can't even begin to understand what it's like for you. But I didn't even know you back then. Yes, I was attracted to you for reasons that weren't about fame or money. You were charming and adorable and, well, so freakin' hot."

He grinned like he always did when she stated her attraction to him.

"But it was one night. A brief night a long time ago. If you want to know if I'm really into you, the real you under all that other stuff, then you'd have to give me a chance to get to know you. Because I don't. I don't know you."

Her words punched him in the gut. Right. She didn't know him. And he'd been wrapped up with this idea that she did, that she saw him for who he really was.

Yet, instead of taking her truth and running like he usually did, he found himself asking, "Do you want to?"

"After what you pulled? I'm not sure."

But she was still standing there talking to him. There had to be something he could say or do to make it work. "If I hadn't been such an idiot, if I hadn't fucked it up royally, what would it take to be with you?"

"It would take *you* being willing to be with *me*. I mean, I wouldn't expect you to become my boyfriend. Or for you to be seen with me in the press. I'd just want a chance to see. See what happens, you know? Spend time together without any presumptions or preconceived notions of what we will or won't be."

"Spend time together . . . would that include time in and out of bed?"

She rolled her eyes. "You are such a horndog."

"These days? Just for you." His grin disappeared as he digested what she'd said. And though his next question tumbled out without much thought, he knew as he asked that it was exactly what he wanted. "I can't take back yesterday, but if you thought you might be able to forgive me, and if I said okay, that I'd be willing to spend time with you without any presumptions or preconceived notions, would you give us that chance to see?"

Confusion and uncertainty crossed her face as she bit her upper lip.

Maybe it was too much to expect, for her to forgive him that completely. But he wanted so much for that chance, he had to ask. "At least consider it." He took her hand.

"I told you not to touch me," she grumbled, but she kept her hand in his. "Okay."

"Okay?" He was sure his eagerness came off as nothing short of pathetic. *Whatever.* He'd rather be pathetic than without her.

"Okay, I'll consider it." She peered at him with intense brown eyes. "But you have to promise to respect whatever I decide."

"Yes, of course." He stroked her hand with his thumb, enjoying the vibrations that traveled through his nerves at the touch of her soft skin.

She stared at their joined hands as if trying to decide if his caress was pleasant or painful. "Why does it feel like I've already decided this a million times?"

"Maybe you keep making the wrong decision."

"Yeah, that's it," she said, her voice laced in sarcasm.

They walked in silence, hands entwined, for several minutes, long enough for Micah to pretend they were an ordinary couple out for a lovers' stroll. It felt . . . nice. Surreal, but nice. He wondered if she felt the same. "What are you thinking?"

She sighed. "I hate you."

"Say that again," he said, throwing the next line in the scene they had read together.

She smiled, catching his reference. Then she said the next line. "I hate you."

Did she want him to continue? If they kept this up, it would lead to a kiss. Did she want that kiss? If his lips were on hers, she wouldn't resist him. He knew it.

But he didn't want to bully her anymore. So he dropped the scene. "I know," he said. "I hate me too." He brought her hand to his lips and kissed it.

"You're going to break me," she whispered, repeating what she'd said to him at the movie theater.

But she was wrong. "You're the one who's going to break me." She would. He knew it now. She was going to break him into so many pieces he wouldn't be able to recognize himself.

And he was totally looking forward to it.

FOURTEEN

MADDIE HAD ALWAYS BEEN SURE. Sure of what to do with her life, sure of who she was as a person. Sure of everything.

The first time she'd really experienced a crack in her confidence had been several years ago when she'd interned for Joss Beaumont. He'd shown interest in her as a director and invested in a project of hers, a short film that she'd written. He had left all the details to her and when the still-inexperienced and fresh-from-school Maddie had overspent and failed to finish the film on budget, he tore her apart.

"You're untalented and incompetent," he'd screamed at her after watching the footage she did have. "You will not work in this town as a director again."

He wouldn't give her the money she needed to finish her film and, since his investment contract gave him full rights, he refused to let her finish it at all. Maddie had worked on that movie for two years, pouring her heart and soul into every frame only to see it get shelved, never to be viewed in the glory she'd envisioned.

A year or so later, when she'd recovered from the blow and began work on another film idea, she sought investors—people who could help her produce a decent movie. True to his word, Beaumont made sure the major players in the city knew his disrespect for Maddie and door after door was shut in her face. She learned the hard way that blacklisting wasn't just an urban legend. Either that or she really was untalented and incompetent. Self-doubt overtook her and she eventually gave up. She took up working as Adam's assistant instead and followed him from set to set, becoming a skilled and unflappable focus-puller. Yeah, she still tinkered with ideas, filming and editing as a hobby, but never letting dreams of career directing cross her mind again.

After the whole Beaumont fiasco, she thought she'd recovered nicely. She remained intrepid in every other aspect of her life, in control and secure.

And then Micah Preston came along. Now she was dizzy and doubtful and undecided. He threw her around like a deck of cards in a game of fifty-two card pick-up. Even when he returned to gather her together again, she still felt shuffled and rearranged, and anything but sure.

She tapped her fingers on the mixer, thinking about him as she waited for the lighting to be set for the next scene. She'd wandered over to the sound table to remain out of the way and to text Bree for advice. But she had no bars in their remote location. She'd have to be a grown-up and sort her problems out on her own.

She closed her eyes and sighed, remembering Micah's words as they'd walked together that afternoon. The reason behind his awful behavior revealed so much insecurity and heartache. *"I wanted you to notice me."* The whole world focused on him and he was concerned about her attention? How could she not want to fold him into her arms and notice him all night long?

But then she'd remember all the women he'd been with, and she'd doubt again. He never had any intention of turning any of his encounters into a relationship. He doomed them from the start. Could he really let her in enough to overcome his natural tendency to remain aloof? Could he really give them the chance he alluded to?

And if he couldn't, should she decide she didn't care and just live in the moment? Or tell him once and for all that she'd had enough?

She wasn't sure.

Chloe's sassy voice pulled her from her reverie. "Did you say something?" Maddie asked.

"Huh, what?" Chloe removed one of the headphones that fed her the sound from the set from her ear.

"I thought you said something."

Chloe broke into a grin. "Ha, no, I was just laughing at the actors. As always."

Maddie glanced toward set. Micah and Heather were chatting by a large prop boulder. They were too far to hear, though. Unless their microphones were still on. "Are their mics hot?"

"Yeah." Chloe appeared to listen for a moment then chuckled again. "Heather's giving Micah a hard time about his mood. It's pretty funny."

"Hmm, really?" Maddie tried not to seem too interested, but who was she kidding? She was interested in everything concerning Micah.

Chloe lowered her voice and spoke in a tone that insinuated good gossip. "I think she's trying to hit on him. They wouldn't be the first costars to hook up during filming."

Every hair on Maddie's body stood up, a storm of jealousy brewing in her blood. "What?"

Chloe twisted her lips and narrowed her eyes. Then, her face eased as if she had come to a decision. "I really shouldn't do this, but here." She handed the headphones to Maddie. "I can't have all the fun."

Maddie hadn't listened to hot mics since she'd worked on sound in college. It was common knowledge that the sound crew was always in the know, constantly overhearing conversations between actors when the cameras weren't rolling and they'd forgotten their microphones were on. It was unethical for the crew to share their inside scoop, and Chloe had never done it as far as Maddie knew. At another time, in another place, Maddie would have politely turned down the offer. But now her curiosity won. She put the headphones on.

"I don't know what you're talking about," Micah's voice came through the cans clearly, his smooth murmur fed directly into her ears sending a shiver down her spine.

"You're distracted and happy all at once," Heather purred. "Who are you thinking about?"

Maddie wondered if he was thinking about her like she was thinking about him. If he'd been sincere during their run that morning, she would bet money he was.

She watched him across the meadow as he ran his hand over his eyes. "I'm thinking about our scene."

Heather tossed a blond curl over her shoulder. "I don't believe you. Our scene isn't happy." She grabbed Micah's shirt and pulled him closer to her. "Are you thinking about us? I am."

Maddie stiffened. Heather Wainwright was totally flirting with Micah. How could Maddie ever compete with Heather Wainwright?

And did she just admit that she wanted to compete over Micah?

Micah removed himself from the actress's clutches. "Uh, Heather, we weren't ever really . . . anything . . ."

Weren't ever really anything? Maddie's heart thumped loudly in her chest. Why would Heather think otherwise?

He leaned back on the boulder. "And aren't you back with your boyfriend?"

Heather shrugged. "I was with him the last time we hooked up."

"You were? I didn't realize . . ." Micah's voice trailed off.

Maddie's thumping heart dropped to her stomach. Micah and Heather had already hooked up. Heather had kissed and fondled and stroked and done all the things that Maddie longed to do with Micah. She wanted to throw up.

It doesn't matter. He had been with so many women it didn't matter if Heather was one of the hordes.

Except that the actress named as one of the fifty most beautiful women in the world by the biggest entertainment magazine in the industry was right there, right now, inches from him. Was he sleeping with her while he hit on Maddie? *Please, oh please, let that be a no!*

Maddie didn't have to wait long for an answer to her questions. Heather's proposition came soft but distinct over the headphones. "Come over tonight, Micah. We have tomorrow off. We could spend all day in the hotel like old times." She leaned into him and whispered, "Doesn't that sound fun?"

He stood up and turned to face his costar, leaving what Maddie considered an appropriate distance between them. "Heather, I'm just, you know, I'm not really feeling it."

Yes! Maddie could have jumped for joy if she weren't afraid of drawing attention.

Heather slumped down on the boulder, pouting. "What a shame. I thought I could always count on you for a roll in the hay. Are you sure you're not coming down with something?"

"Ha ha ha, yes. I'm fine. I'm just—"

"Micah," Joe interrupted. "Let's talk about that moment at the beginning of the scene."

Maddie slipped the headphones off and handed them to Chloe. She was still surprised about the exchange. Micah had slept with Heather in the past and he wasn't sleeping with her now. Half to herself she said, "He totally turned her down."

Chloe raised her eyebrows. "He did? Hmm. Bummer for Heather. Well, I guess that fits his M.O. He's generally a love 'em and leave 'em guy, isn't he? Still, lucky her for getting whatever she got."

Maddie nodded in agreement, but she wasn't so sure. Surprise, surprise! Not sure about Micah. Again. "Chloe, would you sleep with him knowing it was going to be a one-time thing?"

"Uh, duh. Who wouldn't? Girlfriend, if Micah Preston showed even the slightest bit of interest I'd rub myself all up and down him before he could say, 'April Fool's.' That man is fine."

Maddie rubbed her chin. "Really? I mean he's hot." *Super, mega-amazingly eye-blindingly hot.* "But it wouldn't be like just a normal one-nightstand. You'd see his face everywhere after and that would just be—"

Chloe cut her off. "It would be awesome, is what it would be. Every time I saw his face I'd say to myself—and probably everyone I know—'yeah, I hit that.'"

Maddie laughed. Chloe had a point. Sleeping with a super hot actor wouldn't be something most people would frown at.

Oh, hell. Why was she such a frickin' prude? Had she always been this way? Or just with the one guy in the universe that she actually wanted to fuck royally?

"Besides," Chloe added. "You always wonder if you could be the one—the one that the hot guy finally settles for. But you never know unless you go for it. I mean, I'd never go for it. But that's only 'cause I'm all talk."

Maddie sighed. This was crazy. Her and Micah, and chances, and all of it. Absolute madness. She'd read somewhere that the definition of crazy was doing the same thing over and over but expecting different results. Over and over she'd said she was finished with Micah and over and over again she returned to him like a boomerang flung into the wind. If she really wanted to be done with him, she had to do something different.

But what if she abandoned her entire agenda? What if she decided returning to Micah's arms was actually an okay ending? Heaven knew that was exactly where she wanted to be.

What if he really could give them a chance and she was the one who was holding them back?

What if . . . ?

She thanked Chloe for the entertainment and returned to her place at the camera, struggling to hide her sudden giddiness. She'd made a decision and she wasn't backing down. For the first time since Micah reentered her life, she felt sure.

FIFTEEN

MICAH RAN HIS HAND THROUGH his hair as he waited for the hotel clerk to make him a new key card. He thought he'd made progress with Maddie that day. Their run—okay, walk—had been tough to get through, even without the physical exertion, but it had ended on a promising note.

The night's shoot, the last before a much needed day off, had gone well too. Except for a minor awkward moment early in the evening when Heather had tried to resume their occasional sexual activity. Uh, no. If not for Maddie, maybe, but that was hard to even imagine because Maddie was all he could think about.

But after that the shoot had been nice. For the first time since he'd arrived in Colorado, he didn't try to avoid or seduce Maddie. Instead, he'd stood for all his focus measurements, chatted with her between takes, exchanged glances with her when Joe got off track. It was all natural and easy and fun.

On top of that, his acting had been on fire. He'd remembered all his lines and hit all his marks. The scenes had gone so well, they'd wrapped early.

And that was when things started going downhill.

He looked around for Maddie the second they were done, to no avail. He even asked others about her whereabouts, not caring about what they thought or what rumors his inquiry started. No one had an answer. Then he walked down to video village where Adam said she'd taken the camera hard drives. He didn't find her there either.

He decided to hit his trailer and shower, then search for her again. When he couldn't find her after he'd cleaned up, he wondered if she was avoiding him again. He considered calling her, pulled out his phone more than once to do so, but he didn't want to push her. She'd said she'd consider giving them a shot. He had to trust her.

Then to top off his already anxious mood, he couldn't for the life of him find his room key and had to have a new one made at the front desk.

He pulled out his phone again while the night clerk fiddled with the key machine. While he didn't want to be pushy, he wanted Maddie to know he was thinking of her. He deliberated over what to text her for an embarrassingly long length of time. In the end he went with short and simple. *"Sweet dreams, baby."*

She didn't return his text, and he worried. But what could he do?

Nothing. Nothing but wait.

By the time he stood outside his room, he was tired and frustrated. And alone.

He considered knocking on Fudge's door. The idea of entering an empty suite was almost too desolate to imagine. But Fudge had taken off while Micah was still searching for Maddie. He was most likely already asleep. And what use would Fudge be in keeping Micah's mind off a woman?

With a heavy sigh, he stuck the new key in the card reader to open the door.

And there she was. Standing in his room like a vision.

He stood blinking in the threshold.

"Um, hi," she said.

Lost for words, he silently stepped in the room letting the door close behind him. *She's here,* he thought. *She's here.* Everything but that splendid realization dissolved away.

He set his bag down and cocked his head, looking over the beautiful specimen before him.

"I, uh, don't know if it's okay that I'm here." She played with the hem of her tank top. "And I'm sorry if it's not."

He opened his mouth to answer, to say it was more than okay, especially if she was there for the reason he hoped. But she continued talking before he had the chance.

"Actually, I'm really not sorry. I need to be here. I want to be here, too, don't get me wrong. I mean I really, really want to be here especially after everything you said today. Earlier today. When we were running, I mean. And tonight too. Nothing specific from tonight, but just it was really great to talk to you, and you know . . ."

Hmm, so she'd felt it too. Her nervousness was adorable. As if he didn't want her completely.

"Anyway, besides wanting to be here, I need to be here because I'm going to go crazy if things continue like they have. Well, not like to-day—today was good—but before today. And actually, I think I may have already gone crazy, but that's not really relevant to this conversation."

He watched her eyes as she spoke. They were so expressive, changing as quickly as her rambling took a new direction. Beautiful and engaging.

She took a deep breath and he inhaled with her, syncing naturally to her.

"I have to be honest and tell you that it's hard for me to trust that you'll give us a chance. But if I don't give us a chance either, then I'm no better than you. So I have to just throw my hat in and hope. Hope you do too, I mean. Because I have no idea where we'll go after that. I mean, what if I totally hate you? You are an actor and I've always been turned off by the talent."

He covered his mouth to keep from laughing at her delightful rambling.

Her voice dropped to a hush. "And I do want to spend time with you in and outside of bed. And since we've spent all our time together outside of the bed, and since we can't seem to keep our hands off each other . . ."

He almost groaned. *She is here for that.* He shifted his stance to accommodate his tightening jeans.

"I would have waited in the lobby, but I didn't want anyone to see me and since I knew where you kept your key, I took it and let myself in. I was going to wait for you with all my clothes off—"

He raised an eyebrow.

"—but then I realized that would be especially awkward if you kicked me out."

He nodded and switched the dead bolt to the 'do not disturb' position. Even at two in the morning he wasn't taking any chances. They had been interrupted too many times before and nothing was going to interfere this time.

He walked toward her, slowly, purposefully, still not saying anything.

"I'm probably coming off as one of those creepy, stalker girls right now. I didn't really think this through, I just . . . did . . . you know? Without thinking. I just ran to your trailer first thing after wrap and grabbed your key. I'm lucky you keep it in the same place, though maybe you need to rethink that in the future."

She rubbed her hand along her collarbone, drawing his attention to her lovely neck. He'd kiss that first, trace the beautiful line up to her exquisite jaw.

"I'm really not this psycho. I'm—this—everything I do when I'm with you, actually, is really uncharacteristic of anything I usually do— ever—and I don't know why I'm doing it when I'm doing it, but I can't help myself."

Then he'd nibble on that ear. He bet it tasted divine.

"And I know it was really unfair to ask you to stay away from me when I can't seem to stay away from you. You just get in my head and make me insane. Oh, ha ha, I guess I am really this psycho. But it's you who makes me crazy and I'm . . . just . . ."

He stood in front of her now.

" . . . say something."

He cradled her face with his hand. "Stop talking."

He shifted his palm to the back of her neck and pulled her to him. She threw her arms around him and all his plans of where to caress and what to nibble went out the window as his mouth met hers. He kissed her tentatively at first, afraid of the unbridled passion they'd experienced outside his trailer, that it would move them too quickly. He wanted to take his time.

She seemed to have the same idea. Her lips, as they moved and molded to his, still held all the fervor of their last embrace, but none of the desperation. The kiss built and blazed. Soon it absorbed him, her tongue drawing him into a depth of intimacy he hadn't felt in years. He could live on this kiss.

It was Maddie arching eagerly against him that finally reminded him there were so many more areas of her body he wanted to touch and explore. He surrendered her mouth and moved along her neck, licking and nipping as she tilted her head to give him more access. She moaned and he journeyed lower along her collarbone, kissing along the top of her breasts.

Her breasts. He had fondled them, knew they perfectly fit his hand, but he had yet to see them, to taste them. He couldn't wait any longer. "These," he said, his voice tight. "I want to see these."

A shy grin crossed her face as he slid his fingers under her tank top and pulled her shirt up, missing the feel of her hands on his body when she lifted her arms to help him remove it.

Then there they were, pink-tipped and fully exposed for his eyes only. Damn, they were beautiful. Even better than he'd imagined. They were firm and round and her nipples responded immediately as he sucked and tugged at her tender skin. With a soft moan, she collapsed into the crook of his arm under his ardor.

"Goddamnit, Maddie, I need you in my bed."

She squealed as he swept her into his arms, and he reveled in the sound. He carried her through the suite to the bedroom and laid her gently on the king-size bed. There he gazed at her for several long heated seconds. She blushed under his stare and his rock-hard member ached for release. *Not yet.* There was so much he wanted to do to her—do *for* her—he didn't know where to begin.

He leaned over and nuzzled her neck. "Tell me what you want," he whispered in her ear.

Her words came out throaty. "You."

He smiled. She was so innocent. Not a virgin, no. But Micah had a feeling that her previous lovers were self-serving in their sexual exploits. *She doesn't even know what she wants.* Well, he'd have to show her.

He stood again and lifted her leg. He slid off her shoe, then her sock, his eyes locked on hers as he did. "Such a pretty foot," he said. He kissed each toe. When he reached the biggest, he sucked it then grazed the pad with his teeth. She shivered. He lowered her leg and repeated the process on her other foot, enjoying the sparkle in her eyes that his attentions brought.

When he had finished cherishing her feet, he bent over her and drew down the zipper on her pants. He watched her, ensuring she was willing for him to continue. He didn't know what he'd do if she wasn't. He couldn't stop now if he tried. He needed her.

Fortunately, her eyes mirrored the lust and desire he felt. He shimmied her pants past her hips and down her long legs, replacing the fabric with a trail of kisses. She was curvier than most of the models and actresses he usually spent his nights with, one of the reasons he was so attracted to her. He could already imagine how soft and lush she would feel wrapped around him. His cock pulsed at the thought.

He trailed his hands up her legs to return for her panties. "Such pretty panties," he said. "I almost hate to remove them. But for what I have in mind, they'll only be in the way."

Her breath caught and his erection grew harder, if it was possible. He leaned down and placed a gentle kiss over her sweet spot, then hooked his fingers under the black lace, sliding them down past her ankles and threw them to the floor behind him.

She pressed her knees together, instinctively, he guessed. "No, no, no," he teased, placing his hands on her knees to separate her legs. He sighed at the beauty of her naked in front of him—her nicely trimmed pussy, her pink swollen desire. "You're so beautiful," he groaned as he crawled into the v of her legs, holding her open with his body.

He lowered his mouth to her stomach and swirled his tongue around and inside her navel while she moaned underneath him. Then he moved south. Her legs tensed around him as she sat up suddenly, propping herself on her elbows. Astonishment and uncertainty clouded her eyes.

"Please," he caressed her with his voice. "Let me taste you."

She paused. Then let her legs fall open for him.

He trailed his lips slowly over her sex. She exhaled and surrendered to his mouth, all tension leaving her body. God, she tasted so good. He tapped his fingers fast and light on her skin where her thighs met her center as he licked and adored her, circling and stroking her clit with his tongue. She quivered as he surprised her with a gentle nip and he took pleasure in her delightful reaction.

When she bucked underneath him, begging for more, he responded by slipping two fingers inside her. "Ah, you're so wet," he murmured. He tugged and stretched her as he continued to kiss and massage her sensitive bud. She writhed, lifting her hips to meet his probe, her hands buried in his hair. She made the sweetest sounds he'd ever heard and he relished each groan and gasp, recognizing that she didn't offer her vulnerability to just anybody.

When she shattered around him, he continued his assault, drinking in her salty taste until her whimpers softened and her body stilled. Then he returned to her lips. He kissed her softly and tenderly, smoothing her hair behind her ear while her breathing calmed. He knew that she'd exposed herself to him more completely than she had to anyone else before.

And he startled himself by hoping she'd never open up like that to anyone but him again.

———— ♦ ————

HOLY CANNOLI, SHE WAS LYING naked on Micah Preston's bed. And he had gone down on her. And she'd enjoyed it.

Maddie couldn't wrap her mind around it. She couldn't wrap her mind around anything at the moment, actually. Her orgasm had left her numb and delirious and shaking and now he was kissing her again. Micah-from-the-party-Preston was kissing her and doing unspeakably amazing things to her naked body and goodness sakes alive, did he have a present for her. She could feel it, thick and hard against her leg, straining against his pants.

Now, why did he still have his clothes on? She'd have to remedy that.

She pulled herself away from his delicious lips and twisted so she was straddling his hips. "My turn."

He smiled slyly. "And what will you do with your turn?"

"Explore." She grabbed the hem of his shirt and he lifted his arms so she could peel it up and over his head. Oh, the rock-hard chest that had taunted her all during the shoot the night before. She ran her hands up his abs and over his pecs, then down the sides of his torso. *Mighty fine indeed.*

Micah inhaled sharply as her exploration reached the trail of hair leading down underneath the waist of his jeans. She moved herself lower and palmed his erection through the material. He moaned.

"My, this has to be awfully uncomfortable," she teased. "Let's see if this helps." She unbuttoned and unzipped, discovering the tip of his head poking under the band of his boxer briefs. "Well, what do we have here?"

In one motion, he flipped her so she was underneath him. "Why don't I show you?" he growled. Within seconds he'd removed his jeans and briefs and retrieved a condom from the nightstand drawer.

Maddie's mind wandered for the briefest moment to the reason for the condom supply—had there been other girls on this shoot? Other girls in this bed? But she pushed away the thought. She was the girl in the bed now. She was the girl watching as he unrolled the condom over his thick, hard shaft. Her tummy tightened at the sight.

Then he was stretched out on top of her, kissing her with deep need. She wanted to fulfill that need, to satisfy his hunger. In turn, she knew he would slake her own longing.

She wriggled underneath him until she felt him hot against her entrance. She bucked, begging him to enter. "I want you inside me," she whispered.

Micah gazed at her with hooded eyes. Then, in one swift stroke, he plunged into her.

She cried out as he filled and twitched within her. This was so . . . so . . . so much better than she had ever imagined, and she had imagined it quite a few times over the past weeks. She felt beautiful, desired, special. She felt perfect.

He stilled as her body stretched to accommodate him. "My God, you're so tight."

Maddie rocked her hips up, urging him to keep on.

And then he began to move. Long, deliberate strokes pierced her, each bringing more heat and electricity, driving her mad. It was too much and not enough. She simultaneously wanted release and to never, ever stop.

She wrapped her legs around him, granting him deeper access. "Oh baby," he groaned. Her senses heightened at his exclamation. This was because of her—she had brought him here.

His pace increased and he moved longer, deeper. She lifted her hips to meet each thrust, the new friction threatening to send her over the edge. Tightening her grip, she dug her fingernails into his shoulders. Pressure built and grew inside her, pushing her further, further, further until she knew she was close, so close.

"Come for me, baby," he commanded.

And she did, exploding gloriously around him. Her climax sent uncontrollable ripples throughout her body as she cried out. She continued to shudder, milking him as he thrust through her orgasm until he let out a low moan, finding his own release.

He lingered there while their breathing slowed, his ragged respiration matching hers. Reveling in the feel of him against her and inside her, it occurred to her that the other men she'd slept with would have rolled over by now, fallen asleep. But not Micah. He tenderly stroked her neck, holding her in his arms, his forehead pressed to hers. The afterglow was sweet and she savored it.

"You're here." Micah's voice startled her eyes open.

"Hmm?"

"I just can't believe you're here." He stroked the side of her cheek with his thumb. "I'm very glad you're here."

Warmth spread throughout her. "Me, too."

"I looked for you tonight."

"You did?" She had wondered if he would.

"And I texted—"

"Yeah, I got that. It was sweet. I didn't reply because I was already here and I wasn't sure what to say."

"Um, how about, 'Hurry the hell up to your room. Where I'm waiting. Naked.' I know the naked wasn't exactly true, but it would have gotten me moving."

Maddie giggled. "That wouldn't have made a very good surprise."

He rubbed his fingers slowly up and down her arm. "I suppose not. And it was a very good surprise."

They lay silent for a moment. Despite his affirmations, doubt began to creep in. "So, stocked with condoms, huh? Have you had the opportunity to . . . uh . . . use them recently?"

He chuckled. "Someone always stocks my trailer with a box. It's probably written in my contract somewhere as standard protocol. But no, I haven't broken into them at all this shoot. And the few I have here in my room . . . Well, I was hopeful that I might get a certain lady here. Eventually."

Maddie played along. "A certain lady?"

"Yeah, she's really amazing and beautiful and incredibly sexy. She's working on the movie, but I met her ages ago. I wanted her in my bed then, but it didn't work out. Then I got a second chance . . ."

She stared into his deep blue eyes. Had he really only wanted her these past days? Pined for her even? It was incredible and still so hard to believe. But she knew he was telling the truth, had felt it as his body had moved inside her. She saw it now in his eyes, still dilated with desire.

She kissed him, sweetly and tenderly, and for several minutes she was lost again in his mouth.

When Micah finally pulled away he said, "Maddie, I'm sorry."

"For what?"

He furrowed his brow. "I missed my mark."

She clenched around him still inside her. "I think you hit it pretty well, actually."

"Did I now?" His eyes glinted and she felt his staff thickening. "But what I meant—"

She put a lone finger up to his lips, shushing him. "I know what you meant. You apologized already. I don't care anymore. I'm happy."

Micah closed his eyes and let out a deep sigh. "Me too."

She lay in his arms, sated, as he continued to stroke her arm. Exhaustion began to claim her, and she allowed herself to close her eyes and drift.

"Hey, you can't go to sleep!"

Maddie jumped as he shook her gently.

"I've waited for this with far too much anticipation to let this evening end so soon." With a wicked grin, he flipped her over, drew her up to her knees, and reached his hand around to stoke the fire in her loins.

Yes, she thought as her body awoke to his touch, *very happy*.

SIXTEEN

MADDIE'S INNER THIGH MUSCLES GROANED as she squatted to look for the lens cap she'd dropped. And why shouldn't her muscles groan? She and Micah didn't leave his hotel room once in the twenty-seven hours they'd had off from production, and very little of that time was spent sleeping.

She smiled at the memory of this morning's shower together before she ran to her hotel room for a change of clothing. He had sponged and cleansed her so thoroughly, they'd run out of time to take care of other business. Unwilling to let Micah leave for work with such a huge "problem," Maddie had serviced him orally. She'd not given many blowjobs in her lifetime, a handful—mostly in college. They had seemed so impersonal and dirty. But when she placed her lips on Micah's shaft and sucked and licked and moved him in and out of her mouth, she felt powerful and intimately close to him. She'd watched the look of exquisite pleasure on his face, and the knowledge that it was *her mouth* making him feel that way . . . well, she had a feeling she'd be giving a lot more in the future.

The future.

The thought brought her plummeting from her Micah high. Did she even have a future with him? They'd said they would take it one day at a time, wait and see. But that's all they'd said. No talk or plans of any future, including the near future. Would she get to spend time with him at all that day? Should she ask him or wait for him to say something? She could invite him to a late dinner after the day's shoot. Or maybe that was too clingy. Drinks with the crew, maybe.

And heightening the stress of the situation was the knowledge that Micah's personal life wasn't exactly personal. If they were going to have any chance to get to know each other, they'd have to keep their affair on the down-low. If "affair" was the right word.

Dammit, she hated the uncertainty. If she could just look in his eyes. His eyes would tell her.

She looked at her watch. Nine-thirty. Micah was due in costume at nine. Shooting was scheduled for ten-thirty. She wondered where he was now. Probably in makeup.

Her phone buzzed in her pocket.

"Um, details please!"

Crap, she'd forgotten about Bree. While she'd waited for Micah in his hotel room, freaked out by her decision to finally jump him, she'd texted back and forth with Bree for support. Maddie had meant to update her friend but hadn't because, well, she had been otherwise occupied.

She thought about how to answer. What could she say? That she'd had the most earth-shattering, mind-blowing, and beautiful experience of her lifetime? There were no words to capture her feelings.

Besides, it was private. Not just keep-from-prying-eyes-of-the-press private, but also don't-tell-your-best-friend private. She typed a simple reply. *It was nice.*

Bree's response came almost instantly. *"Nice??"*

Maddie sighed. *"More than nice. A lot more than nice."*

Her response had been vague, but she knew Bree would figure she wasn't willing to say more. At least not over text. Besides, the stand-ins had arrived and it was time to get her calculations. She worked around Joe as he blocked the scene, careful to not interfere with his instructions.

She had just finished writing down her first numbers in her notebook when her pocket buzzed again. Guessing Bree hadn't gotten the hint, she rolled her eyes as she flipped open her phone.

But the text wasn't from Bree. *"Come to my trailer."*

Her heart skipped a beat.

Was he asking her to come so they could talk about their situation? Or not talk at all? Or did he want to tell her it was all over and to keep everything mum?

She had no idea. She needed to see him to find out.

Except she couldn't go. She was in the middle of set-up and after Adam had yelled at her the other day, she needed to be especially on game.

Still, he wanted to see her. That had to be good. Reluctantly, she sent her reply. *"I'm working, silly."*

Only seconds passed before his response came. *"Can't u slip away?"*

That didn't sound like an "it's over" text. He really wanted to see her. Could she go? She wanted to. Her panties were already slippery thinking about him. She looked around, assessing how much work was left. She'd only done the calculations for Heather's character and this scene had four characters.

There was no way. *"It would be too hard."*

She held her phone as she waited for his reply.

"Speaking of hard . . ."

Her eyes widened. She had to see him.

But, she couldn't.

Maybe just for a minute.

No, she couldn't. She had to force her fingers to type. *"Sorry!"*

Maddie didn't know if she was disappointed or relieved when he didn't reply. The next twenty minutes were torture as she continued her set-up for the shoot. Wild images of Micah hard and naked filled her mind, making her squirm as she worked.

Then the images grew ugly as she pictured him grabbing the nearest P.A. for a quickie in his trailer since Maddie was unavailable for him.

That's ridiculous. First, he had to be on set soon. Secondly, he'd just spent the last day having glorious sex with her. He didn't need to get some now. Third, he wouldn't do that . . . would he?

She realized that she really didn't know the answer to that question. He didn't have a reputation as a playboy because he never noticed other women, that was for sure. And she had no idea how regularly he got it on, or who with, or anything, really, except that when he got it on he got it on very well.

Dammit! Even after she'd bedded him, she was still mixed-up, shuffled, and a total mess. Wasn't sex supposed to have cleared her head?

They should have talked.

"Maddie." Joe drew her from her miserable thoughts. "Beaumont just called on the headset. He said Micah took full blame for the difficult shoot the other day. Realized he'd made a mistake."

"Good to know. Thanks for telling me." She hadn't talked to Micah about it since their run. She was surprised he'd remembered, and after he'd gotten what he was after—namely her—was surprised he followed through.

"Sure thing. And I guess Micah wants to apologize to you in person. He's waiting for you in his trailer."

Maddie flushed. A hundred warring thoughts ran through her mind. Micah had come clean to their boss, and that was really cool, but had he only done it to get Maddie in his trailer? Did Joe know? Did Beaumont know? Didn't Micah realize she had work to do? Did he think he could just snap his fingers and she'd come running?

And wasn't it incredibly hot if he did?

"It's okay. I've got things here," Adam said when Maddie didn't say anything.

"Are you sure?" Her heart began to race at the idea of being with Micah again. But she felt guilty about leaving her job.

"If Beaumont tells you to do something, you've gotta do it." Adam winked.

God, did Adam suspect?

If he did, she didn't care. She had to concentrate to keep from running to Micah's trailer, energized by excitement. The five-minute walk seemed like five miles. Luckily, it was just enough time for her to get her head straight. This was not right—leaving Adam to do her job. Maybe he was used to having women at his beck and call, but not this woman. Micah needed to know it wasn't acceptable to summon her as he had. And she'd tell him first thing when she saw him.

She knocked on his trailer door.

"Come in." God, his voice was sexy.

She took a deep breath, steeling herself to be firm about what was and wasn't acceptable in the workplace. She opened the door and walked in. And all her determination went out the window.

Because there was Micah, standing in the middle of his trailer, completely naked and fully aroused.

———◆———

MICAH WONDERED IF HE'D GONE too far when he asked Beaumont to send Maddie to his trailer, but as soon as he saw her, his hard and throbbing cock told him not to care.

He'd wanted to take her the minute she'd finished giving him the most incredible shower blowjob. She'd thought she was relieving him, but her amazing gift made him want to give her an orgasm of her own. He'd struggled through the morning, trying not to think about her. Finally, he knew he wouldn't be able to concentrate on his acting if he didn't have her. Now.

He expected she'd turn down his text. She took her work too seriously to drop it for a romp in the hay. He admired her for that. Which was the reason he had to come clean to Beaumont about missing his mark. Plus, he'd promised Maddie he would. Using Beaumont as an excuse to get her to his trailer was just an added bonus.

Losing his clothes came spur of the moment. He was mid-changing into costume when he remembered how turned on he'd been when Maddie had told him she'd considered waiting naked in his hotel room. Maybe this was a good opportunity to reverse the scenario. Hopefully she'd appreciate the gesture.

The look on her face suggested she did.

It took three short seconds for her to cross from the door to his arms. Their mouths met and the kiss was ferocious and fraught, as though he hadn't seen her in days rather than just hours. He grappled with her pants while she roughly ran her hands through his hair, the sensation of her fingers on his scalp heightening his arousal.

When he came up for air, he murmured against her mouth. "Oh, baby, I missed you."

"Um hmm," she moaned, reclaiming his lips.

He lowered her pants and panties to below her knees and lifted her onto the nearby countertop—the same counter he had kissed her against a week ago. Without releasing her mouth, he tore open the condom he'd laid out in anticipation of her arrival and rolled it over his shaft. He scooted her forward until she was on the edge of the counter, and then spread her as wide as she could manage with her pants still hooked around her ankles. With his thumb, he rubbed the length of her pussy, pausing to enter her hot opening, testing her readiness. Christ, she was so wet for him.

He removed his thumb and moved his pelvis toward her. "Here I come." He plowed into her. Fuck, she felt good. Even after more than a day of repeated sex, she still felt hot and heavenly as that first time. He paused for a second to admire that.

Then with a punishing rhythm, he began thrusting, hard and fast. His panting matched hers as she gasped at each stroke, thighs slapping against his hips. He could fuck her like this for hours, forever even, though he knew this would be quick. He was too aroused, and she was too, already clenching around him, warm and tight.

He placed his hands on her hips to help move her back and forth over his cock, and increased their tempo. *Wait, wait,* he told himself. *Wait for her.*

"Maddie, I want you to come," he growled.

She arched and released at his request. "Ah, I'm coming!" She covered her mouth to stifle her cry.

"I am too." Blind, flashing light crossed his vision and he released with her, leaning forward, pushing her back against the cupboards behind her to support the sudden loss of feeling in his thighs. "Mmm, baby, you're incredible."

He gave her a quick kiss and pulled out, noticing her wince as he did. "Are you sore?" he asked.

She waited while her breathing slowed. "Somewhat."

He smiled. "Fantastic." He leaned in to nuzzle her nose before pulling off the condom and disposing of it in the toilet.

"Waiting naked. Wow." She wriggled off the counter and brushed past him. From the bathroom she called, "But what if that hadn't been me who knocked?"

He pulled on a pair of briefs. "Hell, I bare my ass in every movie I'm in. Who hasn't seen my stuff?"

She didn't close the door as she cleaned up. He liked that. She felt comfortable around him. Hell, he hoped so after all they'd done in the last two days.

He leaned against the doorframe, watching her. "Besides, I knew it was you."

She washed her hands and dried them on the hanging towel. She faced him, unable to leave the bathroom with him in her way. "Pretty certain I would come, were you?"

She was frisky, but he sensed she was serious behind her tease. He played along. "Oh, I work hard to make sure you come."

She blushed, her skin turning even pinker under her just-fucked hue. He had to turn away. He loved it when she colored and he couldn't be certain he could stop himself from taking her again.

She took the opportunity to leave the bathroom. She crossed her arms and leaned back against the countertop. *The fucking, amazing countertop.* "I'm supposed to be working."

Ah, that's it. She was irritated at him for interrupting her job. He deserved that. He stepped into his jeans, zipping them before he responded. "This was work related."

"How do you figure?"

"Beaumont told me I should apologize to you. He, of course, didn't know that I already had." He walked over to her and placed his hands on her hips. "It was also a thank you for this morning." He kissed her lightly on her nose then sat on the bench across from her to put on his socks.

She glared at him.

"Hey, if it were really an issue, you didn't have to come." He grinned, emphasizing the word "come."

She rolled her eyes. "I came *to your trailer* to tell you that I couldn't just be summoned for sex."

He chuckled. "How's that going?"

"Hmm." She sighed. "Depending on how you look at it, rather well, actually."

He returned to her, wrapping her in his arms. "I'm glad you came," he said softly. "And I'm glad you came to my trailer."

She hit him softly.

He leaned his forehead against hers. "And I hear you—I won't summon you for sex again." He shouldn't have done it in the first place. Sex on set was unprofessional. Though the sneaking around part was especially fun.

"Promise?" she asked, throwing her arms around his neck.

He nodded. "No."

She smiled against his lips. "Thank God." She kissed him deep and slow in stark contrast to their earlier frenzy. Too soon, she pulled away. "As much as I hate to, I have to get back to work. And so do you, I'm sure."

"Yes, I'm late for makeup."

She started for the door and a sudden aching overtook him. He didn't want her to leave, couldn't bear to be without her for even the short time before he joined her on set. It was a new emotion for him—stifling and suffocating and wonderful and freeing all at once.

He grabbed her hand, stopping her from leaving. "Spend the night with me?"

She grinned, lighting up the small space. "I thought you'd never ask."

SEVENTEEN

M ADDIE GRABBED A FRENCH FRY off the dining cart next to
the bed and dipped it in ketchup. She twisted to face Micah who
was stretched out next to her studying his script. She leaned over
and fed the fry to him.

"Yum," he groaned. "French fries and sex . . . now that's what I call
a perfect evening."

"Post-coital fries are the best. You sound like you don't get that very
often. I'm going to assume you don't usually eat French fries."

"Not on my diet plan. But I figure we've been burning enough
calories that I can indulge."

She giggled as she stuck a fry in her own mouth. "No French fries, no
girlfriends . . . you kind of make it seem sucky to be a Hollywood star."

He gave a dramatic sigh. "You have no idea." He resumed reading
his script.

She picked up another fry and chewed on it slowly, watching Micah
as he closed his eyes and silently mouthed his lines. It had been a great day,
waking up with Micah, sex in his trailer, a perfect shoot. Then, after she'd
cleaned up the set and stopped by her hotel room for a change of clothing
and some personal items, she'd arrived at Micah's room. They ordered
burgers and fries from room service, and while Micah was supposed to
be reviewing his lines, occupied their wait with more physical activities.

They still hadn't talked about their arrangement, and even though that's what they agreed on, she still couldn't help feeling anxious. Was all of this new for Micah or had he been with a woman longer than one night before? What was the best way to balance getting to know him under the covers with getting to know him outside of the bedroom? How should she act with him around others? Could she expect that she was with him until further notice or would she have to wait each day for an invitation to his bed? They were standard new relationship questions, but because of who Micah was, they felt heavier.

He reached up and stroked her arm. "Hey. What's going on in that pretty head of yours? You seem to have gone someplace serious."

"Not too serious." She decided that if she didn't share her thoughts she'd never get to know him. "I was wondering how long you've had your no-girlfriend rule."

His hand rested on hers. "Wow, not too serious at all. I must not be very entertaining."

She slipped her hand out from under his and poked him in the ribs. "Oh, you've been plenty entertaining. Now answer the question."

He sighed. "Seven years. Right about when I signed with my manager, Stu. That was just after I met you, actually."

She bit her lip. "And in seven years, you've had no long-term anything?"

Micah tossed his script on the nightstand. "Now I didn't say that." He spoke carefully. "I dated a model about four years ago. For several months. It was all over the tabloids. Maybe you read about it."

Maddie's breath caught. She vacillated between jealousy and hope. Who was the bitch? And did that mean he was open to a relationship again?

"I don't read the gossip mags." She spoke as cautiously as he had. "What happened?"

"I . . . do you really want to hear this?"

"Yes, I really do."

"Okay. Nichelle was her name. And she'd just started getting some major jobs when I met her. Then we started going out and I decided to break my rule and give the whole relationship a try." He blew out a heavy breath. "That's when I discovered yet another reason Hollywood relationships don't work. You can never tell who's into you for you, and who's into you for what you can get them."

She tensed, realizing that whatever this Nichelle had done to Micah had made an impact. "What did she do?"

"Turned out she wanted a part from a director I was working with. She pushed me to introduce them, so I did. Then when he didn't give her the part, she dumped me."

"Are you kidding me?" Maddie felt a wave of nausea, but she kept it to herself. The man had such a jaded opinion about romance in the first place, then to have someone use him like that? It would make her goal of getting close to Micah that much more difficult.

"I'm dead serious." He stared at her, sensing her anxiety, perhaps. After a moment he asked, "What about you?"

"No one's ever used me to get a part in a movie." She took another French fry and fed it to him, hoping to remind him of the awesome things about girlfriends, such as post-coital French fries.

He sneered at her. "Have you had anything serious?"

"Who says I don't have a boyfriend right now?"

"Ha ha ha."

"What?" She tried to hide the hurt from her voice. "Does it seem utterly impossible that I'd have a boyfriend?"

Micah gave a genuine laugh this time. "No, it seems utterly impossible that you don't. You're incredibly smart, beautiful, creative, sexy as hell . . ." He waggled his eyebrows suggestively. "But you wouldn't be here with me if you had a boyfriend."

"I don't know." She smiled coyly. "You could persuade a girl to forget her man for more than a minute."

"But you wouldn't do that. You're too decent."

Her cheeks warmed. Why did that make her blush? Yes, she was decent. No, she wouldn't cheat on a boyfriend. Even for Micah.

She'd break up, then jump him.

Micah's eyes twinkled, enjoying her discomfort. "Plus, I think you're secretly a hopeless romantic."

She lowered her eyes. "No way." But she really was a hopeless romantic. She wanted the whole thing, the awesome guy who loved her and only her, the ring, the wedding cake. . . .

And Micah knew it. "Yes way," he said. "And perhaps the fear that you won't ever actually find 'the one' is what keeps you so emotionally unavailable."

She gathered the comforter around her, suddenly feeling very exposed. How did this conversation turn to her, anyway? "I'm not emotionally unavailable."

"You so are."

"I'm here with you."

"Yes, you're here with the guy who declared he was also emotionally unavailable. Way to prove your point." He grabbed a handful of French fries and stuffed them in his mouth.

Maddie furrowed her brow. His remark about his unavailability stung. Didn't they say they weren't putting preconceived barriers on their relationship?

But more than that, was he right? About her? She didn't feel emotionally unavailable. Yet, how many guys had she dated since college? Not very many. Besides the casual fling here and there, there had been almost no one.

Because I hadn't met anyone.

As if reading her thoughts, Micah countered, "Look, you have multitudes of men falling at your feet and you don't even have a clue."

"Whatever." He was so dramatic. "Like Sam?"

Micah shrugged. "Sam's a good guy."

She cocked her head and looked at him curiously. "I thought you said he was a douchebag."

"I may have spoken falsely."

His sudden endorsement of Sam put her on edge. Sam was . . . was . . . She actually didn't know what Sam was. She hadn't taken the time to find out. What she did know was what Sam wasn't. He wasn't Micah.

She wasn't brave enough to say that, though. "Sam's, like, barely twenty-one."

Micah shrugged. "Young enough to train."

"And he's always so in the way."

"He's a pleaser." He lowered his voice. "He'd probably try really hard to please you."

Maddie fought to hide the tears that were threatening. Did he really want her with someone else? "So are we done now, is that it? And you're trying to softly hand me over to Sam to ease your guilt?"

"Fuck, no!" He pulled her into his arms, wrapping her tightly against him. "Imagining any guy, let alone Sam, with you—touching your incredibly soft skin, fondling your adorably perky breasts—feels like I'm being stabbed in the gut." He unrolled her from the comforter so their skin met. "And now I have to fondle your breasts since I was talking about it."

She giggled as his palm found her bosom. "So you'd be jealous?"

"Incredibly."

Awesome. "And you aren't trying to get rid of me yet?"

"Not a chance."

Even more awesome.

She relaxed under his soothing massage, her nipple hardening under his fingers. She was exactly where she wanted to be with the kind of guy she wanted to be with. Didn't he know that?

Head pressed against his chest so she wouldn't see his face, she told him. "I don't want to be with multitudes of other guys. I want to be with you."

"I know," he whispered. He kissed her forehead and then nuzzled his face against hers.

He feels it too. Even though he won't say it. Her chest warmed at the realization.

Then she started to sink again as she recalled the complexity of their situation. "How do we do this? Get to know each other, I mean. With you being you, and all. What do we do?"

He returned his hand to her breast. "I don't know about you, but I'm fondling. I can give you some suggestions as well."

"Micah, I'm serious."

He sighed. "I know." He was quiet for a moment and she wondered if he wouldn't answer her. But then he did. "I don't know. I haven't done this either. Not successfully. The press like to connect me with every woman I come into contact with. They'll say that I'm with someone or another, and they will have pictures, but you can't believe it."

"I told you, I don't read gossip magazines."

"Good. Don't start. And the minute they find out I'm seeing you . . . it will be tough, Maddie, I'm not going to lie."

"So then we should try to remain media free. Don't you think?"

"If we want to stay media free, we have to sneak around on set."

She swallowed. "I realize that." She couldn't deny that it made her more than a little sad to be Micah's secret. The way she was feeling about him, she wanted to tell the world. But they were still so new, and she really did want to give their relationship a chance. "I suppose I can live with it."

He tilted up her chin so he could look her in the eye. "It won't mean anything, Maddie. What other people say or know. It's between you and me. If you wonder at all, you ask me. You have to promise."

His seriousness was so startling she took a moment to answer. "Okay, I promise."

"Thank you." He released her chin and stroked her cheek. "If we stay low on set we'll have a better shot of staying out of the media's eye. It won't be easy. But while we have the excuse of working together I think we could pull it off. That gives us . . . what? Four weeks left to figure the rest out."

"Four weeks . . . ," she repeated. It felt like she was saying 'four minutes.'

"To figure it out," he added.

It was a step in the right direction. Nothing permanent, but at least she knew where she stood with him for now.

Micah shifted, turning his whole body toward her. "But we're not figuring it out right this minute. Right now I seriously have some suggestions of things you could be doing while I resume my fondling."

She grinned. "Naughty things, I hope."

"Extremely." He growled as his mouth found her neck, nipping along her throat.

Her heart flip-flopped at the primitive sound. "Tell me," she hissed. "Tell me what to do."

He lifted his head and gazed at her considering. "Touch yourself."

"Hmm, what?" She wasn't naïve, she knew what he meant. He wanted her to play with herself. But she'd never done that in front of anyone, and while she wasn't saying no, she wanted him to tell her how to do it.

He circled her nose with his own. "I want you to touch yourself." He licked at her upper lip. "As if you were thinking about me." He kissed her once. "Do you make yourself come while thinking about me?"

Holy hell, did she ever. How many nights had she slept on wet sheets because of the orgasms she'd brought herself to with him on the brain?

"Yes." She met his eyes.

"Show me."

"Okay."

His breath hitched and she felt a fresh pool of liquid between her legs. She was nervous and embarrassed as she pulled away from him, but she was also excited. Incredibly excited. Though she had never been turned on by the idea of playing with herself in front of another person, she was more than aroused by the thought now. She propped the pillows up behind her and centered herself on top of them. Slowly she dragged her legs up until her knees were bent in front of her. Then, she let her knees fall open into a lotus position.

Micah's eyes widened ever so slightly. He moved himself to a spot with a better view and focused on her intently.

She was tempted to move her hands directly to her clit. She was already turned on and it wouldn't take long. But he wanted to see what she did when she thought about him, and her more intense fantasies of him started elsewhere.

She watched him as she ran her fingers through her hair, several times, pulling and tugging at the ends. "First, I think of you doing this." She was surprised how sultry her voice sounded. "Then, your hands would move." This time when her hands reached the bottom of her hair length, she continued gliding them down to her breasts.

His breath grew heavier as he watched her squeeze and crush her tits, his reaction emboldening her. She pinched at her nipples, tugging the buds until they stood erect.

"And then your tongue would arrive." She licked her index finger then circled a nipple with the wet pad. Next, she brushed against the tip in a zig-zag motion. She repeated the pattern on her other breast, the one closest to Micah.

He leaned in, eyes large and dilated and blew across the top of her wet bud.

"Uh uh," she chided. "You don't do that in my fantasy. Not that it wasn't nice, but you're supposed to be watching."

He pouted but sat back.

"After you thoroughly enjoy my breasts—"

"I want to thoroughly enjoy your breasts now."

She ignored his interruption. "—You'd move your hands again. Lower this time." She trailed her hands along the sides of her torso and down to her hips, then to the outside of her thighs. When she reached her knees, she slid her fingers back up her legs, this time moving up the inside, toward her core.

Just as her hands reached her center, she swept them up to splay her belly instead of letting them touch her where she ached for him. "You'd tease me like this."

He grinned. "I'm such an ass."

"You are. But eventually . . ." One hand moved up to grope her breast while the other descended ever so slowly until it sat just above her slit. She was so turned on by showing him this, by sharing this most private act. "Eventually you'd arrive where I want you most." She skidded a finger past her nub, moaning at the sensation. She repeated the movement, this time with two fingers, stretching her outer lips.

Micah sucked in an audible breath as her two fingers circled her clit, little by little increasing speed. Her body thrummed with a new wave of electricity at each round.

"Are those my fingers?" His eyes blazed, fixed on her movement.

"Or my tongue?"

"Your fingers." Her other hand journeyed from her bosom, drifting past the motion at her nerve center stopping at her tight, wet opening.

"Yes," he hissed as she plunged two fingers deep inside her. When she pulled them out, she dragged her hot liquid up to moisten her clit.

"Now it's your tongue."

"Yes, baby." His voice was husky with need. She moved her gaze from his face and saw he clutched his hard shaft. *So hot.* He stroked his penis, his rhythm echoing her fingers as they plunged again and again inside her.

"Ah, that's it baby. That's it." His encouragement, combined with the sensations of her moving hands and the intense heat of his stare, brought her to release. She quivered as she threw her head back and shouted her release.

While she was still mid-climax, she felt the bed shift underneath her, and heard the rip of a foil packet. Then he was on top of her, inside her, with one deep thrust he filled her to the hilt.

"Ah, baby," he growled as he pounded into her. "You are so beautiful. I'm going to come so hard. I'm going to make you come so hard."

He continued his vigorous assault, hitting a spot deep within her, one she hadn't known existed. "Oh, fuck me!" Her orgasm crashed over and over, long beyond what she thought possible, exhausting and elating her. By the time he joined her, coming in one long stroke as he called her name, every muscle in her body was already limp from her prolonged release.

He fell next to her, his ragged breath becoming even as he drifted to sleep. She drifted into her own slumber, tingling in the warmth of her waning orgasms and the weight of his body tangled with hers and the promise of four more weeks.

EIGHTEEN

THE SUN PEEKED THROUGH THE trees and glared down on Micah's script, making it impossible to continue reading. He tossed it into the grass beside him and glanced around, taking in the scenery. It was beautiful. One day he'd maybe buy a cabin out here in the Rockies. Not anywhere as crowded as the star-populated Aspen, but in a quiet place like this Golden recreation area, not too far from Denver.

Of course, half the reason he was fond of Colorado had to do with the girl lying on her stomach next to him. Would he still be attracted to these mountains if Maddie wasn't with him? Probably not so intensely.

He sprawled out on the blanket and propped his head up with one hand bent at the elbow to watch her struggle with the light, adjusting the top of her laptop down to see better. It was an unusual blanket to use for a picnic, a beige hotel standard they'd found in his closet, but it did the job. The sandwiches Maddie had picked up for them at a local deli had been devoured earlier and the remnants were gathered at his feet in a trash bag, also swiped from his room. Now, he was ready for dessert.

As if sensing his hungry stare, Maddie looked up from editing on her computer. "What are you thinking?" she asked.

"That it's our one week sexiversary."

She chuckled as she shut the lid of her laptop and pushed it to the edge of the blanket. Then she also propped her head in her palm to stare at him face to face. "One week, huh?" She furrowed her brow. "What do you get someone for that? Paper? China?"

"Condoms." He wished he had one now, knew his wallet was empty. "We're out at the hotel. We need to grab some from my trailer."

She traced the line of his nose with her finger and tapped it once when she reached the tip. "You know, I am on birth control."

Condomless sex. His cock pressed tight against the zipper of his jeans at the thought. He couldn't remember the last time he'd had unprotected sex. He knew Maddie well enough to know she was clean. He was too, had regular check-ups for STDs, but her trust astonished him, especially since he had a reputation.

It also astonished him that he wasn't horrified at the idea like he could have been. It suggested a step forward in their relationship. Where was he going with Maddie? Why did it feel so nice? He hadn't forgotten the reasons that relationships in show biz didn't work, but he was willing to admit that maybe he'd been too black and white about the whole thing. Maybe there were instances where his career wouldn't get in the way of a romance.

Maybe.

At least for the duration of the shoot.

She searched his eyes, seemingly trying to read his silence. "What?"

He shrugged. "I haven't had sex without a condom in years. I'm hard just thinking about it."

"No you aren't." She reached her loose hand down to his crotch. Her eyes lit up. "Oh. You are." She scooted herself closer to him and wrapped her arms around his neck, bringing him in for a lingering kiss.

When she leaned away minutes later, her face was flushed and her eyes dilated. "Happy sexiversary. I can't believe I ran from you . . . I wasted so much time."

He smoothed the hair behind her ear. "I liked the chase." Then he remembered the days he'd spent alone and wishing for her. "Well, parts of it."

And he'd needed time. If she'd slept with him the day he'd made his first move, they'd be done with by now. But she'd pushed him for something more and here they were with a week under their belt.

"Parts of it were really nice." She rubbed her lips together as if remembering something particularly juicy. "I'm going to have to thank Adam again for begging me to come out here."

He wanted to take her mouth again, but an old question niggled at him. "Why didn't you do the show from the beginning? You said something about personal issues on the ride from the airport. At first, I thought those issues might be me."

"Like I hadn't gotten over our fleeting night from the past? Narcissistic as always," she teased. "I turned the movie down because of Beaumont. I didn't know you were on this film until I saw you at the airport."

"All these years we could have ended up working together. I have to admit, if it had happened at a different time or in any other way, I might not have been ready for this." He pulled at her earlobe, noticing she didn't have any earrings in. There was a pair sitting on the counter in the bathroom of his hotel—their hotel, really. She'd spent every night there since they'd first slept together. He should invite her to bring all her stuff over. He bet she had more earrings back in at her own hotel.

Sharing space. The concept warmed him. And terrified him. Mostly warmed.

"Would it have been Wham Bam Thank You Ma'am?" She pulled his hand from her lobe and sucked on the pad of his index finger, causing his cock to jump. "Could you really have resisted me after you'd gotten in my pants once?"

"I would have pretended that I could. And I might have been quite an asshole in the process."

"Then I'm very glad it happened like this."

He traced the outline of her mouth, knowing he would take her soon. Still, he had time. They had the whole day off, and he'd already had her once that morning. With their exhausting workdays and their insatiable longing to fuck like bunnies, what they didn't get much of a chance to do was talk. He wanted to know her, all of her, and he was taking the opportunity now while he had it. "So Beaumont? You've worked with him before?"

She stiffened. "I did. Years ago. It was a fiasco." She chuckled to herself at some private joke. "A Beaumont fiasco."

He wrinkled his forehead. "Tell me."

She did, though he sensed her reluctance. He listened to her story, imagining her excitement when Beaumont initially invested and, when she got to the end, feeling an intense hatred at his director for what he'd done to the talented angel in front of him. His chest ached with her disappointment while every muscle in his body burned with an overwhelming desire to beat the guy to a pulp. "He really blacklisted you?" He gritted his teeth. "That fucker."

"Whatever. I've moved on. I like what I'm doing now."

"I have a feeling that's not a reference to doing me." He waited for her to deliver the playful smack that he knew she would before he got serious again. "But Maddie, you might like what you're doing, but you love your movie. I never see you as excited as when you're behind that monitor. Except when you're beneath me. And on top of me." He planted a kiss on her temple. "Anyway, it's your passion."

She shrugged, averting her eyes. "I don't have to make a career out of my passion."

He knew that was her pain talking, understood how much she'd rather be calling the shots than focus-pulling. "But if you can, why wouldn't you? Why are you even making your movie if you don't plan to do anything with it?"

"I'll enter it in film festivals or something. People will still see it."

"Like a handful. It deserves to be seen by more. And it's good enough to get picked up. You just have to fight for it a little."

"I can't." She seemed to truly believe her words. "I tried. I fucked it up." Her eyes brimmed with tears. "Beaumont fucked it up."

"Hey," he whispered, wiping at the tear spilling down her nose. "You made a powerful enemy. That sucks. But you also have powerful friends." He kissed the spot where he had wiped her tear. Without any hesitation he hinted at the offer he'd made before. "I'm a powerful friend."

She bucked her hips against him playfully. "You're right on the powerful."

"I'm actually talking about something besides sex. For once."

"I know." She snuggled deeper into his arms and laid her head on his chest. "I don't want to talk about it anymore. Is that okay?"

He inhaled the delicious smell of Maddie. "Of course." He would put the subject away for now, but he vowed to himself he would help her in the future. He hadn't been feeding her bullshit when he said he had been looking to invest in someone. He wanted to diversify, build a future that didn't rely on fads and good looks. Producing was a logical career move. And Maddie's film was good. It made sense and he meant to pursue it.

Did he really mean that promise? He did. It was a huge step for him, and he didn't fail to notice its implications. He'd been burned in the past by Nichelle when she used him for his connections, and maybe Maddie wouldn't be any different. But besides the fact that he trusted her, knew that she was different, he also didn't give a shit if she used him. He just wanted her happy.

What was that about?

"Can I help you with your lines?" she asked, interrupting his heavy thoughts.

"Please." He should make sure his lines were solid. Then he could put away the script and spend the rest of his day focusing on nothing but Maddie.

She rolled out of his arms and sat up to grab his script. He'd left it open to the scene he was studying and he watched as her eyes scanned the page.

When her mouth tightened into a straight line and her brows creased sharply, he guessed he knew the source of her reaction, but asked anyway. "What's wrong?"

She sighed. "I forgot you had the sex scene this week. I sort of blocked it out."

He rubbed her lower back, hiding his pleasure at her jealousy. "Is it going to bother you?"

"No." She paused. "Yes." She sighed again. "I don't know."

He continued to draw lazy circles on her back. "Talk to me."

She looked toward the horizon, thinking about what she wanted to say or trying to decipher her emotions. "It bothered me when you did the kissing scene. Until you reassured me. That helped. But since then I found out . . ." Her voice trailed off.

"What?"

She looked back at him. "That you've slept with Heather."

She kept her voice level and he focused on making his response the same. "Huh." *How did she know?* He and Heather had always been on the down-low.

But that wasn't important. Putting her mind to rest was. And how they handled this would be a major milestone in their . . . whatever it was they had. One common pressure on Hollywood romances was costar jealousy. "I'm not sleeping with her now. I have no interest in sleeping with her now."

"I know."

Good. Yet he could sense that knowledge wasn't enough. "But . . . ?"

She shrugged. "But doing this scene, you might recall other times with her."

It wasn't a ridiculous worry. For the most part, love scenes were so clinical and uncomfortable that he rarely became emotionally involved. But it did happen with some actors. Spending weeks, or months wrapped in the mind of a character, making their actions believable, and then adding physical contact on top of that—yeah, he'd be jealous if it was her kissing another guy.

At another time in his life, this conversation would have been enough to make him run. But with Maddie, he wanted to work it out. There was no way he could get out of filming the sex scene. But maybe he could make it more tolerable for both of them. "What if there was a way to ensure that I was definitely not recalling her?"

She studied him. "What do you mean?"

"I have an idea." He sat up, wrapping his arms around her from behind, his face against hers. "Let's do the scene together. Now. The whole thing through to the parts that are only hinted at and not filmed. And then, I promise you, there will be no way that you or I will think about anything but each other when we're filming. We'll be the real thing. Heather and everyone else will only get a lame reenactment."

"That sounds . . ." He waited for her to say it was a stupid notion, but she surprised him. "Like a great idea, actually."

She turned to him, her face lit up with excitement. "Should I start at the top of this page?"

"Yeah. That would be perfect." She opened her mouth to begin, but he spoke before she could. "I won't know the blocking until we get on set. So you should direct it. Tell us how we should move."

"Hmm," she said, a gleam in her eye. She read the page again and he knew she was visualizing it in her head. His heart swelled at her enthusiasm.

She moved to a kneeling position. "Okay. You start there and walk by me, brushing my shoulder. Kind of rough. Then walk to that spot at the corner of the blanket." She pointed to where she meant. "Pretend that's the pump. You can be washing your hands at the pump because this scene is right after you skinned that rabbit, right?"

"Yes," he said. He adored watching the director's hat come out. He'd only seen it before in the results—in her footage. Never in actual motion. He could feel her thrill and it excited him. He listened through the rest of her blocking. It would look good if it were being filmed. Beaumont would be lucky to come up with something half as good.

"Places, please."

He stood and crossed to where she had indicated.

"Wait." She rose and searched the woods around them. "Are we really going to, you know? Out here? Do you think we're out of the way enough? To not be caught or anything?"

He couldn't help but smile at her sense of propriety. He liked that they were just far enough away from the hiking trail that they probably wouldn't be seen, but were close enough that they *could* be. "Would you care if we were?"

She gave him a wicked grin. "No. Except that it might invite media into our lives."

"Yeah, there is that." He considered. They hadn't seen anyone all afternoon. "We'll keep most of our clothes on. It'll be fine."

"Well, then. It will be easier if I dispose of these now." She reached her hands under her skirt and pulled down her panties. She stepped out of one leg hole, and with her other bare foot, she pitched them to the grass.

Fucking hot.

She winked at him, knowing full well what effect her action had on him. Then she turned somber. "Places." *Director hat back on.* "Go sound. Camera rolling. And scene."

Micah closed his eyes. When he opened them, he was Billy Winter—his character. With a heavier step than usual, he walked toward where Maddie stood with the script in hand and brushed past her gruffly.

He continued to the spot she had told him was the water pump. He felt her approach him from behind. Then she spoke.

"Billy, why are you so angry?" She was acting her lines more than when she'd read with him in the past. He knew acting wasn't her thing, but it roused him that she was getting into this role-playing.

"Do you have to ask?" He spun toward her. *"They're gonna come for us, Izzie. They got Danny's print and it's going to lead them all—"*

She put one hand up to calm him, the other still clutching the script. *"You don't know that."*

"I know I have no future anywhere but lost out here on this mountain."

"Then I'll be lost out here with you." She took a step toward him and reached for his arm. Softly, she delivered the next line. *"I'll be your future."*

It was scripted, not really Maddie saying the words, but Goddamnit if it didn't feel good hearing them in her voice, said to him.

"Damn it, Iz." He pulled away from her, but didn't turn. He paused, not sure if he could say the next line without choking on it. It was too close to the truth—too close to how he felt about her in real life. *"I don't want to love you."*

"Then don't." She tossed the script on the ground and reached for him again, wrapping her arms around his neck. *"Let* me *love* you.*"

She kissed him. Slowly, tentatively. She had directed him to not pull away, but also not give into her. She told him to let her seduce him, rather let the character she was playing seduce the character he was playing.

Fuck. That was hard. Because Micah was already seduced, long before Billy Winter was supposed to be.

She licked around his mouth, teasing him, inviting him to respond. With great difficulty he didn't react. His resistance began to weaken, though, when she sucked on his top lip, gently at first, then with increasing fervor. Soon, he couldn't take it any longer, opening ever so slightly. She took advantage of his weakness and slipped her tongue in, tasting him with long licks. Her hands ran through his hair, her body pressed to him, breasts heavy against his chest, as she sought deeper access.

She mewled against his mouth and that was when he couldn't hold out any longer. With a heavy sigh, he put a hand around the small of her back and pulled her even closer, if that was possible. He fell into her kiss, surrendering to the tango of her tongue, filling her with such soul-wrenching passion that he only dared show her under the guise of his character.

He was so lost in her embrace that he startled when she pushed him to the ground, as she had said she would. She straddled him, hitching her short cotton skirt up to expose the beige skin of her thighs. Then, pulling at the bottom of his T-shirt, she coaxed him to sit up so she could remove it.

"Yummy," she hissed, running her hands up his chest. His skin burned in the wake of her touch, and he recognized that they were no longer on script, no longer playing characters, but were just Maddie and Micah, about to make love in the woods.

He eased his own hands under her cotton tee, wondering for a moment if he should take it off. His desire to see her breasts as he caressed them won over his need to shelter her from spying eyes. "Lift," he commanded, and she raised her arms for him as he undressed her. He flung her shirt to the ground beside him and lay back down, reaching his hands up to fondle and rub her tits through her thin bra. He paused to gaze at her above him, hair mussed, nipples sticking up under white lace. She was an angel, gorgeous and heaven-sent. He could look at her like that forever.

Except that Maddie seemed set on more than looking. She rocked her hips urgently against the ridge in his pants. "Help me," she pleaded.

He reached beneath her skirt and found her clit, found her legs already soaked, wet for him. His breath hitched. "Jesus, Maddie."

"I'm ready for you. Help me with your pants."

He hesitated, wanting to enjoy her, wanting to feel her clench around his fingers before she clenched around his cock. But her look was insistent, so he complied, undoing his jeans and freeing his penis.

She grabbed him eagerly, and positioned him at the mouth of her desire. She slid onto him and he let out a sound that seemed foreign to his ears, half groan, half guttural cry. Fuck, she felt incredible. So tight, and so wet around his naked cock. *Fucking amazing.*

She put her palms flat on his chest for support and began to move. Up and down, quickly. Too quickly. Without a condom, he'd come in no time at all. "Slow down, baby," he urged.

She curbed her speed for about half a second.

"Maddie." He grasped her hips, attempting to control her rhythm. She wriggled against his grip, maintaining her pace. It was too much, too fast. In one swift motion, he maneuvered her beneath him, pinning her hands above her head. "I said slow down," he rumbled.

She moaned as he took over, moving in and out of her in long, leisurely strokes. Each pass of his penis against her vaginal walls felt more exquisite than the last.

"Is this how you like it?" she murmured as he kissed along her jaw. "Real slow?"

He licked at her neck. "I like it slow and sweet." He nipped her earlobe. "And I like it fast and frantic." He grinned against her ear. "And I like it when there's a chance we might be caught." He pulled his head up so he could look directly in her hooded eyes. "But mostly, I like it with you."

She moaned again as he pulled himself out to the very tip before plunging in again. "That was very sweet to say," she said. "And this is very slow."

"Relax, baby. I'll get you where you want to go. But I'm not wearing a condom and this is the first time I'm getting to feel you. Let me enjoy you." He crushed his mouth to hers, resuming their passionate kiss from earlier. Soon their tongues moved frenetically around each other and he could no longer hold back the passion in his thrusts. She quivered as he let his need take over, plunging into her relentlessly. Her hips met each drive and then she was clamped around him, shuddering through her orgasm, milking him while he pummeled toward his own release.

And when he came, it was a long, violent eruption that he filled with her name. "Maddie, ah God, Maddie."

He collapsed on top of her, still inside of her, sweaty and out of breath. The words from their scene echoed in his head. *"I don't want to love you."* He almost said them to her again, as Micah Preston this time.

But he didn't.

He closed his eyes, as if he could squeeze out the L word like he could the light. "You can't know what you do to me," he whispered into her hair. "You can't possibly have any idea at all."

NINETEEN

MADDIE PULLED A BUTTON-DOWN BLACK shirt out of the closet to drape over her tank top, and glanced at Micah still half-asleep in the bed behind her.

As if feeling her gaze, he stirred. "What are you doing?" he mumbled.

"Getting dressed."

"Stop it. Take your clothes off and get back in here with me."

She grinned. It took every ounce of strength she had not to obey him. Not just because he made her horny as hell, but also because she liked being with him. Loved being with him. No matter what they did. In fact, after two and a half weeks of secret kisses during the day and passionate lovemaking at night, she was beginning to hope the two of them had something that would last beyond the shoot.

But since she couldn't be sure he felt the same, she desperately wanted to hold on to each moment, including this one.

Unfortunately, she had to leave for location in twenty minutes. "You know I can't." She relished in his pout then leaned over the bed to give him a swift kiss. "So, lover boy, what are you going to do with your day off?"

"Actually . . ." He paused, stretching his beautiful naked body.

Maddie's eyes widened as if by a will of their own they wandered to the delicious v of his lower torso that peeked above the sheets. She was so distracted she almost missed his answer.

" . . . with Lulu."

Lulu? Did he say he was spending the day with his mother? "Excuse me, what did you say?"

"My mother. She's coming in this morning. Fudge is picking her up from the airport after he drops you off on the set."

"Oh." Micah's mother was flying in. And this was the first she was hearing about it. "Oh," she said again straightening.

She turned to the mirror and redid her ponytail, even though it looked fine already. "How long is she going to be here?" Maddie hoped her voice didn't sound as choked as it felt.

Out of the corner of her eye, she saw his reflection sit up and lean back against the headboard. "Today. Then I'm sending her off to a spa in Estes Park first thing tomorrow morning."

She watched her brows furrow in the mirror. "That's not very long. You won't get to spend any time with her." But what she meant was that she wouldn't get to spend any time with Lulu. And as her interest in Micah was growing exponentially every day, she had a strong desire to meet his mother. She didn't even know much about Micah's mother except that she'd been a former actress and that she'd helped push his career. There was so much more to glean from knowing her.

And she wasn't going to get the chance.

"I have all of today with her. Believe me, that's enough."

Realizing that she couldn't pretend to fuss in the mirror forever, Maddie sat in the room's armchair and tugged on her sneakers. Still unable to meet his eyes, afraid he'd see she was upset, she kept her focus strictly on her shoelaces. "How long have you been planning this?"

"Um, a couple of days. I'm taking her to the fundraiser thing to-night."

He meant the Evening with Joss Beaumont, a charity event sponsored by the Denver Film Society. Beaumont had decided to wrap early that day and bought tickets for all of the cast and crew. Actually, it had been Bree's idea, but the director took the credit. Though all of the crew had been invited, the focus would be on the VIPs. Bree had arranged for a red carpet at the theater for their entrances and publicized their attendance, hoping to draw more interest in the event.

Maddie stood but sat back down to redo her shoes when she realized her laces were too tight. Or maybe that was her chest. Everything felt tense and off. "Maybe I should go to Beaumont's thing after all."

"I thought you decided last week that you didn't want to go." Even Micah's voice sounded tense. Had he picked up on her vibe?

She heard him moving and she turned to see his backside as he climbed out of the bed. "I don't want to." She didn't. Not with even an ounce of her being. Sit through a night listening to the asshole talk about himself while a room full of people oohed and ahhed? She'd rather shoot herself.

Besides, she hadn't packed any dresses for Colorado. Bree had overnighted one to her for the event, but it was more formal than she was used to. Though the thought of dressing up for Micah had almost changed her mind. He'd never seen her in anything but tanks and jeans and sweats. And naked. He'd definitely seen her naked.

"Then don't go." He walked over to her still in the chair and pulled her up to stand in front of him, then ran his hands up and down her arms. "Stay home, take a bath. Enjoy the night off."

Now that sounded like a good time. Except, not so much without Micah there. And was he trying to keep her away? "Do you not want me to go?"

"I didn't say that." He sighed and pulled her into his arms. "It's just, like you said, why would you go to honor a man you hate?"

"That's why I wasn't going to go." Even as he comforted her she could feel the truth in her fear. He didn't want her there. She didn't like that. She wanted him everywhere with her. That he didn't feel the same—was that an indication that he didn't feel the same about where there relationship was going as she did?

She couldn't think about that now. It was too big. One day at a time. And this day, his mother was coming into town. "But now your mom is going to be there."

"Why does that change anything?"

Maddie pulled back to study him. Was he really going to pretend that his mother's visit was insignificant?

He met her eyes then sighed. "Look, I don't want to go either. But I have to go, because I don't know, somehow people will give more money if I'm there. And you and I decided no press events, so I thought it would be easier to take Lulu. It was either that or go as Heather's date."

"No way." She brushed past him and busied herself with gathering her computer into her bag.

"And that's why I invited my mother." His voice changed, as though he suddenly understood. "Does that bother you, Maddie? Did you want me to ask you?"

"No, no that's not it." She zipped her bag and spun to face him. "It's that you didn't tell me you invited your mother. You'll be at that all night and I'm going to be on set all morning and then she's going to be gone. I won't even have a chance to . . ."

And then it clicked.

He'd planned the timeline of Lulu's visit on purpose. He didn't want them to meet.

The tightness in her chest increased tenfold, like a boulder was crushing against her. "Oh. I see."

"Maddie . . ."

He stepped toward her, but she stepped back. "No, it's fine." God, how had she been so stupid? They weren't committed to each other, why would he want her to meet his mother? "It's a big deal. Introducing someone to a parent. I get it. Seriously, I wasn't thinking. It's fine."

"Really?"

"Yes. Totally fine." Though the tears gathering in her eyes would beg to disagree. She turned back to mess with her bag so he wouldn't notice.

"Okay." She heard the resignation in his voice. "I'm jumping in the shower. We have reservations in Denver for dinner at five so I won't be here when you get back."

"Okay."

She heard the door to the bathroom close and the first tear spilled.

Then at the sound of the door opening again, she swiped quickly at her face.

"Maddie." He waited until she turned to look at him. He knew she was hiding tears, it read all over his face as he leaned against the door-frame. "I also really want you to know each other."

The weight in her chest loosened. "You do?"

"Yeah. I do."

"Then do I get to meet her?"

"I . . . don't . . . know."

The relief she'd felt a moment before was replaced with bone-deep hurt. Another tear trailed down her face, her voice gruff. "So what do you want me to do? Pretend I don't know you? Do I need to get another hotel room?"

"No!" He crossed to her and wrapped her in his embrace. "No, I want you with me."

His arms made her feel better. She could feel in his touch what he couldn't say, that he was torn, that he didn't know how to handle the situation any more than she did.

He pressed his lips to her forehead before tilting her chin up so their eyes would meet. "And I don't want you to pretend anything. I can barely handle restraining myself on set. But my mother . . . it *is* big. For me. And I just thought we could maybe take it the way we've been taking everything else. See how things go. Maybe we can do breakfast tomorrow."

"Okay." She smiled. Surprisingly, a genuine smile. "We'll see how things go. If breakfast happens, it happens. If not, I won't take it person-ally. As long as I still get to sleep here tonight."

"If you don't, I'll come find you and molest you in your sleep."

"Promise?"

He kissed her deeply. When he broke away he said, "What do you think?"

"I think I need to be going." She reached her hand around to fondle his ass. "And you need to get in the shower before I'm tempted to be late."

They lingered a few more minutes in each other's arms before saying their goodbyes. By the time Maddie stepped out in the hall she felt better. A lot better. Even though she longed for Micah to be certain about them, as certain as she was becoming, she couldn't expect him to be there yet. Not after less than three weeks. Not when he was so relationship phobic to begin with.

She met Fudge in the lobby and together they walked down to the car he'd rented for Micah. He opened the passenger door for her like the gentleman he was, and she wondered if the photographer that she spotted sitting across from the hotel assumed she was hooking up with Micah's bodyguard. She came and left the hotel more with Fudge than she ever did with Micah. And there were always photographers.

"Sounds like you have a busy day off," Maddie said as Fudge strapped himself into his seat.

"Day off my ass. My days off are when Micah's on set. Days away from set, he turns me into his driver, his errand boy, his personal shopper. So annoying." But he smiled and Maddie knew his complaining was mostly talk. "You're still not going tonight?"

"No." She still had doubts about her decision to stay behind, but she'd made up her mind.

As if the conversation had cued it to go off, her phone buzzed with a text.

"I want pics of u in that dress!"

Maddie grimaced as she typed her reply to Bree. *"Not going."* Bree was going to be pissed. She'd believed she was doing the crew a favor getting them invites to the shindig.

"I'm calling u."

Her phone rang before she'd even finished reading her text. "Sorry about this," she said to Fudge. Then she answered her call. "I hate Beaumont. Why would I go?"

"Free drinks." What had she expected from Bree? She had always been the quintessential party girl, had always believed life was better with liquor.

"The free drinks is a good draw," Fudge agreed. Leave it to Bree to talk so loudly that Fudge could hear her through the phone.

"I don't want to go," Maddie said firmly to both of them. "And Micah doesn't want me there."

Bree gasped. "Then that's exactly why you have to go!"

"Your friend has a point," Fudge added. "You can't let Micah get away with acting like chickenshit."

"Exactly!" said Bree. "Who is that awesome advice coming from anyway?"

"Fudge. Micah's bodyguard. I told you about him." Realizing she was going to be ganged up on whether she wanted it or not she put her phone on speaker. "Bree this is Fudge. Fudge, this annoying voice is Bree. My whacko best friend."

"Hello, Bree," Fudge said.

Instead of exchanging a greeting, Bree said, "Don't you think Maddie should go, Fudge?"

"I don't know. I can see benefits to both options."

"Fudge, don't say anymore unless it's to agree with me."

Maddie gave Fudge her best I'm-sorry-about-my-friend look. She'd perfected it over years of knowing Bree.

"But his mother will be there," Maddie said, back on topic. "I really won't be able to talk to Micah at all. It'll be awkward and not any fun."

Fudge nodded. "Well, that might be true."

At the same time Bree said, "No, it will be highly informative and you need to go."

"What do you mean by informative?"

"His mom, Maddie!"

"He's not ready to introduce me to his mom, Bree. We've barely been dating."

"He doesn't have to introduce you as the love of his life or anything. But just being there and seeing her—you'll find out stuff."

"Meeting Lulu could actually be a real trip," Fudge said. "She's made a big impact on his relationship mumbo-jumbo shit."

"Thank you, Fudge," Bree said. "Listen to him, Maddie. Fudge knows. And also, Maddie, you've only ever been with Micah in one setting, and it's not a permanent one. There's so much more to his life than that. Not your life, but his."

"Uh, thanks." But that wasn't far off from the truth. Maddie's life was always working on a film. There was no press, no big celebrity events, no fans. There were wrap parties, of course, but that wasn't the same as big charity fundraisers or award show receptions.

"I'm sorry, Maddie, but that's the truth. You need to see Micah in his realm. You know, the world of flashbulbs and red carpets, and pretty people saying pretty things to pretty people with microphones."

"It's a totally different side of Micah," Fudge agreed.

Maddie chewed the inside of her lip, considering. Though she was certain she'd still be attracted to Micah in his realm, she didn't have any idea where she fit into it, if at all.

"You need to know what it would be like," Bree continued softly. "If you stay together."

And that was the real reason Maddie hadn't wanted to go. She was happy being Micah's secret girlfriend on the set, but that didn't translate to girlfriend in real life. She was afraid to find out what that would be like. Afraid it would be awful. Afraid that he wouldn't be able to make room for her there.

"I get that you're scared, Maddie. But you have to find out. Please respect yourself enough to know what you're getting into."

Maddie's resolve was diminishing despite her protest. "We haven't even discussed a future." But she thought about it constantly, despite her one-day-at-a-time promise. And now that their time on the shoot was running out, they'd have to make a decision about going forward. Could she handle his real life?

She needed to find out.

"All right," Maddie sighed. "I'll go.

TWENTY

M ADDIE TOOK A SIP OF rosé wine as she scanned the doors of the Buell Theater lobby for the millionth time. Still no Micah. Who made up the stupid rule that actors were supposed to show up to charity functions so late anyway? Probably the same person who decided that production crew had to show up on time.

God, she was nervous. She had thought about texting Micah to tell him she was coming, but she wasn't sure what his reaction would be. At least she looked good. Even though she wasn't a girly-girl, she could clean up. The silver organza baby-doll dress Bree had sent her hit mid-thigh and, thanks to running, she had nice legs. The sweetheart bodice embellished with rhinestones did awesome things for her boobs and matched the rhinestones that decorated her black stilettos. Yeah, she looked damn good.

"You have to try these crab cakes." Joe balanced a handful of hors d'oeuvres he had swiped from one of the trays.

"I'm not really hun—" He popped one in her mouth before she could finish. The cake melted in her mouth and surprised her at its deliciousness. "Okay, that was good," she said after she swallowed. Truth was she hadn't been able to eat much of anything. She was too anxious about the evening, about spending the night with hundreds of people she didn't know and the one person she was starting to know pretty damn well. Especially because she had to pretend she didn't know that person so well.

"The bruschetta is awesome too," Joe said around a mouthful of crab cakes. "Grab some when the next tray comes along."

Maddie felt a hand at the small of her back and she turned, hopeful, to face the owner.

"Wow!"

Sam. Not Micah.

If Micah had arrived, there'd be more buzz. And he wouldn't touch her in public. He didn't on set, and he definitely wouldn't here.

"You look stunning." Sam's blue eyes sparkled, not in the lustful way that Micah's did when he looked at her, but in a way that spoke volumes about his admiration for her.

She blushed, unsure how to handle his crush. "Thank you. You look great in a tux."

"Ah, this old thing?"

He said more, but Maddie didn't hear it over the commotion at the front doors. Cameras flashed and people pressed against the ropes that created a mock red carpet for the VIP attendees to enter. She had a good view from where she stood at the bar, and crowds began to gather around her as Heather Wainwright made her entrance.

Maddie tensed. Fudge walked in wearing black sunglasses in full-out bodyguard mode. He held the door open for Micah, who strode in with a beautiful brunette on his arm. He was as handsome as ever in his black tux and tie. He seemed untouchable and Godlike. Like the president or a celebrity.

Of course that was exactly what he was—a celebrity. Sometimes Maddie forgot.

It wasn't hard to forget now. Micah posed and waved as he walked down the carpet, his smile wide and his eyes twinkling. Lulu stepped aside with Fudge to let Micah have his glory alone, though Heather stood by him in many of the shots. She looked beautiful at his side, her blonde hair standing out against the red floor-length gown that hugged her tightly around her curvy parts.

Maddie felt an undercurrent of jealousy sparking under her calm exterior as she watched the spectacle over Joe's shoulder, despite all that she and Micah had worked through. Their tryst in the woods had worked to make filming the sex scene a non-issue. Maddie knew she'd had the real deal and that everything on set was acting.

But she couldn't say that now, because even though Micah had brought his mother, Heather was the one who got to walk down the carpet with him. Heather was the one who could lean over and whisper in his ear and laugh at some interviewer's question, her arm casually resting on his shoulder. Heather was the one who could be photographed with him.

Maddie got to admire from a distance. Like a fan. Like a mistress.

"Hey, was that shrimp cocktail?" Joe followed the caterer, stepping out of Maddie's sight line, giving her a clear view of the man she was fucking on a regular basis.

She recognized the minute he saw her. He was joking for the press with a fellow actor, when he stilled mid-laugh, his brows raised in surprise, his stare piercing her like a hot laser. Jaw set, his eyes swept up and down her body, devouring her.

She straightened as the electricity that passed through his heated gaze ignited every nerve in her body, warming her. Her face flushed with desire, her lower belly tightened, and she'd bet money he was hard under his black pants.

But it wasn't just sexual energy that passed between them. It was more—something intangible and impossible to name. The lobby that had held hundreds of people just a moment before now held no one but him and her, and the raw emotions that encompassed them. It frightened and excited her, that he could affect her so with just a look, that she could affect him in the same way.

Then a flashbulb went off and the spell was broken. Micah was back in character, charming and charismatic for the crowd.

"It seems the talent has arrived," Sam said leaning into her so she could hear over the din. His body heat lacked in comparison to Micah's penetrating eyes and she shivered in their wake. "For once I think the crew got the better end of the deal."

"Hmm, what?" She was distracted. How did Micah confound her so completely? How could she feel totally bereft of him one moment and then consumed by him the next?

And she still didn't know if he was glad to see her there. How had he seemed? Surprised. Appreciative of her attire, maybe. What else, she couldn't guess. And she wouldn't be able to find out for hours, probably, since she couldn't have a real conversation with him until they were alone at their hotel.

Yeah, the secret thing sucked.

But if they decided to keep seeing each other, eventually it wouldn't be secret. And then Maddie could walk in with him, though she'd likely still have to watch him pose with his costars while she stood off to the side as Lulu did now. No two ways about it, dating a celebrity was tricky.

Maddie moved her focus to Lucille Preston. Not surprisingly, she was as beautiful as her son. Her dark hair was coiffed short, framing her oval face. Her body, from what Maddie could see through the crowd, was trim and fit for a woman her age. She appeared completely at ease in her short black formal dress, her son the center of attention.

Could Maddie be like that? Could she stand aside and watch her lover be pursued and pounced on by the press? It seemed . . . awkward and kind of a drag.

"It just doesn't look very fun to be all paparazzi'd like that," Sam said continuing a conversation that Maddie kept forgetting they were having.

No shit.

Joe returned then with a plate full of shrimp cocktail and a few other members of the crew. "Look who I found."

Maddie let the group surround her, grateful for the number so she could dissolve into the background. Minutes passed where she smiled and nodded automatically to whatever was said, not knowing what she was smiling and nodding at. All the while, she snuck peeks at Micah and his mother, always aware of where he stood and who he stood with—more often than not with Heather.

Maddie wanted to poke Heather's eyes out with her stilettos. It would be a shame to ruin such a nice pair of shoes though, so she shut the thought out of her mind.

"Are we all sitting together?" Sam asked no one in particular.

"We're together in the balcony," Joe said. "The actors are in the orchestra, I think. Or they have box seats."

Surprise, surprise. Segregation of cast and crew. Again.

Usually she wouldn't think twice about it. Now it felt like a punishment.

"Oh look, it's our production crew!"

Maddie looked to the source of the voice and saw Heather pointing at their group.

"Familiar faces, Micah. Let's go say hi." Heather pulled Micah toward them, with Fudge and Lulu following close behind.

Maddie's heart pounded and her palms began sweating as they approached. She couldn't decide if she was jealous or nervous or excited, or all three mixed up into one impending anxiety attack. Whatever it was, Micah was getting close and her skin goosed as it always did in his presence.

But Micah didn't look at her once. Not even a sideways glance. *Shit.* Was he mad?

"Hey, guys," Micah said, jabbing at his phone. "Excuse me just a minute, please."

And he was gone, stepping aside to privately take or make a call. She wasn't sure which.

She closed her eyes, squelching threatening tears.

Her phone buzzed inside her clutch and she scrambled to grab it. Normally she'd ignore it, but Micah was on his phone—was it ridiculous to think he was calling her? She looked at the caller ID. *Micah-from-the-party.*

She swallowed then answered, her body tensed in preparation for his anger or disappointment or whatever he was about to deliver. "Yes?"

"Baby, you look so fucking hot, I'm struggling to not pull you into the coat room and take you right now."

Well, she hadn't been prepared for that.

His voice was tight and full of need. She flushed, searching the crowd for where he'd wandered off to, and found him standing alone, eyes locked on her.

"Turn around," he said, hungrily. She did and he groaned. "Fuck, those shoes . . . As amazing as you look in that dress, later I hope to see you wearing nothing but those shoes."

She was never taking off those rhinestone stilettos again. God, he made her hot.

"Gotta go." He pocketed his phone and gave his attention to a couple that had just approached him for an autograph.

Relief mingled with her arousal. Really, what had she expected? That he would be angry that she attended an event she had every right to be at? He hadn't wanted her there for the same reason she hadn't wanted to be there—because it made them ache to be together. That was all.

"You look like you're enjoying yourself," Sam said, bumping her shoulder with his.

Maddie realized she'd been beaming since her phone call. She relaxed her smile. "It's probably the wine. I'm a lightweight. I should follow it with some coffee."

"I'd be happy to get you a cup."

"Thanks, but I'll get it. I'm very particular about my mix of cream and sweetener."

She returned to the bar and ordered her coffee. Then she crossed to the condiment area to dress her beverage the way she liked it. As she filled her cup with creamer, a familiar arm reached around her for a packet of sugar.

"Excuse me," Micah's voice hummed.

Maddie glanced sideways at him, saw the mischievous grin he wore and the twinkle in his eye as he prepared his own cup of coffee. They were alone, as alone as they were going to get. She risked a hushed conversation. "So you're not mad that I'm here?"

He reached around her again, this time for a stirrer. She leaned back into the momentary closeness of him, inhaling the musky scent of Micah—a mixture of his aftershave and body wash and his own unique odor. Maybe secret wasn't so bad.

"Not at all. I always want you near." She felt his hand lower behind her to shift his bulge. "Even if it makes me a bit uncomfortable in the pants."

Maddie smiled as she busied herself with stirring her coffee longer than necessary in order to prolong their interaction. "Your mother is beautiful. You look so much like her."

He swiveled to view Lulu. "You think? I mean, I think she's beautiful, too, but I don't know how much I look like her." Lowering his voice he added, "And thank you for mentioning my mother. You've effectively cured me of my semi."

She giggled. "One way or another, I'm always glad to relieve you."

"Let's not even continue this line of conversation," he laughed. He turned his focus again to Lulu. "She loves these things. Look at her milking up all the attention my manager is giving her."

Maddie followed his gaze. "That's your manager?"

"Yeah, Stu."

"She does look awfully comfortable." And a little bit smitten. Did Micah realize his mother had a thing for his manager? From the oblivious look on Micah's face, she guessed not.

They watched Lulu and Stu for a few seconds in silence. Then Micah cocked his head. "Do you want to meet them?"

Maddie's heart stopped. *Them.* Stu and Lulu, two of the most important people in Micah's life. "Only if you want me to." Her response was barely louder than a whisper.

"I do." His eyes lit up with excitement, verifying what he said was sincere. "But I'm warning you now, I'm going to be vague about our relationship."

"You don't want to tell your mother and manager all the amazing things I do to you on a nightly basis? I guess I can live with that."

"Thanks for understanding." He waved his hand to catch his mother's eye, then summoned her toward them.

Maddie braced herself, hoping she appeared casual despite her sudden overwhelming anxiety about meeting Micah's mom. *His mom!* It had been years since she'd met a boyfriend's parent.

Of course, Micah wasn't her boyfriend. Not technically. But he was much more than just a lover. Somehow she had to keep all of that from showing on her face, in her body. Though how could she when her entire soul lit up like a firecracker in his presence?

No time to figure it out. Lulu was there. In front of her. Micah's smile was easy, casual. He gestured nonchalantly at Maddie. "Lulu, Stu this is Maddie Bauers. She's a camera assistant on the film."

Maddie offered her hand first to Stu. His shake was firm but brief, the manager seeming to be more interested in speaking with Micah. No matter. Impressing Stu wasn't high on her list of goals.

Then she swiveled to greet Micah's mother. Lulu's eyes, Maddie noticed, were exactly the color of her son's, less piercing, but equally as bright. Her hand was warm and smooth, her grasp firm though not as tight as Stu's.

Instantly Maddie loved her in a way she would find difficult to explain if ever pressed to do so. Loved her for bringing Micah into this world. Loved her because Micah loved her.

Loved her because, Maddie was beginning to suspect, she also loved her son.

When she took back her hand, Maddie was breathless from the waves of emotions that had accompanied the simple contact. She was also keenly aware that all of it had been one-sided.

Which was fine. More important was the widening of Micah's eyes that suggested he'd understood and that he was pleased.

"It's always a pleasure to meet people Micah works with," Lulu said in a voice that hinted she was good at mingling. Sincere enough to be charming, but not personal enough to make a real connection.

"Adam LaForgeon's on camera, right?" Stu asked. "He's excellent."

"He is," Maddie said, grateful for the easy subject. "I've been lucky to be his assistant for several years now."

"But she's also a brilliant director," Micah interrupted. Maddie didn't miss the pride that tainted his words. "I was telling you about her film earlier, Mom."

He told her about me!

Goosebumps clothed Maddie's arms. He'd told Lulu about her. And even though she'd rather the talk had been on a personal level instead of about her film, she was moved. He'd thought about her.

Lulu's eyebrows raised and her interest in Maddie sparked. "Oh, the one you want to invest in?"

Micah brought a finger to his lips. "Shh, Mom. That's not common knowledge. But if you're a good girl, maybe we can talk Maddie into showing you some of her footage over breakfast."

"That sounds wonderful."

And just like that their breakfast date was a reality.

Stu seemed to have something on his mind. "Maddie, would you care if I steal Micah and his mother for a moment? I need to talk business."

"No, of course not." She would have loved to be included on a personal business conversation, but she barely cared at the moment. Right now she was soaring. Despite his reservations and fears, Micah had introduced her to his mother. Under his own conditions, yes, but she was grateful for the compromise. Relationships were about compromise, after all, and his actions proved he understood that.

Proved he might even be thinking about the two of them in exactly those terms—relationship terms.

Even as Stu led Micah and Lulu away from her into the doors just outside the auditorium, Maddie felt closer to Micah than she ever had.

TWENTY-ONE

T TOOK ALL OF MICAH'S strength to not glance back at the woman behind him as he and his mother followed Stu to discuss whatever was apparently too important to keep. And how he'd be able to concentrate on anything Stu said, he had no idea. His mind was all on Maddie.

When he'd first seen her in the foyer, he had to admit, he'd been startled. Maybe even a little irritated. Then he was turned on. How could he not be with her looking like that, all dolled up and sex on heels? Seriously turned on.

And then he felt relieved.

A blanket of serenity that he'd never felt at these sorts of public events fell over him just knowing she was in the room. After seeing her, his smiles became easier, his laughs a little less fake. Yeah, she'd done that to him.

And when he'd introduced her to Lulu . . .

Why did his insides feel so warm and soft with their meeting? As though he'd just finished a glass of bourbon but ten times better. Not at all nerve-wracking as he'd expected, but pleasant.

More than pleasant. Perfect.

But leaving Maddie to talk to Stu? That wasn't easy in the least. That was one of the reasons he had wanted her to stay home. It was too hard to be in the room with her, especially looking so fuckable in her short silver dress and high heels. He wanted to be with her, to never leave her side.

Never?

Maybe he was being dramatic.

Steel up, man. Stop acting so fucking pussy-whipped.

Stu led Lulu and Micah just inside the theater doors but far enough away from the crowded foyer to speak in private. Micah abandoned his full cup of coffee in a trash can—he'd only ordered it to get himself near Maddie, anyway—and tried to ignore how he felt like a total asshole leaving her alone like that.

This was his job. This was his life. What else could he do?

Micah's focus returned full force to his manager when Stu clapped a hand on his shoulder, excitement animating his features. "Listen, kid, sorry to bother you with business tonight, but I knew you'd want to hear this immediately. Santini saw that Affleck film you did and wants you for the lead in his next film. No read-through or anything. Just yours if you want it."

The floor gave out underneath Micah. A Martin Santini film? He'd been dreading the next movie on his calendar—a sappy romantic comedy—but Santini? That was exactly the kind of thing he'd been working toward, where all the years of sacrifice and sweat and solitude had been meant to take him.

He didn't know what to say, his words fell out jumbled. "Really? Wow! That's . . . incredible!"

Lulu's eyes gleamed with proud tears. "You know what that means, Micah? Santini is almost a guaranteed Oscar nom."

"I know, Mom. I know." He was speechless, breathless. He leaned back against the wall of the dark alcove, needing the support. "What's the movie? I haven't even seen a script."

"Epic western revenge film. I'll have the script sent to you ASAP. Shitload of fighting sequences. He wants you in New Zealand the minute you finish the romance thing to start training."

Something in Micah's chest tightened. "New Zealand?" His romance was being shot in L.A. on a soundstage. And many of the other projects he was looking at were near home as well. Not that he minded going out of the country. New Zealand was just so far from . . .

He couldn't think her name. She had nothing to do with this conversation.

"You know Santini," Stu said. "He loves filming in New Zealand."

"They have great studios there," Lulu added, her face still beaming. "And cheaper than a lot of alternatives."

Micah nodded, hoping the anxious feeling could be loosened with the motion. Maybe he wouldn't be gone long. "What's the production schedule like?"

"Three to four months prep and another four months filming."

"Right." Eight fucking months. It was a lifetime. His next project was scheduled to be over in two months. When he left for New Zealand, he'd have been with Maddie for less time than he'd be away.

If they were staying together, anyway.

He couldn't shake the cold chill that had settled over him since Stu had said the words *New Zealand*. He knew this was coming, it shouldn't have hit him like a ton of bricks. It was just that he hadn't expected to have to decide about where things were going with Maddie so soon. He didn't think he'd have to make such a deliberate choice. Because taking the part could effectively end him and Maddie.

And hadn't he known that would be the outcome all along?

No, they could work it out. If they talked about it, if they made a plan . . .

He couldn't think about this right now, not with Stu waiting for an answer on a critical career decision. Not with his mother looking at him with expectant excitement in her eyes. "When do I have to decide?"

Lulu's eyebrows shot up. "Why do you even have to think about it?"

Stu also looked surprised, but at least he tried to hide it. "He'll want an answer soon. I can probably buy you a couple of weeks."

"Micah?"

Micah ignored his mother. "Thanks, Stu, I'd appreciate that."

"Micah, why do you have to think about it?" Lulu's surprise had turned to confusion. He'd always been open with her about his plans and projects. She knew how much he admired Santini, how this film could change his entire life. Of course she wouldn't understand.

And Micah couldn't explain it. How could he? She'd left her marriage to pursue her career. How would she understand Micah's hesitation over a woman he'd been seeing for a handful of weeks?

Stu seemed to sense the conversation Micah needed to have with Lulu was personal. "I'll leave you to discuss this. Just let me know, kid."

"Thanks again, Stu."

Stu had barely stepped out of earshot before Lulu was questioning her son again. "Micah, why—"

"I just do." He ran his hands through his hair, trying to come up with a reasonable excuse to give his mother. "It's a long time out of the country. And I was looking at that Soderbergh project."

"Soderbergh is nothing compared to this offer. This is Oscar material, Micah."

"Soderbergh could be Oscar." Now he dragged his hand over his face. *Maddie.* That's all he could think of. Maddie. How hard it was not to give that as his defense, his every excuse. Maddie, Maddie, Maddie.

Unable to keep her name off his lips he said, "There's also Maddie's film. Her movie is brilliant. And I want to be involved in more than just acting."

"That's the great thing about working on investment projects. You give your money and you're done. You don't have to be present for it."

Micah turned to study Lulu, searching for some clue as to how he could explain his conflict. "But I really want to be here to see it picked up. I'm invested in it." It would help if he thought he could be honest with his mother. If he could have just told her how he felt about the woman in the other room, maybe she'd understand.

"Micah Drew Preston. Are you sleeping with her?" Or maybe she wouldn't understand. "Is that what this is about?"

He cringed at his mother's questions. "That's not what this is about, Mom." Yes, he was sleeping with Maddie, but that wasn't what his New Zealand hesitation was about. Not entirely, anyway. What he had with Maddie was so much more. Wasn't it?

"You were a mess after that Nikki woman, I can't believe you'd get yourself involved in another situation like that."

"Maddie is nothing like Nichelle."

"I'm just so surprised, Micah. I know you're considered a ladies man, but I've never seen you make career decisions with your Peter."

"Jesus Christ, Lulu. I am not making any career decisions tonight. I need some time to think about it, that's all. And, frankly, I'm really uncomfortable talking about this with you."

Lulu's face bunched up and he feared she might cry. God, please don't let her cry. "But you always talk to me about your film projects."

Great, he'd officially hurt her feelings. "I didn't mean my projects. I'm not comfortable talking to you about my sex life, Mom." He put his hands on his mother's slim shoulders. "Just give me some time to think about it."

"Okay, okay. I just don't want to see you throw away all the time and energy you've invested in your career. Not over some girl."

The sympathy he'd felt for her a moment before disappeared at her flippant dismissal of Maddie. "We're done talking about this."

"Fine." She rolled back her shoulders and patted the sides of her hair, composing herself. "Do you have my ticket? I need to use the restroom before the show starts."

Micah dug in his pocket and found his mother's ticket.

"I'll meet you inside."

He watched his mother follow the path Stu had taken and let out a breath he hadn't realized he'd been holding. What the fuck now? This wasn't the time or place for the introspective thinking he needed to do, but he couldn't help the conflicting thoughts of career and Maddie that mingled in his mind.

Maddie. She was probably waiting for him to reappear. He stepped out of the corridor and glanced to where he had stood with her before at the condiment table by the bar. She wasn't there, but he sensed her near. He turned and found her pressed against the wall at the theater entrance. He met her eyes and knew she'd heard everything.

Quickly, he replayed the conversation in his mind, imagining how it sounded to her ears. Christ. Some of it probably sounded pretty damn shitty.

He searched her face, reading her expression. She was an open book, a book he didn't want to read right now, her eyes sad, her posture broken.

He couldn't talk to her, not now. He set his jaw, and straightened his lips into a firm line, giving nothing away. He left her like that, resuming his role as a personality at a high-profile fundraiser, shaking hands with rich people who had impressive names, and Botoxed foreheads and significant others on their arms.

The serenity Maddie Bauers had given him earlier was gone. In the highly crowded lobby, hundreds of people swarming to his side, he was alone.

Only a few minutes passed before the lights in the lobby flashed, indicating it was time for people to take their seats. Micah hung back until Maddie and the other crewmembers walked up the stairs to the upper level.

Heather sidled up beside him and slipped her arm in his. "Where's Lulu?"

"Already inside."

"Shall we find our box?"

"Sure," he mumbled. They walked up the stairs to the second level where the box seats were accessed and gave their tickets to the ushers. The rest of the cast from the movie were already seated, and he and Heather sat in the back box seats.

When the lights dimmed he sank into his chair, relieved to have the spotlight off of him. Finally, he let himself think. The whole time he'd been with Maddie he hadn't let himself imagine this far ahead in his plans with her. He'd hoped he might get over her by now. Stupid, since he'd coveted her since the night he met her. And now he was more into her than ever.

So he could keep seeing her. And so what that he'd be in New Zealand? He could bring her with him. It would be just like Colorado. He might even be able to get her a job on set. He could make it part of his contract.

But he couldn't just drag her around while he worked. She had her own films to make. Good films. Even if she didn't yet believe it. And he wanted to be the one who helped her discover herself.

But he couldn't turn down the Santini opportunity. It would be ridiculous to give up years of sweat, blood and tears for a woman he'd been with for less than three weeks. He'd been dreaming about an Oscar nom since he was sixteen. And even without the Oscar lure, Micah admired Santini more than most directors in the biz. Besides, it wasn't only his dream—Lulu would be so proud.

That left trying to work out a relationship with Maddie over miles and between shoots. The thought of being away from her like that killed him, yet the alternative was not being with her at all, so it would have to do.

Except, it was the miles and time apart that destroyed all the couples he'd known in Hollywood. Jealousy crept in. The press took advantage. Too much distance, too many rumors, too impossible to manage. It always ended in heartache.

There had to be some way to sort it out. Some way to be able to choose Maddie and his career. He closed his eyes and tried to come up with a solution to bridge the two.

But with his eyes closed he only saw Maddie.

And when he opened his eyes and saw Joss Beaumont on stage and clips from his movies playing on the projector behind him, and all he thought about was how much he loved making good movies.

He had to get out of there.

Without telling anyone where he was going, he wandered out to the balcony lobby, in search of a drink, but found the bar had been left unattended. He contemplated reaching over the counter and making his own drink—what would they do to him? He was Micah Preston, one of the stars of the evening. They should be falling at his feet to please him.

Those were bitter self-absorbed thoughts and he knew it.

Instead, he leaned against the counter and scanned the lobby.

Then he saw her. Maddie. She sat alone on a bench at the other end of the lobby, and even at that distance, he knew she was crying. Her body shuddered with each wave of sobs.

For half a second he wondered why she was so upset, wanted to run to her and fix it. Then he realized with certainty that it was him.

Fuck. It broke him to see her like that. What was it that had pushed her to this place? The idea of being separated from him? Or was she finally understanding the impossibility of their relationship?

Or had it been his mother's callous behavior? Because that was what had hurt Micah the most.

If he had to make a guess, he'd say it was Lulu's comments that had probably stung Maddie most, too. He'd seen how Maddie had wanted to connect with Lulu. Funny how he'd wanted that, too.

He wanted to make it better, but he felt helpless. He didn't have an answer to their situation, didn't have words to take their pain away. Besides, if he went to her now, and she cried like that in front of him, he wouldn't be able to hang on. He'd give everything up for her right on the spot. And that wasn't the answer.

He had to reach out, though, had to tell her not to give up on them. He sent her a text. *"Counting the seconds til I have you in my arms."*

It was several minutes before she dug in her purse, seemingly looking for a tissue, and opened her phone. He watched her read his message, a small smile crossing her lips, then she typed her reply.

"You shouldn't text in the theater. It's rude."

Ah, sweet Maddie. Crying her eyes out in the lobby and she wasn't letting on at all. He hated that he was glad. Wished she could be honest with him. Wished he wanted her to be honest with him. Wished he wanted to be honest with her.

He sent her a text that matched the tone of hers. *"Neither should you."*

"I'm not in the theater."

"Neither am I." He hoped she'd look for him now.

She did.

She stood and crossed to the railing to look down on the lobby below her. Then she peered across the lobby on their level and their eyes met. His heart skipped a beat. She was so beautiful. Even tear stained and mascara streaked she was still the most beautiful woman he'd ever met.

He took a deep breath and walked to her.

"Congratulations on the Santini film," she said as he neared her.

He shrugged, his hands in his pockets. "I haven't accepted yet."

"You will."

This was good. She'd opened the door for him to agree. He could just say it and that would be that. They could skip the more serious aspects of his conversation with Stu and his mother. He could take the out she was giving him so freely. It would be so easy . . .

She leaned on the railing next to him, close enough for him to touch her, and he did, reaching a finger under her eye to wipe at her mussed make-up. "What if I don't want it?"

He met her eyes, tumbling into them as he always did when she gazed at him so trusting and soul piercing. "You do."

Ah, she knew he wanted that role. Of course she knew. She saw him. Always. "I do."

Her breath hitched as he put a hand around her waist and swiftly pulled her to him. "I want you, too," he whispered, his nose circling hers.

"I know." She wrapped her arms around his neck.

He cupped her face and kissed her lips, sweetly and softly. She tasted of tears and makeup and something else—sorrow or heartache, maybe. He didn't want to taste that on her mouth, wanted to take her away from all his bullshit. Wanted to escape with her. "Let's get out of here?"

"You can't abandon your mother, silly." She smoothed his black silk tie, and he wished she was removing it instead.

"Then let's find some place more private."

She glanced around, and he followed her gaze. There was an usher behind them and a woman leaving the restroom.

"There're too many eyes here."

Yes, too many eyes. Eyes that could make their moment a scandal in a minute. They shouldn't even be holding each other like this, in public, not if he wanted to protect her from that. Still he couldn't let her go.

After they'd held each other for much too long, she pulled away. "You should get back. You'll be missed."

In her words, he felt the chains that bound him, the constant monitor of the public that he wore like shackles. "Yes."

She stepped to leave him, but her hand lingered in his, and he pulled her back to him, not wanting to let go. Ever. "Maddie, I—"

She searched his face and he almost finished his sentence, told her how he felt about her. But saying those words, there would be no going back from that. That would be his decision and he just . . . couldn't.

"Kiss me again," he said instead.

She delivered a light kiss. But he seized her lips with his own, his tongue possessing her with demanding need, claiming not only her mouth but her soul. With his kiss, he marked her as his, reserved her for a future that he wasn't able to give her. *Yet.*

When he separated his mouth from hers, he leaned his forehead against hers, his chest rising and falling in her rhythm. "Maddie, I'm glad you're here."

Lame. He had given her nothing tangible, nothing that told her how he felt, no hint that he was confused about her—that he wanted what they had to become something more. The only words he had for her were, "I'm glad you're here."

Totally lame.

He vowed he'd give her a clue. And while he sat in his box seat pretending to watch the rest of Beaumont's interview, he made his plans.

TWENTY-TWO

MADDIE TWISTED BENEATH HER SEATBELT so she could lean against the backrest and watch Micah as he drove the rental car. She had never seen him drive. Even on the rare occasions that they shared a call time, she always rode up with the crew or Fudge, maintaining the secrecy of their affair.

He enjoyed driving. She could tell. His body relaxed behind the wheel and he wore a silly boyish expression on his face as he jammed to the music coming from his iPod over the car's speakers. She liked seeing him this way.

She liked seeing him period.

She smiled, recalling a conversation from a few nights before. They had gone for drinks and pool with the crew, and afterward as they walked down the hall of his hotel, buzzed from beer and the company of friends, Micah had taken her hand and said, "Is this what normal people do? Come home every night and be happy?"

And for a minute she believed that they could be normal people.

But that was before the Joss Beaumont evening. Before the conversation she'd overheard between Stu, Lulu, and Micah. She'd been so thrilled for Micah the minute she heard he'd been offered a role as coveted as the lead in a Santini film. Then, when Stu said that Micah would have to be in New Zealand for the better part of a year, she felt crushed. Absolutely and completely crushed.

How had she let herself forget that was how the business worked? Films took actors and crew all over the world, to different parts of the world. They'd be separated. Of course they would be.

And then Lulu had encouraged Micah to take the part, as she should, and Maddie agreed with his mother's stance. But the exchange still hurt. A lot. Especially when Micah was unwilling to tell his mother that his hesitations revolved around the way he felt for Maddie. If he couldn't tell Lulu, if he couldn't admit it even to himself, how could they have any hope of making a real go of it? If they had any chance of surviving long periods of time apart, they'd have to be strong enough to declare their feelings openly. At the very least, declare them to each other.

Micah glanced at her from the driver's seat, interrupting her thoughts. "What are you thinking about?"

"Your sad choice of music," she answered, steering clear of the topic they'd avoided in the three days since the Joss Beaumont night. Not that they'd ever talked about a future, but now their avoidance of it was heavy and glaring at the periphery of every moment together.

He grinned. "Hard rock's no good?"

"No good at all. In fact, it's seriously making me reconsider our relationship." Inwardly she cringed at the word relationship, hoping it didn't sound like she was putting pressure on Micah to discuss their situation. With less than one week left of production though, she should have been putting pressure on him. Eventually they would have to talk about it. She knew she should bring it up, but every time she had the chance, she pushed it off, not wanting to ruin the moment.

"Fine," Micah said, turning off the music. "Let's talk instead."

"Okay." *Now. Talk about it now.* "What do you want to talk about?" God, she was a chicken.

"I don't know. Uh, how's your movie going?"

Maddie frowned. That was an odd question. He was with her every time she worked on it, and he usually watched and gave her feedback whenever she completed a section. He'd viewed everything she had done so far with his mother two days before. Maddie had backed out of their breakfast date at the last minute. She didn't think she could spend another occasion pretending she wasn't head over heels for Micah, especially not one so intimate.

"I haven't done anything since the last time you saw it. Why?"

"I just love the theme of the movie. And so did Lulu, I know I told you that already. Freedom through flying. It's really good."

"Okay," she said, drawing out the word. He had told her Lulu'd been very impressed, and Maddie had been proud of herself for it. But every time she thought of Lulu and her movie in the same sentence, she recalled Lulu's comparison of Maddie to Micah's ex. And she couldn't bear that anyone might think she was using Micah for his film connections.

But all of those thoughts were miles off from whatever Micah was talking about now. She just couldn't quite follow his direction yet.

"And how about heights? Do you have a fear of heights?"

"No," she answered tentatively. "Do you?"

"Nope. Not at all."

She narrowed her eyes at him. "Why are you being so weird?"

"Weird? I'm not being weird. I just realized I didn't know if you were afraid of heights or not. You know. Standard get-to-know you question. I really should have already known this."

"Uh huh." Maddie didn't believe him. He was up to something.

"Do you have anything you'd like to know about me?"

She'd learned a lot about Micah in the last few weeks—things she never gleaned about him from the countless interviews she'd watched and read over the years—but she knew there was still more to discover. Everything. She wanted to know everything about him.

Like, for example, what would happen with them after the shoot ended on Friday? And where the heck was he taking her?

But she didn't ask those questions. He'd told her that today was a surprise, had woken her at four in the morning on their day off, and told her to dress warmly. He refused to say anything else about it. After twenty minutes of probing, she'd dropped it.

Maybe that was why she couldn't bring herself to steer the conversation to their relationship—she didn't want to ruin his carefully planned surprise.

"Let's see." She searched for a safe but meaningful query. "Oh, I know. Did you always want to be an actor?"

"Seriously?" He turned off the main road they'd been following onto a smaller winding road. "That's what you want to know? You can find that out from a good Google search."

"In every interview I've read you've said 'yes.'"

"There you go," he said, throwing his arm out dramatically.

"But I've always sensed you were hiding something."

He peered at her. "How do you do that? How do you know me so well?"

Because we're meant to be together. She shrugged.

"No. I didn't always want to be an actor." He looked at her as if gauging her reaction. "My mom was an actress, so she got me acting in commercials when I was about thirteen. And I hated it. We didn't live in the film industry part of the city and no one in my school was into anything artsy. Kids picked on me, called me a fag, beat me up on a regular basis. In fact, that's how I met Fudge. He stepped up for me and has been protecting me ever since."

Wow. She had no idea.

"Do you know how he got his nickname?"

She shook her head.

"Because he used to scare kids so bad, they'd fudge their pants."

She giggled.

"Anyway. Then I turned sixteen. My high school was putting on *David and Lisa*. I didn't really want to do it, but my girlfriend—"

"Girlfriend?"

He ignored her. "—thought it would be super sexy if I was in it. So I tried out and I got the part of David."

"Which is a great part. Definitely super sexy."

"Yes, it is." He slid his free hand over to grab hers. "But on top of that, my high school theater director was amazing. She taught us more than just memorizing lines and blocking. She taught us process, how to make choices in acting, how to create a character internally and externally. I fell in love."

"I'm assuming you fell in love with the acting, not the girlfriend."
Not that she was jealous of a high-school sweetheart. Not in the least.

"Totally the acting. I broke up with the girlfriend before the show
even went up."

"Awesome." She grinned.

"I started taking classes outside of school—speech, movement,
acting for the camera. I got a personal coach. Then an agent. Then I
started doing indies, which I loved. Then I got Stu."

"And the rest is history."

"I suppose so."

He was silent for several seconds. The morning light brightened,
the sun just coming over the edge of the horizon. She let go of his hand
and rummaged through her purse until she found her sunglasses.

When Micah spoke again his voice was low and serious. "That break-
up was because of the show, actually. Even back then acting interfered
with my relationship."

"With your teenage girlfriend? How so?" She didn't like what he
was hinting at and was grateful for the dark of her glasses so he wouldn't
see the glare in her eyes.

"We broke up because she was jealous of my acting. She said I
spent too much time away from her. We fought and fought about it. It
was awful."

Maddie cocked her head to look at Micah's profile. Was this the reason he was so convinced he couldn't have a girlfriend now? Because of a
silly break-up when he was a kid? It was a ridiculous idea, but a bubble of
hope began forming in her chest. "But you were in high school. Kids are
selfish and self-centered. Most teenage relationships end for those sorts
of reasons with or without acting involved." Surely he could see that.

"It's not just because of that girlfriend. There were others after.
And then there's my parents."

"Your parents?" She was taken aback. What did his parents have to
do with anything?

"All my life my mother tried to be an actress and it always put a strain on my parents' marriage. When I was twelve she realized that all the compromises she'd made to be a wife and mother had kept her from being as successful as she'd dreamed of being as an actress. So she left my dad."

"Ouch." The bubble of hope burst as pieces of the puzzle were beginning to make sense. Lulu had chosen career over family. No wonder she was so eager for Micah to do the same.

"It destroyed my dad. He loved her so completely. He couldn't understand why Lulu had to give up on their marriage. I didn't understand either until later." He paused and gave Maddie a quick side glance. "Now I understand completely."

Her body tensed, but before she overreacted, she needed clarification. "Are you saying you still have no faith in Hollywood relationships?"

"I've never said any differently."

Tears sprang to her eyes. All the time they'd spent together, she'd thought it meant something. And now he was saying it didn't change anything. "Then what are we doing, Micah?" Her voice was choked. "We said no preconceived notions about where we were going, but clearly you've already decided we're doomed. So was I just something to fill your time?"

"No! Of course not, baby." He took one hand off the wheel and ran it through his hair. "When we take one day at a time, yeah, it seems possible. But long term? I just . . . I still haven't seen any evidence to change my mind."

She closed her eyes and swallowed, stemming the pain before it could overwhelm her. Didn't he realize how much his words hurt her? Or was that his intent? Was he breaking up with her?

No, he couldn't be. Or, if he were, she wouldn't let him without a fight. She opened her eyes again and she slid her glasses on top of her head, turning to face him. "There are people who make it work, Micah. Successful people. Look at Tom and Rita. Didn't Julia Roberts marry her cameraman? They've been together for ages."

"But Angelina and Brad do a whole lot fewer movies than they used to. And Julia practically retired."

"They chose to scale back."

"Exactly. They chose their relationships over their careers." Micah's knuckles went white as he gripped the steering wheel. "Everything I say and do, Maddie, is a choice between my career or not my career. From deciding to take a shoot in another country to answering a question in an interview to sending a tweet on Twitter, to whether or not I send flowers for Valentine's Day."

"If you send flowers to a woman your career will be affected? Come on, Micah. That's dramatic." She didn't even bother to hide her eye roll, she was so annoyed.

His eyes narrowed and she could feel his frustration rising, fueling her own. "It's reality. If sending those flowers initiates a scandal, the director on the next film I want might say he doesn't want to deal with that type of drama."

"That's ridiculous."

"It's how it is. You don't know." He gestured between the two of them. "This little life we've been living? This is a fantasy, Maddie. This isn't how it is all the time. It's not this easy. If I want to keep this career, the choices I have to make are hard and they're painful."

"Why do you have to choose your career every time? There has to be room for compromise without throwing away your career goals."

"Not in this business. You have to fight every day. Even when you're on the top."

He *was* breaking up. Or he might as well have been. Every word that fell out of his mouth said he could never believe in them. That he didn't choose her. She wiped at her damp face with her palm. "So you're telling me that every day you choose your career? Everyday you'd choose that over me?"

He didn't answer. He didn't have to. Because as Maddie curled up against the door and stared out the window she noticed the landscape for the first time in several minutes. The mountainside they'd been following had ended, opening to an enormous field that was empty except for a van, three men, and a huge hot air balloon with a rainbow chevron pattern.

Micah slowed the car.

A hot air balloon.

"Oh, Micah!" Emotions whirled and warred inside her as the full realization of his surprise settled in. Her movie. Freedom through flying. His questions about fear of heights. He'd done this for her. Today, he'd chosen her.

Too overcome with emotion, Maddie couldn't speak. Micah pulled the car up next to the van and turned off the engine. Eyes focused on the colorful balloon, she stepped out, chewing on the knuckle of her hand to keep from crying again.

Still silent, Micah got out and came to her side. She met his eyes and he took her hand and squeezed it. "I'm scared," he said quietly and she knew he didn't mean about flying.

"I know," she whispered.

The next half hour was a blur of emotions and sensations. The quick thrill at the balloon's lift off, the fire hot at her back, the pull in her stomach as the basket skimmed the South Platte River, the pounding of her heart as they soared higher and higher. All of it intensified by the feel of Micah's arms around her.

When she'd finally gotten her air legs and was no longer over-whelmed by the spectacular view, her mind drifted to the possibilities that lay between her and the man embracing her. Micah had taken a lot of risks to allow for their flight to happen. The crew that set up the balloon, the pilot . . . anyone of them could spread news of the star's morning adventure, even though he'd required all of them to sign a confidentiality agreement. What did it mean for them that he'd done this? Because he'd chosen her that day, did it mean he'd be willing to choose her again?

Eventually, at almost two thousand feet in the air, riding the wind, the silence was so stark that the noises in her mind struggled to be voiced. Finally, she couldn't hold them in any longer. "Micah," she said, not turning to look at him, hoping that the pilot truly couldn't hear anything with his thick headphones on. "Please, tell me the truth. Are you even considering giving us a chance after this shoot is over?"

He was quiet for a beat. Then he buried his face in her hair and whispered near her ear, "More than you know. More than I ever could have believed I would."

She took a deep breath in, memorizing the moment, so focused on his words she almost missed what he said next.

"What about you?"

She twisted her head so she could look at him, surprised by his question. Was he seriously asking? She thought her opinion on the matter was a given. How crazy that he didn't know. "Yes," she said simply.

Still, even though her heart burst inside with a much more emphatic acknowledgment, she knew there was more to overcome. "But I heard what you said, Micah. I get it. I'm scared, too."

She turned in his arms to face him with her entire body, letting him wrap himself so entirely around her she felt joined to him. Resting her forehead against his chin, she spoke into his neck. "If we did continue to see each other, would you ever believe that we'd have a shot at making it?" This question scared her most. Or rather, its answer did. Because if he said he didn't, then there would be no reason to keep seeing him.

He pulled back so he could look in her eyes, and his gorgeous smile took her breath away. "Maddie, look at us." He spun her around so she her back was to his chest again. Then he nuzzled his head against hers, his arms tight around her waist. "We're flying, Maddie. Flying! How can we not believe we can do anything?"

She melted into him. It was the perfect thing to say. Romantic, and maybe a bit vague, but in the words, she felt truth. As long as they believed that, how could their relationship not survive?

Beyond sentiment, his statements held weight. They showed a depth to his emotion that he'd never revealed in words. He still may not have been ready to say exactly how he felt about her, but she knew now that she meant more to him than a simple fling.

She also knew for certain how she felt about him. That night she told him, as she straddled his cock, burying him inside her. She slid herself up and down and when she quickly built up the pace, he sat up and steadied her. One arm wrapped around her waist, the other tangled in her hair, he taught her a new rhythm, slow and merciless.

Eyes locked on his, she moaned her surrender to him.

"Come for me," he urged.

And she did. Over and over her orgasm rolled through her, overtaking her so fully that he had to support her.

"Shh," he whispered. "I've got you."

With her steadied in his arms, he impaled himself into her, again and again, until she released anew. Then he joined her, as she gasped and burst around him, and she cried what she finally could say without doubt, "I love you."

TWENTY-THREE

MICAH ROLLED HIS HEAD, PAUSING at each side to crack his neck. Ah, that felt better. Not great, but better. He needed a massage and a week of sleep. He made a mental reminder to make a spa appointment for when he got back to L.A.

Ariahn Jessler, the blonde journalist from Faire Play Magazine furrowed her brows. "You seem tense," she said, pressing the red button on her digital recorder. This was the second leg of their interview. The first session had started the minute he'd arrived on set for the day, ending only when he had to shoot his scene. Now they were filming one of the other actor's close-ups so Micah was on break from acting and back on the interview.

"It's a tough week," he answered, careful not to sound too negative about his job. "We're going to have to work hard to stay on schedule."

"You finish up Friday?"

"That's the plan. We're behind schedule so we'll probably have some late shoots to make it up."

Ariahn jotted a note on her paper. What could she be writing? He hadn't really said anything. *Shake it off.* Best not to worry too much about what she wrote.

He put his arms on the rests of his director's chair. "Heather starts another movie on Saturday. It doesn't give us much wiggle room for finishing."

"Heather Wainwright?"

"Yeah." He casually moved his hand to his knee to stop his leg from twitching. God, he was on edge, had been since he'd woken up that morning. The end of production was only part of the reason. This interview was another. It had originally been scheduled for his day off, but he hadn't wanted to lose his free time. It would have thrown a serious damper on his hot air balloon surprise. He couldn't cancel altogether since Faire Play had promised a cover article. It was great exposure for him and his upcoming movie release, a sci-fi thriller. But a cover article of this length meant he'd be spending a lot of time with Ariahn. It made for an exhausting work day, playing his character for the film one second and then having to present a different character, his public self, during his off-camera time.

"What do you have lined up next?"

Surely she already knew. Six weeks ago he would have said that, would have flirted his way through the interview. But now, with Maddie nearby, it seemed wrong. Instead, he remained matter-of-fact and forthcoming with his answers. "Let's see, I'm presenting at the America's Choice Awards in a couple of weeks. Then I'll be promoting *Night in Space*. I start my next project in the late fall."

"And what is that?"

Micah had to work not to cringe. "It's called *Love Lessons*. I play a teacher who falls in love with his student." He couldn't believe he'd agreed to do a romantic comedy. He really hoped the Santini thing went through. If not he'd push to get in with an actor's director like Soderbergh or Branaugh or Van Sant.

Or Bauers. He'd love to be directed by Maddie, and not just in the bedroom.

Maddie. There was another cause of his tension. So many complicated thoughts and feelings arose with her around. Their day off together had been the best of the last six weeks, but they'd said things to each other, things they couldn't take back, some things he didn't want to take back.

He couldn't quite explain why he'd provoked her on the drive. He'd repeated the main points of an argument he'd made for years—why he couldn't have a girlfriend and his career—even though he wasn't sure how convinced he was anymore. But he stood firm and pushed her, almost hoping it would scare her away so that he wouldn't have to deal with the repercussions of madly adoring the woman.

Except it hadn't worked. And damn, he was grateful for that. So grateful that though he couldn't tell her how he felt, he'd hinted at a future that he still didn't know if he could deliver.

He wanted to deliver, that wasn't the problem. The more time he spent with her the more he realized how much he loved being with her. She was smart and fun. She inspired him creatively.

The sex was incredible.

All right, sex in general was incredible—women were usually intent on gratifying him, willing to do anything to get their one night with Micah Preston. But he'd forgotten what it felt like to be on the other side, wanting to satisfy someone else with such an ache that his own pleasure became irrelevant. How long had it been since he'd gotten to know a woman's body so intimately that he could play her like an accomplished musician, knowing exactly where to stroke and caress to make her sing?

And then she learned him too, and he didn't have to tell her what to do. She pleased him out of a genuine desire to share and connect, not because he was a Hollywood star.

It was the emotional component that boggled him. It frightened and thrilled him to feel whatever it was he felt for Maddie. He cared for her, appreciated her, adored her. She changed him. Made him believe things about himself, about the possibilities of a future that he hadn't believed in before.

He'd almost said he loved her. And then she did say it. In bed—did that count? With Maddie, he was pretty sure it did.

Though he hadn't told Maddie yet, he knew that the end of the production wouldn't be the end of them. It couldn't be. He had to be with her beyond Colorado. He'd talk about it with her soon. That night, maybe. It was such a major move for him, he had to prepare for it. And he still had five days to work it out. He didn't need to worry about it right this second. Especially not with a reporter sitting in front of him, watching his every move.

Had she asked him something? "I'm sorry. I'm not usually so distracted. I had a late night." *A late night of lovemaking.* He shifted, recalling it, giving himself more room in his pants.

"Oh, a late night?" Ariahn abandoned whatever question she'd just asked and redirected. "That's right, we were originally scheduled to meet yesterday, but my assistant said you had something come up. Sight-seeing, wasn't it?"

Micah stiffened. He hadn't mentioned his adventure with Maddie to anyone. He answered cautiously. "Yeah, I did some sight-seeing. Figured it was my last chance since the shoot's almost over."

"A hot air balloon is certainly the way to see Colorado."

Shit. Thank God his sunglasses hid his panic. *Who let it leak?* It had to be a member of the balloon's crew. How much had the source said? Had they mentioned Maddie? How could they not mention Maddie? What should he say now?

He took a swallow of his coffee and looked over at the set nearby, hoping it was time for filming to resume. Bruce was still adjusting lights, though. Damn, he wasn't getting out of this interview yet.

He moved his attention back to Ariahn who was peering at him intently. He cocked his head, deciding to play dumb. "Oh, are you waiting for me to answer? I didn't realize it was a question."

"I guess it wasn't." Ariahn picked up her bag and rifled through it. "Here's a question though." She pulled out several sheets of paper and laid them on the table between them. "Who's this attractive young woman that Hollywood's most eligible bachelor has been hanging out with recently?"

Micah felt the blood drain from his face as he examined the papers in front of him. They were low-quality photos, obviously printed off the Internet, four of them in total. Three pictures were of him and Maddie getting into the basket of the hot air balloon. One of the crew must have taken them with his phone. How had he not noticed? The fourth was from the Breckenridge Film Festival. That one didn't surprise him. In fact, none of it surprised him. He knew the press would find out about her eventually. They always did.

Fuck.

He wasn't ready for this.

Several possible responses whirled through his mind, each with a different set of consequences. A big part of him said he should just claim her as his. Tell Ariahn that Maddie was his girlfriend and deal with the aftermath later.

But he hadn't talked to Maddie about it and that wouldn't be fair to her. He needed to have this conversation with her first. Tell her how he felt. Work out with her how they would move forward.

Besides, there would be an inevitable media circus. Once it was out that they were a couple, every decision they made would be under the microscopic eye of his fans and the paparazzi. It would add an incredible amount of strain to their relationship. Maddie's private life would be destroyed. They'd pounce on her, follow her wherever she went, dig up all of her past, lie about her. Hurt her.

They'd find out about her history with Joss Beaumont. That could harm her chances at a directing career. Hell, it could harm his own career.

Did she even realize that's what dating him meant? Why hadn't he talked to her about the press? Prepared her? He was such an idiot, trying to keep their romance in a bubble.

And when her movie came out—and it would eventually, he'd see to it—her brilliance would be overlooked because she was Micah Preston's girlfriend. People would say that was the only reason she'd gotten her movie picked up, before they even saw it.

At that moment, he hated the press more than he ever had. Because they forced him to keep Maddie a secret, whether he wanted to or not.

He processed all of this in a matter of seconds so when he answered Ariahn it didn't even seem like he'd skipped a beat. "Ah, Maddie Bauers. Yeah, she's on the crew of this show." He removed his sunglasses and met the reporter's eyes, hoping to come across sincere. "She's also a writer/

director and we've been talking about working on a project together."

Ariahn looked skeptical. "In a hot air balloon?"

"Only place I'm not followed by paparazzi." Yeah, it was vague, but it was also charming.

"Yes, the paparazzi." Ariahn smirked. "Oh, I forgot—I have one more." She uncovered another sheet of paper she had tucked under the others. This one was taken in the lobby of the Buell. He and Maddie were lip-locked in one of the most heart-searing kisses of his lifetime. *The usher.* It had to be.

Goddammit! Why did everyone have to have camera phones nowadays?

Though he liked the look of them together like that.

This one was the hardest to deny. This one almost made him ignore all the reasonable arguments and claim Maddie as his right then and there.

Almost.

"This looks like more than a meeting about a project," Ariahn prodded.

He swallowed his surprise, his frustration, his desire to come clean about the woman he adored and improvised. "All right, Ariahn, you caught me. I made a pass. Hot girl at a hot party? I've been known to do that."

Ariahn raised an eyebrow. "Let me put it this way: Micah, are you off the market?"

"Come on, am I ever off the market?" He added a wink. Time to bring out flirtatious Micah.

It worked. She smiled coyly in return. "So you're still Hollywood's most eligible bachelor?"

"Definitely." He leaned back in his seat, putting on a relaxed air contrary to the uneasiness he felt at dismissing his relationship with Maddie. "Without a doubt. Free and single as ever. In fact, I'd ask you if you were busy later, but I see you're wearing an engagement ring."

"Hey, you got that hard drive for Beaumont?" Joe's voice drew Micah to peer behind him to see who he was addressing.

His heart stopped.

Maddie.

She was standing right behind him, clearly in ear shot, hard drive in hand as Joe approached her from the set. Micah didn't have to wonder if she had overheard his interview. Her face said that she had heard every word.

And that every word hurt.

Fuck!

But this shouldn't matter, he told himself. They'd agreed no media. A shift had occurred between them, he couldn't deny that, but they hadn't said they were ready for this. He would remind her of that. He'd tell her how he felt about her and that would make up for this. It had to.

Except the pain in her eyes said that nothing could make up for this.

Maddie didn't speak, but she turned and waved the hard drive at Joe.

"Cool," Joe said. "I'll tell him you're on your way."

Micah almost rose to follow as she left briskly toward video village. He almost called after her.

But he couldn't. Not without negating everything he'd just told Ariahn Jessler. Not without inviting chaos into their relationship.

No, he had to sit and watch her walk away, hoping he wasn't watching her walk out of his life forever.

TWENTY-FOUR

MADDIE'S EYES WELLED, AN INFURIATING inconvenience since she was only steps away from video village. *Dammit!* She couldn't let Beaumont see her cry. She blinked, clearing her tears.

She hadn't meant to eavesdrop on Micah and his interview, hadn't even really been interested in it. Beaumont had summoned her to bring him the footage from that morning, a job that should have been relegated to a P.A. or one of Adam's other assistants. So she shouldn't have even been walking past Micah in the first place. And then she'd heard her name. How could she not be intrigued?

"So you're still Hollywood's most eligible bachelor?"

"Definitely."

The words stung more than she could have imagined. And then he'd flirted with the journalist . . .

Dammit all to hell! She was definitely hurt, but more than that she was embarrassed. What had she expected? Did she think that he'd proclaim his love for her in some entertainment magazine when he hadn't even said the words to her? *Stupid, stupid, stupid.*

And okay, she shouldn't care what he said to the press. She knew it was all fake.

The problem was she did care. Fake or not, she couldn't stand it. Maybe if he'd given her some indication of what he really felt for her she could deal with whatever lies he told others. But since he hadn't, the words he'd told the reporter were the only ones he had to cling to.

"There's Maddie," Sam said as she reached video village. Beaumont had been antsy waiting, she could tell.

"Here I am." She was surprised at how controlled her voice sounded. Inside she was reeling. *Shake it off.* "If you scoot over, I'll load it."

An assistant sitting in front of the main monitor relinquished his seat. Maddie slid into the chair and connected the hard drive into the USB slot of the computer. Micah's words rang in her ears as she pulled up the contents of the drive. *"Without a doubt. Free and single as ever."*

She shook her head and redirected her focus to her job. She dragged the folder to the computer's desktop and a warning box came up. *The file already exists, do you want to replace the existing file?* Maddie paused. There shouldn't be a file with the same name. She squinted at the file's title. It should have said which scene they had filmed that morning, but it didn't. The file name still said the date and scene from the previous shoot. The second assistant must have forgotten to change it.

What scene had they shot that morning? She closed her eyes, trying to clear her head. *"Free and single as ever."*

"Get outta the way." Beaumont pushed her out of her chair. "You're taking too long."

Numbly, Maddie stepped aside. She watched as Beaumont grabbed for the mouse in front of him. "Wait," she said. *Scene fourteen.* That was the scene they'd filmed. Beaumont needed to change the name to say Scene Fourteen. "You need to save as—"

But Beaumont had already clicked.

Panic coursed through her veins. "What did you just do?"

"I saved the file."

"But it had the wrong name! You just saved it over the last footage!" Hoping she was mistaken, she leaned over the director and grabbed the mouse from his hands. She clicked open the file on the desktop with the previous scene's date and watched in horror as that morning's footage played. "No, no, no." She scrolled through more of the files. All of the footage from the last shoot was lost. "It's gone. Scene twenty-four is all gone."

Beaumont furrowed his brow. "What do you mean it's gone?"

Maddie's words came soft and measured. "You just clicked 'yes' to replace the file and it had the same name as the other day's shoot." A lost scene was a disaster. They would have to hold actors over, adjust the shoot schedule. And they were already behind schedule.

"Fuck!" The director stood abruptly, knocking his chair over in the process. "Is this some kind of sick joke?"

"No! I wouldn't do that!"

Beaumont's face reddened. He swept his arm across the table in front of him, throwing a stack of papers and clipboards to the ground. "Fuck!" He turned to Maddie. "How the fuck could you make that kind of a mistake?"

Maddie usually kept her cool, no matter what her boss threw at her, but she'd reached the end of her emotional rope. "I was the one who was fixing it when you pushed me out of my chair. If you hadn't been so goddamned anxious and just let me do my job—"

Beaumont screamed so loud that Maddie wouldn't have been surprised if they could hear him on set. "It shouldn't have had the same name in the first place! You are incompetent, unprofessional, and completely out of your league! I should never have agreed to let Adam bring you on. "

"No, *I* should never have agreed to come on." Out of the corner of her eye, Maddie saw Sam take a step toward her, trying to stop her. She ignored him. "You've been an arrogant bastard since you fucked me over years ago. My coming here saved your ass."

Beaumont laughed. "Add cocky to the list. Assistants like you are a dime a dozen. Do you even realize how much your mistake is going to cost?"

"I don't know how much *your* mistake is going to cost. And frankly, I don't give a shit. You deserve it."

His eyes narrowed. "Get your things, Bauer. You're fired."

Maddie took her tape measure off her belt loop and threw it at

Beaumont's feet. "Fuck that. I quit."

She'd never been so angry in her life. Accused of making his mistake? She didn't have to take that shit. She stormed off, high-tailing it to the trailer where the crew kept their personal items.

"Maddie," Sam called after her.

Sam was the last person she wanted to deal with. Well, maybe not the last person. She didn't want to deal with anyone.

He called again, running to catch up. "Maddie!"

She spun around. "What?"

He put his hands on his hips, panting. "Do you need a ride?"

Sam's voice was kind and gentle, and it broke her. Tears welled up again in her eyes, this time she couldn't stop them from falling. "Yes," she mumbled. She nodded to make sure he understood.

"Go get in the car. It's unlocked. I'll get your things."

She climbed in the front seat of his car and slumped down. *Fired.* She had been fired. She'd never been fired from anything in her life. She was an exemplary employee, devoted to her job. Now she'd been fucked over by Joss Beaumont twice in one lifetime. Christ, she'd be lucky if she worked anywhere in film again.

She wiped at the tears falling down her face. There would be some serious crying later when she was alone. She knew that. She just had to hold on until then.

Her phone buzzed alerting her of a text. *Micah from the party.* She stared at her phone, not sure if she wanted to read it at the moment. Sam's arrival helped her make the decision. She pocketed her phone and curled up next to the window. *Please don't make me talk,* she willed silently. *Please, please, please.*

"Don't worry, you only have to talk about it if you want to," Sam said as if reading her mind.

As they drove in silence, Maddie replayed the scene with Beaumont over and over in her mind. She didn't want to think about it, but as soon as she stopped, thoughts of Hollywood's most eligible bachelor crept in its place. Those thoughts were too much to bear.

When they'd nearly reached her hotel, she found she could no longer stay trapped in her mind. She peered over at Sam. He really was a nice kid, not a douchebag at all. "Won't you get in trouble for leaving the set?"

Sam stole a glance at her before answering. "I called Joe's cell phone. He agreed I should drive you."

"You called Joe?"

"Yeah. I told him what happened. I'm sure Beaumont's version of the story will be different than yours and I wanted him to know the truth."

How thoughtful. And irrelevant. "Beaumont's version of the story is the only one that matters."

"On this film, maybe. But Joe and Adam—they'll make sure you get hired again."

She nodded. Sam had never experienced the joy of being blacklisted by Beaumont. "I don't even know if I want to be hired again."

"You might feel differently later. I mean, Beaumont's a dick. And you're good. You don't want to give that up."

Maddie stared at Sam. He was sweet. Would Micah say the same thing to her? Would he comfort and reassure her?

Yes and no. He'd tell her to get the hell out. Tell her to take this as a sign to move on, to direct her own stuff. And he wouldn't say it because he was reckless and irresponsible. He'd say it because he knew that was what she really wanted to do.

Sam pulled into the front circle of the Comfort Inn and let the car idle. She looked out the window, suddenly realizing he didn't know she wasn't at this hotel anymore. What should she do? She couldn't walk to the other hotel. She was exhausted—emotionally and physically. She could call a cab after Sam drove away. What a pain.

Fuck it. "Sam, I'm not staying at this hotel."

He nodded and put the car in drive. "I know."

Shocked, she soaked in his response while he pulled out on the road toward Micah's hotel. He *knew.* "Does everyone know?" Just what she needed, for her love life to be the talk of the production crew.

"I don't think so. I didn't know if you wanted me to know, so I took you here first. No one else has said anything."

"That's good, I guess. Especially considering how incredibly fucked up that situation is right now."

"I bet it's not as fucked up as you think."

She studied him again. There were so many thoughts and emotions running through her that she found it difficult to make her brain work. "Why didn't you say something?"

The lips of his mouth curved slightly. "I didn't think you wanted me to."

She looked out her passenger window, knowing she'd break again if she met Sam's eyes. She'd dismissed him so easily, put her sights on the unattainable Micah Preston, what the fuck had she been thinking? Micah was right—she was emotionally unavailable.

They pulled into the circle at Micah's hotel and Sam again let the car idle. "I could come in, if you want me to."

She pictured inviting Sam into the hotel room she shared with Micah. "That might be weird."

"I suppose it would be."

"Thanks, though. For everything." She got out of the car and waved goodbye as he drove away.

Inside the room, the tears Maddie had expected to fall generously didn't come right away. She'd been fired. And she felt like shit about it. But Beaumont had fucked her before. She had survived then, she'd survive now.

But Micah . . . *Micah* . . . Just the thought of his name shot like a bullet through her heart. She was such a fool. She couldn't even be mad. All along he'd said it didn't want a relationship, how had she convinced herself that he had told her anything different?

She pulled out her phone to read the text he had sent her.

"She was just a journalist. What I say to her doesn't matter."

She stared at the screen. He probably hadn't realized she'd been fired yet, but she'd hoped for more in his response. She'd wanted him to say . . . what? What exactly did she expect?

"I'm sorry. I love you." That's what she wanted.

Micah had been right about her here, too—she was a hopeless romantic. She wanted a guy who loved her, who gave up everything for her, who wasn't afraid to tell reporters how he felt, who didn't care that choosing her might jeopardize his career.

She'd told him she loved him. And he'd told the world he was single. *Such an incredible fool.*

She turned her phone off and tossed it on the nightstand. Then she wrapped her arms around herself as the tears began to flow, fast and steady. Even in the generic space of the typical hotel decor, she felt Micah's presence. She wished he were there to hold her and comfort her.

But he couldn't fix her when he was most of the reason she felt so forlorn. She grabbed a T-shirt of his from his laundry pile, threw herself onto the bed and curled up in a ball, clutching his clothing to her. It smelled like him. She stayed like that, sobbing, for more than an hour.

When she'd run out of tears, she shook herself out of her stupor, and turned her phone back on. She scrolled through two more texts from Micah. The first said, *"Are we okay?"* The second read, *"Where are you???"*

She erased both messages and dialed a number from her favorites list. "Bree, can you book a flight for me tonight? I want to come home."

TWENTY-FIVE

H E SHOULD HAVE GONE AFTER her.

All through the eight tortuous hours that followed his last encounter with Maddie, Micah couldn't shake the feeling that he should have gone after her.

She had overreacted, of course. He was a famous actor, and telling stories to the press was part of the job. She worked in the biz, didn't she get that? Maybe she'd be fine when she calmed down.

Except Micah didn't really think she would be fine. First of all, he'd felt sick as he told Ariahn that he was free and single. Though he didn't have any official commitment to Maddie, he was tied to her. He'd been sharing a room with her—sharing a bed—for three weeks. That made him anything but free and single. And, all right, even if he didn't want to tell everyone via magazine article about his complex feelings, he should have at least told Maddie.

Her disappearance from the set was perhaps even more convincing proof that he'd screwed up royally. When Micah filmed his next scene, Beaumont had taken over the camera and Adam had filled Maddie's spot. That wasn't unusual behavior for the director, but it was odd that Maddie wasn't around at all.

On top of going M.I.A., she wasn't answering his texts. Or the few phone calls he'd managed to make. Had she walked out on the show because of him? No, she would never do anything that unprofessional. Still, Micah was apprehensive.

By the time filming wrapped for the night, he was crazy with worry. He needed to get back to the hotel, see if Maddie was there, ease his mind. He made a beeline for his trailer only to be met by Joe outside his door.

"Whatever you have for me, talk while I'm changing."

"Uh, sure." Joe followed Micah into his trailer. "I just wanted to let you know we lost some footage from the other day so the call schedule's been adjusted." Joe held out a sheet of paper.

Half out of his shirt, Micah didn't take the schedule. "Lost footage?" That was unusual. And not good at all. Was Maddie involved?

"Don't worry about it too much, man. Technical difficulties can happen even to the best shows." Joe set the schedule on the counter. "I'll just leave it here. It's going to be a tough week. Sorry."

Joe started to leave, but Micah stopped him. "Does this have anything to do with Maddie not being on set today?"

"I'd rather not say anything. I wasn't there."

Joe's vague response increased Micah's anxiety. Something bad had happened, and he needed to find out what.

Joe left, passing Sam as he entered the trailer.

Micah groaned. Did no one understand he wanted to get out of there? "What do you want?" he snapped.

Sam shifted from one leg to the other. "Beaumont fired her."

"He what?" Surely he hadn't heard right. But it made sense. Micah cursed under his breath. "Where's Beaumont?"

"Why? You gonna get her job back for her? I don't think she wants that."

"Why wouldn't she?"

"Because she quit. Just not before he fired her. Besides, that's not what she needs right now."

Micah's eyes narrowed. How dare this kid tell him what his girlfriend needed? Okay, not girlfriend, but that wasn't the point.

Maybe that was the point. Right now Sam was more in tune with what was going on with Maddie than he was. She should have come to him. She should have been able to come to him.

He took a deep breath and looked Sam in the eye. "Do you know where she is?"

"I drove her to her hotel." He regarded Micah. "Your hotel."

The wind left Micah's lungs, but he kept his features even, not giving anything away.

Sam pointed a finger at Micah. "And before you go assuming that she said anything to me, she didn't."

Micah raised his eyebrows, impressed by the boy's bravado. He considered. Sam liked her. Micah had known that since the airport. He should have expected Sam would have figured it out. If Maddie had hooked up with anyone instead of him, Micah would have known. When you liked someone, you noticed.

He hated asking Sam what he should have known himself, but he had to know. "Is she okay?"

"She's pretty shaken up, but I think there's more to it than just the job."

Shit! Just what had Maddie told the P.A.? And how far had Sam gone with the info? He'd just curbed a major media blowout with Ariahn Jessler, would he need to worry about stopping another?

Sam answered his unasked question. "I offered to listen, but she didn't want to talk about it."

Micah blew out the air he'd been holding. "Thanks, man."

"I didn't do it for you."

"I didn't mean to imply that you did. But it means a lot to me that you were there for her." He leaned against the door and did something he never did—opened up to someone. "She hasn't been answering my texts or calls."

Sam shrugged. "She probably needs some time to herself."

"Yeah." Micah ran his hands through his hair. Sam was probably right. But he couldn't let her retreat from him completely. He had to get back to the hotel. He needed to be there for her, to comfort her. "Thanks for telling me."

Sam started to leave but turned back at the door. "Micah, don't fuck it up."

"I'm trying not to." But he was afraid he already had.

———◆———

MICAH KNEW THE MOMENT HE opened the door that the room was empty. It felt too quiet, and void of the presence that filled any space Maddie occupied. He looked anyway, in the drawers, in the closet, for traces of her. But there were none. Not even a note. Just the faint cling of her apple scent that seemed to be everywhere—in the bed sheets, in the closet, in the air.

His chest tightened. He sat on the edge of the bed—the bed that felt too big for just one person—and lay back. He'd done it. He'd fucked up. He'd known she was upset when he saw her, her eyes filled with tears, pained by words he'd said. Why didn't he fucking go after her?

He slid his phone out of his pants pocket and pushed redial for the hundredth time that day. He didn't expect her to answer, but he couldn't give up. Not yet.

It rang four times. Then, just as he was about to hang up, she answered.

"Micah?"

He sat up. "Maddie!" Relief washed over him. "Thank God. I've been trying to get ahold of you all day."

"Oh." She sounded distant, far away. "I'm sorry. I didn't mean to worry you."

"No, Maddie, I'm sorry." He needed to apologize, he just wasn't sure what to apologize for first. "I didn't know about Beaumont. Do you want me to get your job back?"

"No!" She softened. "Please don't. It's fine. He's a prick anyway."

"He is." *Say it. Tell her you're sorry about the reporter. Tell her you didn't mean it. Tell her you love her.* "Maddie—" This was so awkward over the phone. He paused, suddenly aware of echoing background noises. "Where are you?"

"I'm at the airport. I'm going home, Micah."

"Oh." *Shit.* The weight on his chest returned.

She cleared her throat. "Look, I'm sorry I didn't call earlier. I just wanted to get out of there, you know?"

"Uh, yeah." He rubbed his hand over his face. Why should she stay? Her job was the only reason she was in Colorado.

But he'd hoped she'd stay for him. Instead she'd run. Did he blame her? Hadn't he run from her first? "Yeah, I get it."

"But I wanted to say thank you for the past few weeks." Her words were stiff and rehearsed. "I had a really fun time."

Fun? Micah resisted the urge to throw his phone. Sure, they had fun together, but they had experienced so much more than that. He knew he hadn't imagined it.

Fuck, he wasn't trying hard enough. "It doesn't have to be over, Maddie," he said softly. "What I said to that journalist—"

He heard an intercom announcement in the background. "Hey, I have to go. They're boarding my flight."

"Wait, Maddie!" He paused, making sure he could still hear her on the line. Stay. He wanted to ask her to stay. But he chickened out. "Can I call you?"

"Of course." Her voice cracked, but she recovered. "Talk to you soon."

Then she was gone.

He threw his fist into the bed. Hard. Even though her words said differently, she'd just shut him out. That phone call, the reason she'd finally answered—she was telling him goodbye.

He should have gone after her.

TWENTY-SIX

E VEN AFTER A TWO-AND-A-HALF-HOUR FLIGHT and a long delay at baggage claim, Maddie still had Micah's phone call in her head. She hadn't wanted to talk to him, afraid that she'd break down and run back, but he deserved a goodbye. Besides, knowing him, he wouldn't quit calling and texting until she talked to him.

She'd been right—the minute she heard his voice she couldn't remember why she'd left. But why would she have stayed? Her job was over and Micah hadn't given her any reason not to go. He hadn't asked her not to leave, hadn't told her he wanted to keep seeing her. Hadn't told her he loved her the way she had stupidly told him. Leaving was the only thing to do.

The conversation had gone well enough. She'd communicated the things that were necessary: *I had fun* and *I left because I was fired*. She didn't want him thinking she'd left because of him. She needed a clean break.

She'd told him he could call. That was the polite thing to do, though she didn't plan to answer again. Clean. Break.

It doesn't have to be over, Maddie.

That was what gave her pause, the words she'd played over and over again in her mind. What did he mean? Did he mean they could still shack up until the end of the shoot? Or longer? If it was an attempt to continue their relationship past Friday, it was half-hearted at best. And she couldn't stay for a half-hearted invitation. Hopeless romantic Maddie wanted whole-heart. She wanted an "I love you" or "Don't go."

It didn't matter. He had told her over and over he didn't believe in a real relationship. She'd been the fool for thinking she could change him.

She texted Bree, telling her she'd be outside in five, slung her bag higher on her shoulder and headed out to the passenger pick-up exit. Bree had been circling the airport and was already waiting when Maddie walked through the automatic doors to the street.

"Oh, sweetie!" Bree jumped out of her car and threw her arms around her friend. "I'm here for you. I want to hear everything."

Maddie, not normally a hugger, pressed into Bree's embrace, enjoying the feeling of being cared for. Tears started again, and she pulled away, wiping her eyes. "There's a lot to tell."

"Start talking."

After her bags were tucked in the trunk, Maddie climbed into the passenger seat, buckled her belt and recounted the last six weeks. Bree knew bits of it, but Maddie filled in all the holes. By the time she'd told it all, they were back in her apartment in Studio City, curled up on the couch, each with a glass of cheap white zin.

Bree, having said very little, took a deep breath. "Okay, first, Beaumont's an ass. You already knew that."

Maddie nodded. "How can you stand to be his assistant?"

"I'm rarely in the same room with him. We communicate mainly by phone and it's easy to ignore his assholishness. Besides, I don't threaten him. You do."

"I don't threaten him."

"Yes, you do. You're smart, talented, and you have vision—traits that B. has himself, but he's very afraid he's losing or has already lost. Anyway, my point is, don't worry about him. He faxed me a new call schedule today. They'll be able to fit the reshoot in without going much past deadline. I had to change a couple of flights out of Denver and extend a permit, but it's all taken care of with very little cost or inconvenience. The movie's going to be fine."

Maddie let out a breath. She took pride in her work and had been upset about the lost footage, even though it wasn't any of her concern anymore.

Bree looked Maddie in the eye. "And B.'s not going to destroy you. I won't let him."

"Thank you." Maddie took a long swallow.

"That's what I'm here for." Bree swirled the liquid around in her glass. "What are you scheduled to do next?"

"I'm supposed to join the crew in two weeks on the set for a Danny Boyle film."

"Good."

Maddie bit her lip. "But I already texted Adam and gave him my notice."

Bree smiled. "Even better. Are you going to work on your own film instead?"

"Yes." She'd decided this on the plane. She had some money set aside that she could live on for a bit while she tried to get some producers. Micah had thought her material was good enough. Still, she'd been blacklisted for a reason. "Is that stupid?"

"No. Your work is even better now than it was when the first Beaumont fiasco happened. It's gotta get a nibble, blacklisted or not. Besides, he can't rule all of Hollywood forever. Do you have a trailer cut?"

Maddie nodded.

"Get it to me, and a copy of the script, and I'll pass it around to some people I know. It might take a while to convince people that whatever Beaumont has said about you is a lie, but we'll get there."

"Bree, before with Beaumont, I failed. It wasn't just him being a dick."

"You only failed because he didn't give you a chance to succeed. When are you going to learn that?"

"When are you going to start acting again?"

"Ha, ha, we're not talking about me right now." She narrowed her eyes. "Now, about Micah."

Maddie sighed. "I told you everything."

"I'm sure you think you told me everything. But there's some things

I need to clarify because I'm not certain you know what you're doing on this."

Maddie reached for the wine bottle and refilled her glass. "I do know what I'm doing." She didn't want to talk about Micah anymore. She wanted to move on. But Bree wasn't easily deterred. "Okay. You've got five minutes."

Bree moved up to her knees and rested her arm on the back of the sofa. "So he told a reporter that he was single?"

"Yes."

"After you'd been with him for like half a minute?"

"Three weeks," Maddie corrected. "But, yes."

"And you'd both agreed to keep media out of your relationship?"

She lowered her head. "Yes."

"What the hell, Maddie?"

She knew she was being unreasonable, but that didn't change what she felt, what she wanted. "I want it to be more."

Bree's face softened. "Did you ask him to be more?"

Had she? "Not exactly." She thought back over their relationship. "Well, I might have said the L word."

"Maddie!" She lowered her voice. "Did you mean it?"

Maddie paused, not wanting to admit it now, after they were over. "Yes, I meant it. But I only said it once, during . . . you know. Does that count?"

"With you, yes it does. But maybe he needed it spelled out for him. Did you not have any other chance during those three weeks to tell him? Or was incredible sex all you had time for?"

"No." She grinned. "We *were* having incredible sex. But we talked, too."

Bree pressed her. "Then you didn't tell him because . . . ?"

"Because he'd say 'not interested' and I'd get hurt. Or—"

"Or he'd say 'me, too' and give you more."

Maddie scowled at the interruption. "Or he'd say, 'Let's just take this one day at a time.' Eventually you can't do that anymore. You have to make plans. You have to know where you're going."

Bree lifted her hands as if to strangle Maddie. "It's Micah flippin' Preston, Maddie! He's *the* guy. If he wanted me one day at a time, I'd be on that in a heartbeat and he's not even my type."

"He might be *the* guy, but he doesn't think I'm *the* girl."

"But he hasn't said that exactly, right? So you're just running before he gets a chance to. Okay, whatever. Go ahead and be chickenshit."

"He doesn't believe Hollywood relationships can work, Bree." Her voice was raised and tight in her throat. "Until he believes otherwise, there's no point. He'd always be expecting us to fail. He'd always look for reasons to justify why we shouldn't be together."

"Well, that could be true." Bree took a swallow of her wine. "And you think he's totally sold on that stars-can't-date thing?"

Maddie took a moment to think before she answered. Micah had said he was considering a future with her. She hadn't forgotten that. But he'd said that to her in a hot air balloon far above the Colorado landscape. It had been like a beautiful dream, a romantic place that stirred romantic notions. Kind of like saying *I love you* during sex.

God, had he dismissed her words as easily as she was dismissing his?

It didn't matter. Because even if she believed the words he said in the air, she couldn't forget the words he'd said on the ground. "*I haven't seen anything to change my mind.*" And more important were the words he never said—he never said he chose her.

"I don't think he wants to be totally sold on it," Maddie said finally. "But yes, he is."

"Well, that's a load of shit. People in Hollywood date all the fucking time."

"You're preaching to the choir." This wasn't anything Maddie hadn't thought about a hundred times. But she'd also considered Micah's point of view. "You have to admit, though, this town has a higher rate of failed relationships than most places."

"I don't have to admit shit. You're talking about Micah being all self-fulfilling prophecy with his viewpoint and all, but what about you? You sound as convinced that it isn't going to work out as he is." She shook her head in frustration. "If you really loved him, you think you'd have a little more faith."

"I'm kinda all out of faith, Bree. This whole biz has jaded me."

"I get it. But I just have to ask . . ." Bree reached over and tapped Maddie on the nose. "What if he loves you too?"

Maddie traced the bowl of her wine glass with her index finger. "He could have told me during those three weeks."

"Did it ever occur to you that he might be just as stupid at this type of thing as you are?"

Maddie thought back to the hot air balloon ride, when Micah had taken her hand in his. *I'm scared.* That had only been a day and a half ago. Maybe she was short-changing him. Maybe he really wanted to give her more. Maybe he just needed more time.

But that was a lot of maybes, a lot of opportunities for Maddie to get hurt. *Yeah, that's right, Micah, I'm scared, too.* Too scared.

She was done with Micah. She looked at her watch. "Your five minutes are up."

"Madalyn Rae Bauers!"

She threw her head back and groaned at the use of her full name. Maddie knew her friend. If she didn't give something, Bree would harp on her all night. "All right, if I see him again, I'll talk to him."

"Promise?"

"Yes." But Maddie didn't plan on seeing Micah again. Seven years had passed between their first and second meetings. It couldn't be that hard to pass another seven before she saw him again. Now it was time to move on.

TWENTY-SEVEN

"**M**S. BAUERS, RIGHT THIS WAY please. The team is waiting in the private conference room."

Maddie grabbed Bree's hand to steady her shaky knees as they followed the receptionist to the conference room at Three Spot Films. She still couldn't believe that Bree had gotten her a meeting with potential investors only two weeks after her return from Colorado. It had to be a record in the movie biz.

The receptionist, a petite Asian woman, led them toward a small room with glass walls. Inside, Maddie could make out three men and a woman sitting around a table. Two of them had their backs to her. Something about the scene triggered a feeling of familiarity, but before she could analyze it further, Bree put a hand on her shoulder.

"Maddie, hang on a sec."

"Take your time," the receptionist said, stepping aside so they could talk privately.

Maddie took a deep breath, preparing herself for the pep talk she was certain Bree was about to give her.

Instead, Bree turned Maddie so she was no longer facing the conference room and took both her friend's hands in her own. "Um, don't be mad, okay?"

"About . . . ?"

Normally confident and self-assured, Bree seemed flustered. "See, here's the thing. I have names of people that Beaumont works with, of course I do, but none of them care what I have to say about an unknown filmmaker. And, Maddie, the people Beaumont works with are the ones who've heard shit about you from him. They don't want to work with you. I could shop your movie all day long for the rest of my life and still not get a single meeting. Producers need a name attached, someone who is in the biz who's willing to go to bat for you."

Maddie's stomach dropped. "What did you do?"

"He contacted me, Maddie."

Maddie pulled away and looked back over her shoulder, not wanting to confirm her suspicion, but needing to all the same. Yes, the familiar feeling about the people in the conference room—one of them was Micah. She felt faint.

She hadn't talked to Micah since the airport. He had called at least once a day even though she never answered. His text messages were more frequent, but those she deleted right away without fully reading. Because if she didn't, who knew what she'd read into them?

Nights were the hardest. Her queen size bed felt large and cold. She'd toss and turn for hours. Finally, she'd pull out her laptop and Google his name, reading every article ever written about him, watching every YouTube interview. She always ended up staring at the photos of him and her together. Then she'd cry and eventually fall asleep.

She so wasn't over him yet. There was no way she could see him now. All he had to do was smile at her and she'd be putty in his hands. "I'm not going in there."

Bree gripped Maddie's arms at the shoulders. "Yes, you are. This is your dream. Don't be stupid about it." Here was the pep talk. Just not the one Maddie had expected. "It's good business, Maddie. He recognizes your talent and he's been looking for a project to invest in. And it's not just him. Three Spots wouldn't be on board if they didn't think it was good. Take the meeting. Decide then."

"I can't work with him. I can't see him all the time."

"They're just investors. You can demand complete creative control. If you don't want to see him, then kick him off the team. Take the meeting."

Her career, her dreams. Micah had said that every day was a choice—career or not career. If she didn't go in that room, she might never have the chance to choose career again. If he could be so single minded, so could she. She took a deep breath. "Okay."

"Good. Now go get 'em."

Maddie shook her arms out, took another deep breath, and nodded at the receptionist.

"Right this way," the receptionist said, taking them the rest of the way to the conference room. She opened the door and announced them. "Ms. Bauers and Ms. Weber."

One of them, a tall gentleman with salt-and-pepper hair dressed in a light gray suit, stood and crossed to her, extending his hand to Maddie. "Hi, Ms. Bauers, I'm Richard Thurgood. It's a pleasure to meet you."

She shook his hand. "Maddie, please. This is my, uh, associate, Bree "

Richard shook Bree's hand, then gestured to the other man, a younger version of himself. "This is my brother and partner Lance, and the third spot in the Three Spots is our good friend Kelsey Grey."

Maddie shook hands with Lance and Kelsey.

Then she faced Micah. God, oh God, he was hotter than she wanted to remember. He still hadn't shaved his scruff, but it was trimmed and more groomed than he had worn it for the film. His eyes were bluer and deeper, was it possible? And his lips, curved down slightly, taunted her with memories of sweet kisses. Just being near him made her heart pound faster and her eyes misty.

"Of course you already know Micah," Richard said.

Micah took her hand in greeting. The familiar electric spark from his contact surged through Maddie's body, and her knees buckled. Thankfully she had her other hand on the back of a chair so that he wouldn't notice, though something in his expression said he knew anyway.

"I met Micah quite some time ago," Richard said, pulling Maddie from the thick haze of Micah to the reason for their meeting. "And told him we were looking for something just like your film. I was surprised when he brought us your project."

"I have to admit," Maddie said, "I was surprised too."

Micah pulled out a chair for her and she nodded politely as she moved to sit. He leaned in as he pushed her in to the table. "I would have told you if you'd answered my calls," he whispered in her ear.

Maddie shuddered at the feel of his breath on her skin. "Voicemail works for more than just pining," she said through gritted teeth.

"Touché." He sat next to her, then leaned in again, a broad smile on his face. "You're going to be awesome," he whispered. "This is your moment to shine. Enjoy it." He squeezed her knee under the table, which turned her belly molten and made goosebumps run up her arms. But it also gave her the confidence she needed. He believed in her. He was there because he believed in her.

Richard ran the meeting. He highlighted the elements of her film that he and his partners liked the most, as well as their concerns going forward. He worked through all of her budget items, suggesting adjustments and additions. Then he asked Maddie about her vision and ideas for the movie. Occasionally, Kelsey and Lance interjected, adding their own thoughts. When Beaumont had invested in her film, he just handed her a check and expected her to deliver. Maybe, with their guidance, she could actually pull this off.

Micah sat quietly, only speaking when directly addressed. His presence was never forgotten by Maddie, though. The hair on the right side of her body, the side closest to him, stood on end. She wondered if he might touch her again, perhaps bump her under the table. After his knee squeeze, however, he kept his hands to himself.

When the meeting ended, nearly two hours later, Richard announced that they would commit seventy-five percent of her needed funds and would leave all creative control to her. "Don't think that means we wouldn't like to give input. Please come to us often. We want to build this with you, if you'll let us."

"Yes!" Maddie almost squealed. "Yes. Thank you and yes."

Micah cleared his throat. "Maddie, you know I love your film, but I understand if you don't want me on the team—" He paused, making sure she knew exactly what he was saying, letting her know she didn't have to include him on the project. Then to the rest of the room he said, "Since I'm only a silly actor, after all." Richard and Lance chuckled. "I certainly couldn't add the production expertise that Richard and Lance and Kelsey could. But I'm more than committed to providing the additional twenty-five percent."

He met Maddie's eyes. "I'd even be a silent partner, if you prefer."

No, she didn't prefer. She loved his thoughts about film and the ideas he'd given her over the last several weeks had been amazing. He'd been invaluable, stimulating her creatively, inspiring her daily. For a moment, she let herself fantasize about working with him again.

But working with him would only make her want him. And she didn't need to revisit the list of reasons why that would end in heartache. The heartache she was feeling was already worse than she could ever imagine. Spending more time with him could only make it worse.

She put on a smile, mostly for the rest of the room. "I want you on the team," she said to Micah. "But could I think about the silent partner part?"

"Of course." But she saw Micah's eye twitch as he spoke and knew her response hurt him.

Well, too bad. She hurt, too.

"Great!" Richard exclaimed. "I'll have the papers drawn up and a check ready for you by the end of next week."

Maddie exchanged an excited glance with Bree. It was happening, really happening! A real company was making her movie!

Her mind was dizzy as Richard wrapped the meeting up. Goodbyes were said and the next thing Maddie knew, she and Bree were stepping into the elevator with Micah.

Then there was a whole other reason to feel dizzy. Because now she was in a tight space with Micah, with Bree as her only safeguard. And Bree had already sold her out with Micah once that week. She braced herself for the awkwardness to set in.

The minute the doors shut, he turned to her. "We need to talk."

No, not here, not now. She chose to divert him. "Yes, we do. Thank you, Micah. I'm so incredibly grateful that you hooked me up with Thr–"

"That's not what we have to talk about."

"Micah . . ." She didn't know how to handle him, particularly with Bree there.

"I'm not letting you out of this elevator until you agree to talk." He moved toward the electrical panel. "I'll pull the emergency button if I have to."

She put her hand out to stop him. "No, don't do that."

"Then you'll talk?"

"I—" She wanted to talk, she did. She missed him. She had so much she wanted to say to him. She just didn't know if she could bear what he'd say in return.

"You promised, Maddie," Bree hissed at her. "You promised if you had the chance—"

If Maddie didn't agree, Bree would tell Micah all her thoughts and feelings for her. "Fine. We can talk in the valet lounge. Bree, I'll meet you at the car."

"I'll drive her home," Micah said.

"No, I'll meet you at the car," Maddie growled, making sure Bree understood and didn't drive off without her.

Bree nodded as the elevator doors opened to the parking garage. "Take your time," she said over her shoulder as she walked toward her car.

Micah pulled Maddie by the elbow into the small lounge next to the elevator, a waiting area for when valet was available. Her skin burned under his grip, but too soon, he let her go, depositing her on an upholstered bench. He sat on the bench perpendicular to her and met her eyes.

He stared at her without speaking for several long seconds. Finally he spoke. "You're mad at me."

Maddie pursed her lips. "I'm not mad at you."

He cocked his head. "Then why are you avoiding me?"

"I'm . . ." She considered all the answers she could give including the stock *I'm not avoiding you.* She settled on the truth. Why not? She'd told Bree she would be honest with him if she had the chance. "Because I'm afraid if I see you again, I'll never want to not see you again."

He sighed, as though relieved by her response. "Then don't not see me again." He reached over and stroked her cheek. "I miss you."

She leaned into his caress, her skin vibrating under his touch. "I miss you, too."

"I tried to tell you, we can still see each other."

She took his hand from her face and held it in her lap. *There.* She could concentrate better. "But you've already decided we won't work out, Micah. So I didn't see the point."

"Forget what I've said." He put his other hand around hers. "No decisions. No preconceived notions. One day at a time. I want to keep seeing you."

Her heart sped up at his admission. "Then you believe a celebrity relationship might work out?"

"I still don't know that yet, Maddie."

She pulled away before he finished talking, wrapping her arms around herself. "I can't do this, Micah. I can't be a test subject for your theory."

"That's not at all what you are." He brushed his hand through his hair. "This is hard for me, Maddie. Why can't you give me time to figure all of this out?"

"How do you plan to do that? The shoot's over. We can't sneak around so easily. People will see us together and you'll have to admit that we're something. What will you say to the press?"

He answered her with a guilty stare.

"Oh, I get it." Realization dawned on her. "You aren't planning on telling anyone anything."

"It's nobody's business but ours."

"How do you imagine that will work? Do we get hotel rooms? Or do I just act like I'm all into Fudge when we're in public and hope the media just assumes I'm with him? Or do you just not say anything and let everyone think I'm just another one of Micah's many girls?"

"Don't make it sound so disgusting. It's not like that."

"Then what is it like?"

Micah stood and paced the room. "You don't get it, Maddie. The press makes everything a whole other ballgame." He stopped and faced her. "The minute they're involved, they'll descend on us."

"You mean, the minute they're involved, it's real."

"No, that's not what I mean." He put one hand on his waist, his fingers resting at the band of his slacks. "I'm trying to protect you, Maddie. You can't imagine the things they'll say. They'll dig up your Beaumont past. They'll dismiss your movie because you're Micah Preston's girlfriend."

"Or you're afraid that I'll take advantage of you because I'm your girlfriend."

"That's Lulu talking. You aren't like that and I know it. And I couldn't care less what the media thinks about my involvement with your movie. What I do care about is what they say about you."

She stood as if gathering her argument around her before delivering it full force. "But that's what it means to be part of your life, Micah. And I want to be part of it! All of your life, not just the parts you think I'm ready for. How else will I ever know what it really means to love you?"

There. She'd said it. And not during sex. No going back now.

He took a step toward her. He opened his mouth to say something then closed it. Then opened it again. "Why does it matter what I say to journalists when I'm sharing my bed with you?"

Her eyes felt moist. She'd said *I love you* and he ignored her. Again. "It makes me your shameful little secret."

"No." He placed his arms on her shoulders. "It doesn't."

She shrugged out from his grip. "It does. And it's not just journalists. It's charity events where I watch with your fans while you hang on the arm of women you've slept with. It's you lying to important people about who I am in your life. Would you even tell your mother?"

His pause told her no.

"Yeah, that's what I thought."

"You promised me, Maddie, that you wouldn't care what other people thought or knew. That you'd come to me. That you'd talk to me."

"I am talking to you. And I don't care about what they think of me. I care about what you think about me. What it means that you don't want to tell people about me. If you cared about me at all, you wouldn't ask me to be a secret. It's not fair. It's selfish."

The lines of his jaw hardened. "And you weren't being selfish when you decided when and how we were going to end without giving me a chance to respond?"

She hung her head as if she'd been slapped. "You're right. I ran away—I run away, Micah. That's my M.O." She took a deep breath. "But I'm not running now. I'm telling you how I feel and that's not easy for me. Did you hear me? I *love* you. I want to be in your life. For real." A tear escaped down her cheek.

He caught her tear on the tip of his finger. "Maddie . . ." His voice was low and pained.

But he didn't say it back. He didn't love her.

Her heart broke. The dam of tears burst and she swiped as they fell. "I know. You have to choose and all that. You've told me. Well, I choose, too. And I'm choosing this. I . . . can't see you."

He closed his eyes, pain etched across his features. When he opened them again, he'd turned hard. He nodded once.

Maddie choked back a sob. He was letting her do this. Letting her walk away. She had hoped he would fight harder for her. But he didn't.

"Goodbye, Micah."

As she passed by him, he grabbed her and pushed her against the wall. He pressed his body to hers, his stiff member throbbing through his pants against her pelvis. She shook her head, but he put his hands on the sides of her face and held her still, capturing her lips in his.

He kissed her roughly, desperately, and within moments she surrendered to his demanding mouth. Warm liquid pooled between her legs as she melted into him. She loved this like she loved him. She wanted him like this always. He moved a hand down to her breast. His fingers kneaded her frantically, drawing her nipple out easily.

She moaned, and he moved his lips to her ear. "Doesn't this mean anything to you?" His voice was thick with need. "What you do to me? How you respond to my touch?" He pinched her nipple and her breath drew in sharply. "Can you really walk away from this?"

Maddie moved her hands to his chest and, fighting against every aroused nerve ending in her body with more strength than she knew she had, she pushed him away. He dropped his hands and stepped back.

She wiped her mouth, trying to erase the taste of him. "It's sex, Micah," she said when she could speak. "As long as you're officially free and single, that's all we have."

She turned again to leave, but paused in the doorway. "Silent partner, I think."

"I'll tell Richard." His voice was cold and empty, breaking her heart further—she hadn't known it was possible.

Without another word she walked out on Micah Preston, her chest aching, and her pride hurt. It killed her to admit, but she had learned something important: Fairytale endings only ever happened in the movies.

TWENTY-EIGHT

MICAH WOKE UP WITH A hangover from hell. He peered over at the alarm clock on the nightstand. Ten forty-seven am. How come it felt so much earlier?

He lay in bed massaging his temples for several minutes to no avail. Finally, he staggered to the bathroom for Advil, only to find an empty bottle in his medicine cabinet. *Dammit.*

He relieved himself and splashed water on his face, then ventured downstairs in search of pain reliever. Dressed only in his boxers and squinting to shield his eyes from the bright light of day, he stumbled to the kitchen of his Brentwood mansion. Fudge sat on a stool at the island eating a bowl of cold cereal, reading the latest Walking Dead comic book.

"Morning," Fudge greeted around a mouthful of Cinnamon Life.

Micah groaned, heading straight for the stainless steel refrigerator. "Could you crunch a little less loudly, please?" He opened the freezer cabinet, pulled out a package of frozen peas—when on earth had he purchased frozen peas?—and placed the vegetables over his throbbing forehead.

Fudge tsked. "Feeling the effects of last night? I'm not surprised. I think you drank all the Tequila."

"Tequila?" Micah leaned back against the cool stainless steel door. "I thought I was drinking Vodka."

"That was the night before."

The night before, that's right. How many nights had he spent in a drunken haze now? Let's see, since Tuesday after he'd last seen Maddie. What was that . . . five nights ago, now? Christ, if he kept this up he was going to be an alcoholic in no time.

Micah threw down the peas and rubbed his hands over his face. "Do you know where I can find some Tylenol or something?"

Fudge waited until he swallowed to speak. "There should be some in the cabinet under the mini-bar."

"Good place for them."

He made his way to the mini-bar in the dining room off the kitchen. There he found a bottle of aspirin, emptied two small pills into his hand and downed them with the rest of the almost empty bottle of Cuervo Gold. Hair of the dog that bit him, he reasoned.

After tossing the finished Cuervo bottle into the trash, he opened the fridge of the mini-bar and grabbed a bottle of water. "Do I have anything going on today?" he asked as he returned to the kitchen.

Fudge flipped a page in his comic book. "Hmm? I don't think so."

Even the sound of pages flipping irritated Micah. He took a swig of water, wishing it was something stronger. "What time do I have to be at the award show tomorrow?" He paused. "That is tomorrow, isn't it?"

Fudge dropped his spoon in his bowl, causing an annoying clank. "Am I your secretary now?"

His friend had been teasing, but Micah wasn't in the mood. "You're my half-assed bodyguard who lives free of charge in my pool house. Excuse me for thinking you could maybe pull a little weight around here."

"Grumpy." Fudge rolled his eyes then crossed to the kitchen laptop. He clicked on a desktop icon and turned the screen to Micah. "Here. I pulled up your calendar."

Micah massaged his scalp, trying to rub away his irritation. "Ooo, thanks. What effort that must have taken."

"What the fuck is your problem? You've been in a foul mood all week."

Micah ignored Fudge and glanced at the laptop. Yep. America's

Choice Awards were scheduled for the next day. At least he wasn't up for an award. He was just a presenter—a much easier job with very little focus on him from the press.

"In fact," Fudge was still talking. "You've been in a foul mood since that investment meeting you went to about Maddie's movie."

Micah scowled at her name. He didn't want to think about her, hence the recent large consumption of alcohol. "I don't know what you're talking about." He pulled the laptop closer, not really looking at it, but trying to discourage Fudge from conversation.

Fudge wasn't deterred at all. "Come to think of it, you've been a bitch since the last week of filming. Since right around when Maddie left production."

Ow, her name again.

Fudge patted Micah on the back. "Did the standard Preston brush-off not go well?"

Micah let out a groan. Even though the two of them were good friends, he didn't share much emotional crap with Fudge. What he knew about Micah's personal life was from observation and interrogation. Interrogating was today's tactic.

"I didn't give her the standard Preston brush-off. We ended things mutually." Only a partial lie. She wanted one thing, he wanted another. They'd both had a chance to let it not end, and neither of them took it.

"Then why are you moping over her, dude?"

Micah shut the laptop lid. It wasn't like he was really looking at it anyway. "I'm not."

Fudge pulled a near-empty bag of Cheetos from the pantry. "You're certainly moping over something and every time I say the name Maddie Bauers—"

Micah winced.

"—you wince. What's that about?"

Damn Fudge and his inquisition. He crossed his arms and leaned against the counter. "She wants me to be a silent partner."

"So?" He popped a Cheeto in his mouth and grimaced. "These are stale as crap." He put another three in his mouth, crunching noisily.

"They're from before Colorado. I'll put them on the list for the housekeeper. She won't be here until Monday, though."

"That's cool." Fudge ate another Cheeto. "Anyway, I thought you were just helping Maddie out financially. Are you interested in contributing creatively?"

Micah watched Fudge as he put yet another Cheeto in his mouth. "Why do you keep eating them if they're bad?"

Fudge shrugged. "Why aren't you answering my question?"

Micah took another swig of his water, noticing that his head felt the slightest bit better. Talking no longer seemed quite so unbearable. "I'm not interested in contributing creatively." How could he explain how he felt about being sidelined on Maddie's movie? "I just . . . I don't know . . . I really enjoyed talking through the process with her. It made me remember why I loved this whole business in the first place because she's still so fresh about it. She has a good eye, very creative. Super intelligent. And when she gets a new idea or hits a roadblock, she likes to bounce it off someone." He paused, remembering. "She'll get all fidgety and she starts pacing and talking with her hands. And her beautiful brown eyes get all big and bright." He smiled. "By the time she's finished telling it, she's always worked it out herself, but it's stimulating to be near her when . . . what?"

Fudge was staring at Micah, his mouth gaping. "You're in love with her."

"Whatever." Micah crossed to the fridge and opened it, pretending to look for something to eat, even though he had zero appetite.

Fudge slammed his hand on the counter. "You're totally in love with her!" He chuckled. "Does she know?"

"No," Micah answered quickly. Too quickly. He backtracked. "There's nothing to know. Just drop it." He shut the refrigerator door.

Fudge wasn't dropping it. He followed Micah outside to the veranda. "Why the hell did you break things off with her?"

"I have rules, remember?" God, the sun was bright. "No dating. No serious relationships."

"It's your own stupid rule. You can break it."

"The rule exists for a reason. It's not stupid." Micah circled back into the house, out of the blinding sun, Fudge in tow. "It's a proven fact that relationships in this town do not work."

"Then why were you seeing her in the first place?"

He stopped walking and turned to face Fudge. "Exactly. No clue."

Fudge shook his head as if disgusted with Micah's answer.

So Micah amended his statement. "Because she made me think that maybe I was wrong. But I wasn't." Except he hadn't known if he was wrong or not. He'd wanted to see what happened with her. He sighed. "I asked her if she wanted to keep seeing me on the down-low." He wandered into the den and threw himself face down on the couch. "But she didn't want that."

Fudge sat on the couch arm and threw the bag of Cheetos on the coffee table. "She didn't want to see you anymore?" Surprise laced his voice.

"I didn't say that exactly," Micah said into the couch pillow.

"Hmm." Fudge stood and crossed to where he could look at Micah directly. Then he walked toward the kitchen, but returned a second later, his arms crossed.

Micah leaned himself up on one elbow. "Do you have something to say?"

"Yes, I do." Fudge took a deep breath. "You're an asshole."

"What?"

"You're a selfish asshole."

Micah moved to a sitting position. "Selfish. That's what she said."

"Because you are. Dude, you probably don't know this since you've had, like, zero experience with any relationship that lasts longer than an hour, but when you love someone you do things in the best interest of you as a couple, not just you as a superstar. You can't give up your playboy status to see where things go with Maddie?"

Micah leaned forward. "I need more time without the press to see how things go."

"Bullshit."

"What do you fucking know about it?"

"I'm always with you, Micah. I know all about it. I know all about you. You want more time to come up with another excuse about why it's not going to work out. Because heaven forbid things did work out and you found out all your years of self-imposed solitude were a waste of your life."

Micah sat back into the couch and pulled the pillow into his lap. "Whatever. I'm not talking about this with you anymore."

Fudge's eyes traveled to a spot behind where Micah sat. "Fine with me. You can discuss it with Lulu."

"I'm not discussing shit with Lulu."

"Micah?"

Lulu's voice behind him made Micah jump up, the pillow flying from his lap to the floor. "Mom!" Fuck. He looked and felt like shit and now he had to deal with his mother.

Micah circled around the couch to hug Lulu. "You didn't say you were stopping by. What are you doing here?"

"Chris called me."

Micah turned to Fudge and delivered his best death glare. "I wonder why he would do that."

Lulu threw her purse down on a side table. "He was worried, and I can see why."

Christ. Lulu, too? "There's no reason to be worried." As he talked, Micah straightened the room, both because it was trashed and because he needed something to help him avoid his mother's eyes. "I'm a little hung over, that's all. You know how we celebrate when a shoot is over."

"Micah, I know it's not the movie. You don't have to pretend."

He bent over to pick up the pillow that had fallen off the couch. "What do you mean?" He was afraid to find out the answer.

"I told her." And Fudge's tone said he didn't regret it at all.

Micah's eyes flitted from Lulu to his bodyguard. "What exactly did you tell her?"

Lulu's face softened with compassion. "He told me everything, Micah. About Madalyn."

If Micah could kill Fudge with a simple stare, he was sure this was the stare that would do it.

"I told her the truth! That you're hung up on Maddie but you're being an asswipe about it. Excuse my language, Lulu."

Lulu smiled reassuringly. "You're fine, Chris. From what you told me, I think asswipe is more than appropriate."

Micah threw the pillow down onto the couch in complete frustration. "Why are you on his side? You didn't even want me to stay here to work on her film."

"I didn't know you were in love with her. Why didn't you tell me?"

"What do you care about love?"

"What's that supposed to mean?"

"You left your marriage, Mom. You chose your career over love."

Lulu's eyebrows shot up in surprise. "No, I didn't."

"Oh, really?"

Lulu circled the couch and came to Micah's side. "I chose to leave a bad marriage, Micah, and threw my energy instead into a career."

"Yeah, that's not how Dad put it."

"Your father could never admit we had problems. He wanted to blame it all on my acting. But that wasn't it at all."

Micah shook his head. This conversation made his eyes cross. He sat heavily on the couch. Why hadn't he ever discussed this with his mother? All these years he'd just assumed. "But you haven't dated since you left dad. You've been totally focused on your career and then my career."

Lulu laughed as she sat next to Micah. "I have too dated. Just because I haven't shared it with you doesn't mean I didn't do it."

Seriously. Micah's whole concept of life was shattering before his eyes. His mom dated? Like, men? "Are you kidding me?"

"Not at all. Actually—" Her face colored slightly as she looked down at her white linen pants. "Stu and I have been dating casually for the last several months."

No. Fucking. Way.

Micah spun to look at Fudge. "Did you know about this?"

Fudge shrugged.

"Micah, honey." Lulu put her hand on his knee. "Maybe I've been too single-minded about you and your career. And maybe I've lived vicariously through you and that put a lot of pressure on you. But all I really want is for you to be happy."

Micah swallowed. "I'm happy. I like where my life is at."

"That's a total fucking lie." Fudge sat on the chair across from the sofa. "Yeah, you're at the top of your career. You demand top pay. You can pick and choose each project. You've been Golden Globe nominated, for Christ's sake, but you're still a miserable sack of shit. Have you considered that there might be more to life than money and making movies?"

Micah frowned. He had considered it. A lot, lately. Truth was, the only upcoming project he felt completely excited about was Maddie's, and frankly, her movie could have sucked and he'd still feel the same. He relished that he was a part of making her dream a reality. He wanted to be part of every aspect of it just to watch her delight, just to be near her.

And if he was really being honest, he wanted to be part of every aspect of everything she did. He wanted to be her partner and her friend and her lover. Her everything.

Fuck. Fudge was right. He was totally in love with Maddie, and he knew it. Why was he being such a prick about admitting it?

Oh, yeah, that's right. Because he didn't believe that relationships in his world had any chance of surviving. But that idea had been largely based on his parents' failed marriage. And now his mother was telling him that his whole concept of their divorce was a lie? He couldn't even comprehend anything anymore.

He glanced at Lulu beside him.

"Micah, if this girl is what makes you happy, then you should be with her."

He ran his hand through his hair. "But we'll be apart so much. And the paparazzi is not kind."

"But if you really love someone honey, those things don't matter." Lulu patted his leg once. "Who cares what the press says? Who cares what anyone says? They don't know. And as for the distance and the schedules, you make compromises. You work together. As long as you keep communicating and sharing what's going on in your head—and your heart—you can make anything happen."

She turned her head until she met Micah's eyes. "It's not any differ-ent than building a film career. You just choose to work on each other as much as you choose to work on your own stuff."

God, he was such a dick. And he couldn't figure it out until his mother sat him down and told him the obvious. What was he, twelve?

He ran his hand over his eyes, rubbing out the last bits of sleep crust-ies that still clung to his lashes. "Mom, I think I've fucked up pretty bad."

"Then un-fuck up."

He chuckled at his mother's uncharacteristic swearing. "How? She won't answer my calls. I agreed to not go to meetings about her movie." Micah considered. "I could send her flowers."

Lulu shook her head with a frown.

"Nah, that's lame," Fudge agreed. "Your last romantic gesture was a hot air balloon ride. You need to do something drastic to top that. You know what they say, 'Go big or go home.'"

Drastic. Micah's brain started whirring, somewhat slowly due to his hung-over state. "Got any ideas?"

Fudge shrugged, reaching for the Cheetos. "You're Micah Preston," he said, popping one in his mouth. "I'm sure you'll think of something."

TWENTY-NINE

"JEN'S DRESS IS HIDEOUS." BREE curled her leg under her, her eyes never leaving the flat screen TV on the wall.

Maddie kicked her flip-flops off and stretched her own legs out on Bree's couch. "She's just lost too much weight." Unlike Maddie who watched movie awards shows because she loved film, Bree watched to see what the stars were wearing.

Maddie squinted at the television. "She's almost as skinny as you now, Bree."

"Shut up." Bree pretended she didn't love to hear how thin she was.

"She won best supporting actress, right?"

"Yeah."

Maddie marked the box on her makeshift ballot. She had made predictions earlier in the day while she'd run on the treadmill at the gym. This one she'd gotten wrong. Usually she was pretty good at guessing, but her heart really wasn't in it this year. The only actor that permeated her thoughts was Micah Preston. And he wasn't up for any awards.

"Oh my God, Christian looks h-o-t hot!"

"Where?" Maddie looked toward the screen.

"No, don't look now. They just scanned over Micah. And he looks super hot too. Sorry."

Too late. Maddie had already seen him. He did look super hot. As always. Dammit, she had hoped moving on wouldn't be as hard as it was turning out to be. Stupid, broken heart.

"At least he looks like he didn't bring a date. He's sitting in between two guys."

This comforted Maddie. Unless the two guys were merely place-holders. Award shows did that, had paid models available to take the seat of anyone who left their seat for any reason. It made the theater look full. What if one of the guys sitting next to Micah was simply filling in for some hot blonde that had to pee? "Why do we have to watch the America's Choice Awards again, Bree?"

"Because if Beaumont wins Best Director, he's going to immediately get a million phone calls and crap, and I have to be ready to handle them."

Ah, yes, I'm watching this stupid award show because of Beaumont. It figures. "It seems like you should be there then."

Bree didn't detect the bitterness in Maddie's voice. "It does seem that way. But no, I have to be here instead of dressed up all pretty sur-rounded by yummy, yummy hot stars." Bree had her own bitterness. She squeezed Maddie's leg. "I mean, I'd totally rather be here with you."

"Of course you would."

"Tell you what, when you get nominated for best director or screen-writer or cinematographer, I expect an invite."

"Deal," Maddie said. And finally, for the first time in her life, she saw being nominated for an award as a possibility. She actually had a shot, now she that was being funded by Three Spot. Three Spot and Micah. How had Micah managed to make her biggest dreams a reality and then completely break her heart all in the same day?

Nope. Stop. Don't think about it tonight. Focus on why you're here. Oh, yeah, Beaumont. Maddie groaned. "I'm sorry, Bree, but I'm seriously hoping Beaumont loses."

"Frankly, I am too." If Beaumont won, the rest of Bree's night would be spent working. "And must I remind you that you don't have to be here?"

Maddie sighed. "I didn't want to be alone. I'd end up not only watching Micah, but rewinding his segment over and over." She had done that with a million YouTube videos already that week. "And then

I'd cry." She'd done that too. "A lot. I'm tired of crying."

Bree wagged her finger at her friend. "No more crying. Your eyes are going to turn perma-puffy."

"Are my eyes puffy right now?" Maddie thought she had put on enough foundation to hide that.

"Don't think about it baby, you're gorgeous." Bree grabbed two Oreos out of the package on the coffee table. "You don't have this set to DVR do you?"

Maddie took a cookie from Bree. "No." She took a bite. "Maybe."

"Madalyn!"

"I'll only watch it if I'm desperate." When she'd set the record option, she had told herself she was doing so in case she ended up leaving Bree's early. She wouldn't want to miss any of the big awards. Not that she couldn't find any of that info on the Internet.

Maddie leaned her head back against the armrest of the couch and swiveled toward the TV. The best supporting actor, announced while Maddie and Bree were talking, finished his acceptance speech and the voice-over came on. "Coming up after the break. Best Actor and Actress presented by last year's winners Natalia Lowen and Micah Preston."

Bree gave Maddie a sideways glance. "You can close your eyes and plug your ears when he gets on screen."

"I can watch him." She better be able to watch him. He was everywhere, after all. If she couldn't make it through an award show, she'd never make it past the magazines in the checkout stand at the grocery store. Realizing that she knew exactly what he was doing at that moment, though, that made her heart extra lonely. "You better pass over the ice cream." *Yeah, good idea. Eat all the calories I burned off today at the gym.*

Bree passed over the container of Ben and Jerry's Chocolate Therapy. "Be careful, it's kind of melty."

Maddie took the carton, a drop of chocolate oozing onto her white Jersey dress. "Uh, no kidding." She pulled the fabric to her mouth and licked the spot off her dress, leaving a brown smudge in its place. "Good thing I'm not going anywhere."

Bree nodded toward the television. "He's up."

Dishing up a giant spoonful of ice cream, Maddie turned her attention to the screen as the announcer's voice boomed. "Presenting our next awards, last year's Best Actor and Best Actress, Micah Preston and Natalia Lowen."

And there he was looking gorgeous, and more than a bit nervous, in his fitted black tux with a non-traditional black-button down shirt. Seeing him sent a stab to her chest while simultaneously causing her lower belly to clench. He looked so hot, she knew that later, when she was alone, she'd fantasize about taking him out of those clothes. Probably while she was in the shower so she could employ her showerhead nozzle to erase her pent-up horniness.

Christ, would he ever stop having this effect on her?

Maddie fixed on Natalia, trying to pretend she was alone on screen. "Micah, we've worked together so you know how I love gossip."

With nervous charm—Maddie had never seen him so anxious—Micah gave his best smile. "This is true. You're a gossip queen."

Natalia fidgeted with her long, red gown. "Gossip princess, thank you. But anyway. I've heard various rumors about your relationship status. Can you clear that up for us right now? Are you or are you not available?"

Maddie stiffened. Was this seriously the only thing people cared about where Micah was concerned? She couldn't bear to hear this again.

On cue, Bree patted around for the remote. "You don't have to listen, I'm muting."

She found the remote as Micah said, "Nat, I am totally *unavaila*—"

The TV went silent as Bree hit the mute button and threw the remote down.

Unavailable? Maddie dropped her spoon. "Wait! What did he just say?" She must have heard wrong.

"I don't know."

"Unmute." Maddie leaned forward and watched the soundless screen trying without success to decipher the dialogue. "Unmute!"

Bree twisted around on the couch. "Where's the remote?"

Maddie ignored the ice cream melting down her arm. She needed to hear what Micah had said. "You just had it!"

"I know, but I threw—oh, there it is."

The sound returned, " . . . you've broken the hearts of a million women across the world," Natalia said.

"He's broken hearts." Maddie's pulse quickened. "Why are there broken hearts? Rewind, rewind!"

Bree sounded just as frantic as Maddie felt. "I am!"

Keeping her eyes glued to the TV as the show rewound, Maddie instructed Bree when to stop. The show picked up in the middle of Natalia's sentence. " . . . princess, thank you. But anyway. I've heard various rumors about your relationship status. Can you clear that up for us right now? Are you or are you not available?"

Maddie set down the melting carton of ice cream, all focus on Micah.

"Nat, I am totally *unavailable*." He stressed the *un*. "I've fallen in love with an amazing woman."

"Oh, my God." Maddie gripped the edge of the couch with her fingernails. *Fallen in love*. He said he'd fallen in love.

Natalia tossed her black hair. "Wow. I never thought I'd see the day, Micah Preston! Tell us more?"

The camera closed in on Super Hot Micah. "Well, she thinks I'm a total douchebag—can I say douchebag on air?"

"I think you can."

"Good, because she's right. I am a douchebag." He turned to look directly into the camera. "But I love you, Maddie Bauers—"

Maddie sucked in her breath.

"—and, I should have told you earlier, and I didn't. So if this is what it takes to get you back, then fine. I'll say it as many times as you need me to." His voice softened. "Because I choose you, Maddie."

Maddie felt faint. "Oh, my God."

The actress winked at Micah. "Who could still think you were a douchebag after you've just declared your love on national television? You know you've broken the hearts of a million women across the world."

Micah shrugged, not seeming to be bothered in the least about breaking the hearts of women across the world. And why would he be? He was in love—in love with Maddie. Her throat tightened.

The camera turned its focus to Natalia. "Are you ready to break four more hearts? Because we have five nominees for best actress and only one of them can be the winner."

Bree turned down the volume again. Or else Maddie's head zoned it out, because she never heard the names of the nominees. "Maddie, you have to go there."

But Maddie couldn't move. Micah Preston loved her. He loved *her*. "Oh. My. God."

Alarm entered Bree's voice. "Are you okay that he just outed you on national television?"

"I totally am!" *He chooses me!* "Oh my God."

"Maddie!" Bree shook her arm excitedly. "Do you still love him?"

"Yes!" Yes, she did. More than anything. Maybe she always had, since they first met seven years ago in the backyard of that party. She had wished and longed that he would love her back, but in her wildest dreams she never could have imagined he loved her enough to tell the world on live television. *Oh, Micah!*

She stood up. "I have to see him."

Bree nodded vigorously. "Yes. Go."

Panic set in as Maddie looked down at her chocolate-stained white jersey. "I'm not dressed—"

"You can borrow something from me."

Maddie chortled. Bree's waist was thinner than her thigh. "Yeah, right."

Bree looked Maddie over. "Just go like you are." She paused, dabbing at the chocolate stain between Maddie's boobs. Giving up, she said, "You're fine. He won't care."

"But I'm . . ." Maddie didn't have time to change. She needed to get to Micah. "Okay, okay. Whatever." In a daze, she looked around for her purse and spotted it on the kitchen table. She picked it up and slung it over her shoulder, then turned back. "How will I get in?"

Bree bit her knuckle. "Um, who's there that we know?"

A name surfaced through the haze of Maddie's mind. "Fudge. Fudge's there. Micah's, um, sorta-bodyguard. I'll call him." She opened her purse and rummaged for her phone.

"Call him on the way." Bree pushed Maddie toward the door. "It's going to take you forever to find parking."

Maddie nodded. Parking could be a bitch. Good thing Bree's Echo Park apartment was close to the Nokia Theater. It would only be a ten-minute drive.

Taking one more deep breath, Maddie crossed to the door. She trembled as her sweaty palms turned the knob.

"Oh, and Maddie?" Bree gave her two thumbs up. "Yay!"

"Yay" didn't begin to describe how Maddie felt inside, but it would have to do since there were no words for the grand, earth shattering emotions that consumed her as she walked to her car. Her horrible sadness had been, in a matter of seconds, completely diffused in the same way shadows disappeared at the switch of a light. She loved Micah, a fact she had thought would remained buried inside her for the rest of her life. But now she was on her way to see him, to tell him how much she adored him and wanted him and yearned for him.

Tears rushed her eyes. Micah Preston loved her!

THIRTY

MADDIE'S CHEST CONSTRICTED WHEN FUDGE didn't answer his phone. She left a frazzled voice message saying she needed to find Micah and she was already on her way to the Nokia. But what if she couldn't get ahold of him?

Thank God, he texted her half a minute after she hung up. *Of course.* He was probably in a place where he couldn't take a phone call. *Idiot.*

She glanced at his message while stopped at a light. *"Park at the Ritz. Text me when you arrive."*

She tossed her phone down on the passenger seat and turned onto Olympic Boulevard. With the few minutes left of her drive, she centered her thoughts. Micah said he loved her. On national television. But had he changed his mind about the future? Did he believe they might actually have a shot, even in Hollywood?

Micah loved her. And she loved Micah. Still, she couldn't relax in that knowledge without more information.

Though still a block away, Maddie slowed her car as the Ritz came into view, hoping the change in speed would calm her sudden anxiety. But when she turned into the hotel's driveway, her heart seemed to beat even faster.

"You're in luck," the valet attendant said. "A parking spot just came available." He opened her door. "Are you staying in the hotel?"

"Visiting someone who is," she lied.

As the valet drove her car away, she texted Fudge. *"Just parked."*

"I'm in the hotel lobby."

Smoothing down her dress—as if that would help her disheveled state—Maddie pushed through the revolving doors and stepped into the cool lobby.

Fudge saw her first. "Hey, you!" He was dressed in a black T-shirt and black jeans, his "on duty" attire. He enveloped her in a bear hug. "You saw the show? What did you think?"

Man, was that a loaded question. It would take an hour to run through all her thoughts and feelings. She settled on the dominating one. "I'm shocked."

He took her hand, leading her toward the main elevators. "But it was good, right?"

She nodded as he pushed the up arrow on the call panel.

Her brow furrowed. They were staying in the hotel?

Fudge didn't notice her confusion. "I just knew you'd show up after that. Micah wasn't so sure. He was really nervous about it actually. He's gonna be real happy to see you. *I'm* real happy to see you. He's been an ass since Colorado."

"An ass?"

"Total ass. Moody. Mean. I've never seen him like that." An elevator opened behind them and a formally dressed couple stepped out. Was that the guy who just won best screenwriter? Fudge ushered her in the empty car before she could look again.

"But good for you," he continued. "Not letting him force you into less than you both deserve." He pushed the number four on the panel and the doors shut.

Maybe Micah was waiting for her in a hotel room. With nothing on. *Yummy.* She grinned at the thought. "Does he know I'm here?"

"Nah. We're surprising him." Fudge tapped his foot, watching the dial as they climbed.

So no naked in a hotel room. "Um, where are we going? Is Micah here or at the Nokia?"

Fudge hit his head as if he just realized he were in idiot. "Duh. Sorry. He's here in the hotel." The doors opened and he led her down a hall following a sign that pointed toward the hotel ballrooms. "All the presenters and award winners are sent over here to the press room for pics and interviews and stuff."

Maddie halted, panic setting in. "There won't be pictures of me, right?"

"Maybe. Everyone wants to know who the mysterious Maddie Bauers is, after all. Is that not cool?"

She gestured at her outfit. "Look at me. I'm a mess! I'm wearing an Old Navy Jersey. I have a big old chocolate stain on my boobs."

Fudge scanned her over, as if seeing her for the first time. "Hmm. Yeah, we'll keep you out of the limelight then. No worries."

He resumed his trek down the hall. Hesitantly, Maddie followed. He stopped outside a corridor where two security guards stood. Several feet behind them, a sign on a set of heavy double doors read "Ballroom A."

Fudge flashed a badge and pulled her past the guards and through the double doors. "Micah was up next when I left him."

Inside, the room was abuzz with activity. At least two hundred people were spread around the small ballroom. Light bulbs flashed and boom mics bobbed above the photo area at the end of the room. Maddie stood on her tiptoes to see above the heads of the press. There he was. Posed in front of the America's Choice Awards logo, looking like the hot God he was.

"I haven't had a girlfriend in years," Micah said in answer to a question Maddie hadn't heard. "I have a lot to learn."

"Micah, where did you meet Maddie?" a reporter near the front asked.

They were talking about her!

"You'll dig it up soon enough." Micah was all suave and charming. "Some of you are especially talented with that kind of thing."

A few people laughed.

Fudge waved his arm, signaling to Micah.

Maddie raised herself on her toes again and nearly choked on her own spit as she briefly met his glance. Her stomach flip-flopped at the look he gave her, his eyes wide, full of longing and love.

Fudge tugged at her sleeve. "We gotta get outta here if you don't want to get photographed."

Maddie followed as he crossed behind the crowd to a small room off the ballroom. "This is a lounge for while the stars wait for their turn with press." He gestured for her to enter. "But no one's been using it. I'll tell Micah you're here."

Maddie entered the room, finding it furnished in old Hollywood décor. A white couch and two armchairs created a sitting area around a television showing a live feed of the award show next door. The winner of Best Director was giving his award speech. And it wasn't Beaumont. *This night's getting better and better.*

After several minutes of unsuccessfully trying to concentrate on the show, Maddie paced the room. Where was Micah? What would he say when he saw her? What would *she* say when she saw him?

Spotting a sink at the bar on the opposite side of the room, she crossed to wash her hands, sticky from nerves and chocolate ice cream. While drying, she had the eerie feeling she was being watched. She turned and saw him, leaning against the doorframe. Excitement and desire rushed through her and the only reason she wasn't running into his arms was fear that her knees would collapse before she reached him.

Micah looked her over from head to toe. Her body trembled under his ravenous gaze. When his eyes reached her chocolate stain, he chuckled. Maddie cringed. Of course he'd notice all of her. He stepped into the room, still saying nothing.

She had an idea. In what she hoped sounded like a reporter's voice, she said, "Micah Preston."

He cocked his head.

She took a step toward him. "Rumor has it that you don't believe you can have a successful movie career and a girlfriend. Do you care to comment?"

He relaxed, understanding settling on his face. "This is true."

She tensed. Did this mean he still believed they had no future?

"I have historically stood my ground on the idea that romance has no place in Hollywood." He stepped toward her. "But recently I've had a change of heart."

She swallowed, taking another step. "A change of heart?"

"I still think it's a difficult situation, don't get me wrong there." He moved again toward her. "But relationships are about sacrifice and compromise. And as long as we choose each other more often than we choose our careers, I think we might have a shot." He furrowed his brow. "I'm not sure if she's completely thought about the sacrifices she'll have to make for her own career."

Maddie took a deep breath. She'd thought about it, but she knew that wasn't the same as experiencing it. It wouldn't be easy, especially facing her Beaumont past again, but Micah had given up a way of thinking for her. She could give up things for him as well. *It takes two.*

"Do you care what the press says about you? About her?"

"Not in the slightest." He suddenly seemed to remember she was pretending to be a reporter herself. "No offense to you and your kind. But usually whatever you have to say is a bunch of bullshit."

Another step toward him. "No offense taken. I'm sure she knows that as well. And if you can ignore them, I bet she can, too. Since she loves you and all."

His eyes twinkled. "You think she still loves me? Even after I've been such a dick?"

"I'd bet my life on it," she said softly.

He beamed. Then his delight was replaced with a mischievous grin. "I'm not so sure." He took two more slow steps toward her. "She can be pretty hot-headed. And stubborn. And non-compromising. Sometimes she runs away. Oh, and she can be a bit of a tease, so there's that."

Maddie raised a brow. "A tease? No way."

"Yes, yes way. I've taken many cold showers because of her."

"Hmm." She was so near to him now, only a few feet away. She could touch him. But one more question. "With all her negative traits," she said, her eyes lowered, "Are you sure that you really . . . love her?"

He pulled her to him in one swift movement. "Oh yeah," he said huskily, his mouth inches from hers. "I'm damn sure."

His lips found hers, and she melted into his taste, his tongue darting playfully around hers. She clutched him desperately, and his body soaked her with heat from the tips of her breasts to the place where his arousal pressed into her belly, to lower where her own desire burned. She wanted him, and he wanted her, and she reveled in this, as he kissed her so thoroughly that her insides turned into complete mush and her legs could barely stand without his support.

When she thought she couldn't take it anymore, that if he lingered in her mouth a moment longer she'd have to rip off all his clothes and make love to him right there in the ballroom of the Ritz Carlton, only then did he tear his mouth away to whisper in her ear. "Oh, Maddie." His voice was ragged and low. "I've been such a shit. I'm so sorry it took so long for me to come around. I could live the rest of my life without ever seeing another script or movie set again, but I can't live another second without you. I love you. Please tell me I still have a chance, that we have a chance."

"Oh God, Micah. All I needed was for you to believe we did." Maddie blinked back hot tears. "Yes. Yes! I love you so much."

He leaned back to search her eyes. "You really do?"

"I do. I always have. Probably since I met you on the bench in that backyard on my graduation night."

His mouth possessed hers again, this time the heat of the kiss turned her arousal from a simmer to a boil. When Micah pulled away to meet her eyes, his were dilated with ravenous desire. "Oh baby, I'd say we need to get a room, but I don't think I can wait that long."

His sexual promise had her teeming with excitement.

His eyes swept the room and settled on the sofa near them. "Later we'll take it slow and sweet. But I need to be inside you now, and it's going to have to be quick."

Her mouth fell open in surprise as he lifted her and carried her to the sofa. He lay her down and reached under her dress to remove her panties.

Panic swept through her. "Micah! What if someone—?"

"Shh, we don't care about anyone else, remember? I have to have you."

She relaxed, trusting him, letting herself give in to his need.

His hand slid up her thigh to the bud of her want. "God, Maddie you're soaked." He swirled her clit with his thumb sending a shiver throughout her body then dipped a finger inside her.

Oh fuck. She needed him too. Now. She squirmed, anxious for him to fill her. "Come on!"

He unfastened his pants and his cock sprang free, causing a surge of excitement in her blood. "You ready?"

She answered by spreading her legs further and bucking her hips.

He climbed into the v of her legs. "Is this what you want?" He plunged inside her and groaned.

"Yes!" Her memories of him—wonderful, heavenly memories— paled radically to the exquisite reality of his naked cock within her. And he still had further to go. Her body opened to accept him and he slipped deeper inside.

Then he began to move. Not in the creative, circular motions that he usually tortured her with, but with sharp, piercing jabs. Each time, he stroked that spot—the one that made the lights flicker when it was hit just right and oh, was he hitting it right. So right in fact, that despite her concern that she'd never get off with people so close by, she found herself soaring over the edge in record time. Her orgasm was so fierce and so sudden she had to bite into Micah's shoulder to squelch her cries.

"Yes, baby, yes!" He pounded through her release to his own turbulent climax.

Seconds after they'd finished, before her brain could even process a cool-down, voices—or rather *a* voice—drifted in from outside the room. Fudge, speaking louder than usual, said, "Yes, Mr. Santini, Micah's in there. But before you go in—"

Maddie and Micah scrambled to compose themselves as Fudge resumed a normal volume of speech. "It's so great to meet you. I'm such a fan."

"Where're my panties?" Maddie hissed as Micah tucked himself in his pants.

He grinned. "Do you really need them?"

She narrowed her eyes at him.

He joined her search. "I threw them behind me. Oh, they're on the lamp."

But before he could reach them, Martin Santini walked in the room.

Maddie knew she must look petrified. One of the most prolific directors in the history of film had just walked into the same room and here she was with a fresh-fucked face, chocolate-stained boobs and her floral cotton panties hanging from the lampshade.

Thank God for Micah. He moved to the director and greeted him with one hand while deftly retrieving her underwear behind his back with the other.

"Great to see you, Marty," Micah said, slipping her panties in his pocket. "This is my girlfriend, Maddie Bauers."

Girlfriend! After the heights of her orgasm, she was surprised he was able to thrill her further.

She put one hand on her chest to cover her stain and shook Martin Santini's hand with the other. "I'm honored to meet you, Mr. Santini. You've been a huge influence on me."

"Call me Marty, please. Glad to meet you." He winked at Micah. "I'm guessing you're no longer a douchebag."

Micah chuckled. "Well, I'm not sure about that."

She hit him playfully. "No, he's still a douchebag. But it's sort of endearing."

"Good." Marty clapped a hand on Micah's shoulder. "I hope you don't mind me talking business at a social event, but when I heard you were here, I wanted to check in. Did you get the script I sent to your manager?"

"I did, thank you. I loved it. I'm very interested in the part. My only hesitation is the time spent out of the country."

"Micah . . ." Maddie was worried about being away from Micah, too. But she wanted him to take the role.

But Micah shook his head, silencing her.

"Understandable," Marty said. "Might the offer seem more attractive if I agree to move the training stateside?"

"That makes the offer a whole lot more attractive." He winked at Maddie. "I would still have to discuss it with Maddie. I can't do anything without her being on board."

Before Maddie could give her whole-hearted consent, Marty said, "Great way to run a relationship. My wife, as you may know, is a costume designer. And we've been married for over twenty-five years, and in this town, that's a lifetime. We never would have lasted so long if we hadn't worked our schedules out together. Anyway, you two talk it over, but can I at least set up a meeting?"

Micah looked at Maddie who nodded so enthusiastically she thought her head would fall off.

"Yes, let's do that," Micah said.

"Great. I'll have my agent contact your agent. Now I'll get out of your hair." Marty winked again. "I think I may have been interrupting something."

Maddie suppressed a giggle.

Marty turned to leave then stopped at the door. "Great meeting you, Maddie Bauers. I hope to see a lot of you both."

The second the director left the room, Maddie and Micah burst into laughter. God, she loved the sound of his laugh. She loved him, period. And he was about to land a Martin Santini role! "Micah, you have to take the part."

"Only if you're completely on board. We have to work our schedules around each other. We can't be apart for too long. We need to put ourselves first."

"Agreed. But I've already been thinking about it and I have a plan. I can finish up post-production of my movie with Three Spot while you're doing your comedy. Maybe I'll need another month or so, which, if you can get your training moved to the states is perfect. Then, I have a script I've been working on that would be awesome set in New Zealand. I could raise some money, rent another RED camera and shoot my movie while you're shooting yours."

"That is perfect." He wrapped his arms around her. "Leave it to you to always be two steps ahead of me."

She smiled into his neck, enjoying his words and his embrace, and the crazy things he was doing to her lower parts. Again. "Hey, can I have my panties back?"

"No. I like knowing you're bare. It's easy access." He brushed his nose against her ear. "Now let's get out of here so I can take advantage of that."

He took her hand in his and chuckled.

"What?" she asked.

"I was just thinking. I'm Micah Preston, guy who can supposedly get any girl in the world."

She raised an eyebrow, wondering where he was going, not really caring because all the other girls in the world didn't matter since he was hers and she was his.

He put his hand on her face, his thumb caressing her cheek. "Yet it took me seven years and two months to finally go home with Maddie from the party." He paused. "You know what?"

"Hmm?" She covered his hand with her own, enjoying every little touch of the man who was everything—*her* everything—the man that she had grounded while he gave her flight. The man she loved. The man who loved her in front of the world.

He tilted her chin up. "I never want to go home with anyone else again."

You have the right to remain sexy.

Anything you say can and will be used to get you in my bed.

You have the right to use my body to give yourself a delirious, life-changing orgasm.

If you have trouble . . . don't worry, I'm a bit of an expert in that department.

There's nothing 'thin' about my blue line, if you catch my drift, and trust me, I know how to put those handcuffs to good use.

Livia Ward wants a baby before she's thirty. And even though Officer Chase Kelly is exactly the kind of cocky jerk this librarian has sworn off, he is undeniably hot. Both of them think they can give each other what they want—a few nights of fun for Officer Kelly, a no-strings baby for Livia—but this hot cop is about to learn that sex, babies, and love don't always play by the rules.

You know me.

Come on, you know you do.

Maybe you pretend you don't. Maybe you clear your browser history religiously. Maybe you pretend to be aghast whenever someone even mentions the word porn in your presence.

But the truth is that you do know me.

Everybody knows Logan O'Toole, world famous porn star. Except then Devi Dare pops into my world, and pretty soon

I'm doing things that aren't like me—like texting her with flirty banter and creating an entire web porn series just so I can get to star in her bed. Again. And again.

With Devi, my entire universe shifts, and the more time I spend with her, the more I realize that Logan O'Toole isn't the guy I thought he was.

So maybe I'm not the guy you thought I was either.

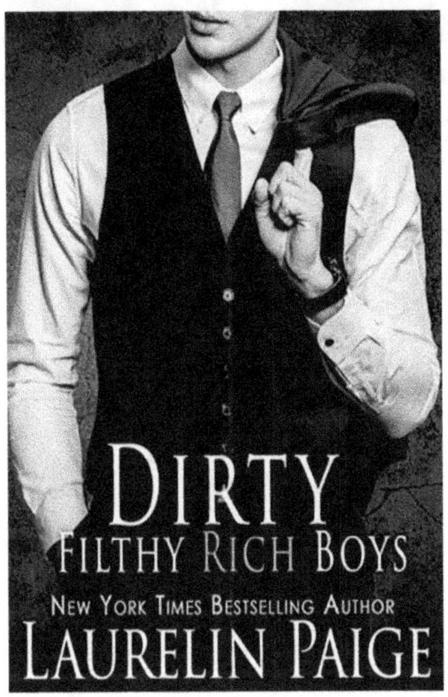

When I met Donovan Kincaid, I knew he was rich. I didn't know he was filthy. Truth be told, I was only trying to get his best friend to notice me. I knew poor scholarship girls like me didn't stand a chance against guys like Weston King and Donovan Kincaid, but I was in love with his world, their world, of parties and sex and power. I knew what I wanted—I knew who I wanted—until one night, their world tried to bite me back and Donovan saved me. He saved me, and then Weston finally noticed me, and I finally learned what it was to be in their world. Because when dirty, filthy, rich boys play, they play for keeps.

From NYT Bestselling author Laurelin Paige, discover a whole new world filled with sex, love, power, romance and Dirty, Filthy Rich Men.

Dirty Filthy Rich Boys is FREE everywhere for a limited time!

ALSO BY
LAURELIN PAIGE

THE DIRTY UNIVERSE

Dirty Filthy Rich Men (Dirty Duet #1)

Dirty Filthy Rich Love (Dirty Duet #2)

Dirty Filthy Fix (a spinoff novella) (November 7, 2017)

Dirty Sexy Player (Dirty Games Duet #1, July 2018)

Dirty Sexy Games (Dirty Games Duet #2, November 2018)

THE FIXED UNIVERSE

Fixed on You (Fixed #1)

Found in You (Fixed #2)

Forever with You (Fixed #3)

Hudson (Fixed #4)

Fixed Forever (Fixed #5, June 2018)

Free Me (Found Duet #1)

Find Me (Found Duet #2)

Chandler (a spinoff novel)

Falling Under You (a spinoff novella)

FIRST AND LAST

First Touch

Last Kiss

HOLYWOOD HEAT

Sex Symbol

Star Struck

One More Time (May 2018)

Written with Kayti McGee
under the name LAURELIN MCGEE
Hot Alphas
Miss Match
Love Struck

Written with SIERRA SIMONE
Porn Star
Hot Cop

ACKNOWLEDGMENTS

MADDIE AND MICAH WERE THE first romance characters I ever wrote, and I'm very fond of them because of that. I'm so excited that I can release them again now and more people can discover their story.

As always, Sierra Simone read this book as I wrote it. And rewrote it. And rewrote it. Thank you for standing by through each rendition, and, even more, for still being here all these years later.

To my team—Candi Kane, Melissa Gaston, and Ashley Lindemann. There's not many people who would put up with a half-assed surprise release the way you all do, and yet you've all been nothing but there for me. Then I threw in an emergency surgery, and you still weren't flummoxed. You guys are good. ;)

To my LARCs. You guys came together quick and were amazing! I can't wait to keep working with you in the future.

To Jenn Watson and Social Butterfly PR for rolling with the punches. Man, I know how to punch lately, don't I?

To Nancy Smay, Wander Aguier, and Letitia Hasser for helping repackage this baby. And to Mr. Melissa Gaston for the title and Michelle Ficht for catching our goofs.

To Serena McDonald who beta read it and reminded me I loved these characters. And to Lauren Blakely who read it way back when and pointed out that Micah was just a different kind of bad boy. You've both been so amazingly supportive throughout my career. Thank you from the bottom of my heart. <3

To Rebecca Friedman, Flavia Viotti, Meire Dias, the most amazing agents on earth.

To ShopTalkers and Order and most most most of all, my Snatches. You teach me and humor me and make me laugh, and those are basically the three things I need from best friends. Oh, and you tell me to nap. I need that too.

To the Sky Launchers! Thank you for all your book love and enthusiasm for what happens in my head. You make it a pleasure to get out of bed and go to work.

To the bloggers and the readers, I'm so lucky to be in this world with you. I appreciate you, even if I'm remiss to say it.

To Tom and my three girls—love is love is love is love is love.

In the end, that's what matters, and we're doing that right.

To my God who looks over us and cares for us. Thank you for the abundant blessings. You know that I'm greedy and still you give me more.

ABOUT LAURELIN PAIGE

WITH OVER 1 MILLION BOOKS sold, Laurelin Paige is the *NY Times*, *Wall Street Journal*, and *USA Today* Bestselling Author of the Fixed Trilogy. She's a sucker for a good romance and gets giddy anytime there's kissing, much to the embarrassment of her three daughters. Her husband doesn't seem to complain, however. When she isn't reading or writing sexy stories, she's probably singing, watching *Game of Thrones* and *the Walking Dead*, or dreaming of Michael Fassbender. She's also a proud member of Mensa International though she doesn't do anything with the organization except use it as material for her bio.

www.laurelinpaige.com

laurelinpaigeauthor@gmail.com